FYODOR DOSTOYEVSKY was born in Moscow on October 30, 1821. He was educated in Moscow and at the School of Military Engineers in St. Petersburg, where he spent four years. In 1844 he resigned his Commission in the army to devote himself to literature. In 1846, he wrote his first novel, *Poor Folk;* it was an immediate critical and popular success. This was followed by short stories and a novel, *The Double.* While at work on *Netochka Nezvanova,* the twenty-seven-year-old author was arrested for belonging to a young socialist group. He was tried and condemned to death, but at the last moment his sentence was commuted to prison in Siberia. He spent four years in the penal settlement at Omsk; then he was released on the condition that he serve in the army. While in the army he fell in love with and married Marie Isaeva. In 1859 he was granted full amnesty and allowed to return to St. Petersburg. In the next few years he wrote his first full-length novels: *The Friend of the Family* (1859) and *The Insulted and the Injured* (1862). *Notes from Underground* (1864) was in many ways his most influential work of this period, containing the wellsprings of his mature philosophy: the hope of gaining salvation through degradation and suffering. At the end of this literary period, his wife died. Plagued by epilepsy, faced with financial ruin, he worked at superhuman speed to produce *The Gambler,* dictating the novel to eighteen-year-old Anna Grigorievna Snitkina. The manuscript was delivered to his publisher in time. During the next fourteen years, Dostoyevsky wrote his greatest works: *Crime and Punishment, The Idiot, The Possessed,* and *The Brothers Karamazov.* The latter book was published a year before his death on January 28, 1881.

DOSTOYEVSKY

The Dream of a
and
SELECTIONS FROM

A SIGNET CLASSIC
NEW AMERICAN LIBRARY
NEW YORK AND SCARBOROUGH, ONTARIO

Notes from Underground
White Nights
Ridiculous Man

The House of the Dead

A New Translation with an Afterword
by Andrew R. MacAndrew

Revised and Updated Bibliography

SIGNET, SIGNET CLASSIC, MENTOR, ONYX, PLUME, MERIDIAN AND
NAL BOOKS are published *in the United States* by
NAL PENGUIN INC.,
1633 Broadway, New York, New York 10019,
in Canada by The New American Library of Canada Limited,
81 Mack Avenue, Scarborough, Ontario M1L 1M8

19   20   21   22   23   24   25   26   27

PRINTED IN THE UNITED STATES OF AMERICA

Contents

White Nights

A TALE OF LOVE FROM THE REMINISCENCES OF A DREAMER

ᕮᘒᘏᘓ

Could he be born from the start,
If only for a fleeting moment,
To be so dear to your heart?
IVAN TURGENEV

The First Night

It was a marvelous night, the sort of night one only experiences when one is young. The sky was so bright, and there were so many stars that, gazing upward, one couldn't help wondering how so many whimsical, wicked people could live under such a sky. This too is a question that would only occur to the young, to the very young; but may God make *you* wonder like that as often as possible!

Now, mentioning whimsical, angry people makes me think how well I behaved that day. A strange anguish had tormented me since early morning. I suddenly had the impression that I had been left all alone, that everyone was shrinking away from me, avoiding me. You are, of course, right to ask who that "everyone" is, for although I've lived in Petersburg for eight years now, I haven't managed to make a single friend. But what do I need friends or acquaintances for? As it is, I'm acquainted with all of Petersburg. And that's why I had the impression of being abandoned by everyone when the whole city rose and left for the summer. I was afraid to be left alone, and for three days I roamed dejectedly through the city, unable to understand what was happening to me. Whether I went to Nevsky Avenue, to the park, or wandered along the embankments, I never came across the people I was accustomed to meet in certain spots at certain hours all year round. They, of course, didn't know me; but I knew them, all right. I knew them intimately, and having studied their faces, I rejoiced with them when they were cheerful and grieved with them when they were downcast. I almost became friends with a little old man whom I met every day at a certain time on the Fontanka Embankment. His face was so dignified and thoughtful; he carried a knotty walking cane with a gold top in his right hand, swinging his left arm, and was constantly mumbling something inaudible. He even noticed me and took a keen interest in *my* existence. I'm sure he must've been quite upset when I did not appear at a given hour on the embankment. That's why sometimes we almost exchanged greetings, especially when we both happened to be in a good mood. Recently, two days went by without our seeing each other, and on the third day, our hands almost shot up to our hats, but thank God, we came to our senses, dropped our hands, and passed by with mutual sympathy.

I'm acquainted with houses too. As I walk up a street, each house seems to have darted ahead and to be waiting for me, looking at me out of all its windows, almost saying: "Hello! How are you getting on? I'm fine myself. And you know what? They're going to add another story to me in May!" Or: "How are you? Well, me, I'll have to undergo some repairs tomorrow." Or: "You know, I almost burned down last night. It gave me such a fright!" And other things of that sort. Among houses, I have my favorites. Some are intimate friends. One had decided to undergo a course of treatment with an architect during the summer. I'll make a point of visiting him every day, in case the treatment turns out to be fatal, God forbid! I'll never forget what happened to one very pretty, rosy little house. Although he was rather haughtily distant with his clumsy neighbors, that little stone house used to look at me so nicely that I always felt glad as I passed by. But last week, as I was walking along that street, my friend looked at me dejectedly, and I heard his plaintive cry: "They're painting me yellow!" Ah, the criminals! The barbarians! They spared nothing; neither the columns nor the cornices, and my friend became yellow as a canary. I nearly had an attack of jaundice myself, and I still haven't been able to go back and visit my poor disfigured friend painted in the color of the Celestial Empire.

So you see, that's what I meant by being acquainted with all Petersburg.

As I said, I'd been uneasy for three days and now I'd discovered why. Things didn't feel right in the street —this one was missing, that one was missing, and where on earth was such-and-such? And at home, too, I wasn't quite myself. For two whole evenings I'd tried to determine what I was missing in my corner, why I was so ill at ease there. Puzzled, I kept examining my green walls with their black soot stains, the ceiling covered with cobwebs that Matryona cultivates with such eminent success. I examined every piece of furniture, every single chair, to see whether the trouble wasn't hidden just there. For I know that I can be badly upset if a chair is not in exactly the same place as it was the day before. I also looked at the window. But all in vain. I even decided to call in Matryona and give her a fatherly scolding about the cobwebs and about her slovenliness in general. But she only looked at me, surprised, and left without answering a word; the cobwebs remained unmolested.

It was only this morning that I realized what was happening. Why, they were deserting me for their summer places. I must apologize for this trivial way of putting it, but I can't be bothered with style just now, because everyone is either leaving Petersburg or has already left it; because every respectable-looking man hailing a cab in the street is thereby, before my very eyes, turning himself into a venerable *pater familias*, who, having taken care of his usual duties, departs, just as he is, to join his family in their country house; because every passer-by in the street has a special look about him that almost audibly announces to the world at large: "I'm only passing through town—in a couple of hours or so, I'll be back in the country." If slender, sugar-white fingers drum on the inside of a window pane, if that window then opens, and a pretty face peeps out to buy some potted plants from a street flower vendor—I immediately imagine that she's just buying them to pass the time and not at all to enjoy spring and flowers in a stuffy city apartment, and that anyway the people in that apartment will leave for the country and take the flowers along. I've become so perspicacious that I can tell with certitude from people's faces what kind of summer houses they live in. Those from the Rocky and Apothecary Isles, or from the places along Peterhof Road, are recognizable by the studied exquisiteness of their manners, the elegance of their summer suits, and the magnificence of the carriages in which they drive into the city. Those from Pargolov and places beyond always impress me with their solidity and their down-to-earth air. A visitor from Krestovsky Island is distinguishable by his imperturbable cheerfulness. Whether I happen to meet a long caravan of movers' wagons loaded with mountains of furniture—tables, chairs, sofas (Turkish or otherwise), and all sorts of household junk, on top of which, moreover, a thin female cook is enthroned, looking after her master's belongings like a nesting bird after her eggs—or watch the boats and barges, heavily loaded with household goods, sliding down the Neva or the Fontanka toward the Black Stream or the Islands—in my eyes, the wagons and barges multiply by tens and hundreds, and I have the impression that everything has risen up and started moving in long files out of the city to the countryside, that Petersburg will soon be a desert. So, in the end, I feel offended, ashamed, and sad. I have absolutely nowhere to go and no reason to go out of town. I long to leave on any wagon, to drive off with any gentleman hailing a cabbie. But no one has invited me. They seem to have completely forgotten me, as if I really were a stranger to them!

I'd been walking for hours and, as usual, I'd lost track of where I was, when I suddenly realized I'd reached the city limits. I immediately felt happy and, without hesitation, passed beyond the barrier and found myself walking between cultivated fields and meadows. I didn't feel tired at all. On the contrary, every joint in me was as relaxed as if a load had been lifted from my shoulders. All who drove by smiled at me engagingly, almost bowing to me. They looked pleased about something and the whole lot of them were smoking cigars. And I too was happier than I'd ever been before. Such was the impact of nature upon me, a semi-invalid city dweller who'd almost suffocated within the city walls, that I felt almost as if I'd found myself in Italy.

There's something inexpressibly moving in our Petersburg countryside when, with the arrival of spring, it suddenly reveals itself in all its might and with all its God-given gifts; when it dresses up, adorns itself with bright, multicolored flowers. . . . It makes me think of a weak, frail, sickly young girl, usually regarded with pity, sometimes with compassionate love, and sometimes not even noticed, who for one moment, as if by accident, suddenly becomes immensely beautiful; and, struck and charmed, you can't help wondering what force could have lighted the flame in those sad, dreamy eyes. What has caused the blood to rush to those pale, sunken cheeks? What has brought this passion to her delicate features? Why does her bosom heave like that? What has so suddenly communicated vigor, life, and beauty to the poor girl's face; given it that radiant smile; produced that glittering, sparkling laughter? You look around, you try to guess. But then it's all gone, and the next day perhaps, you'll meet her usual pensive, abstract gaze again, recognize her pale face and the timid humility of her movements; you'll even detect remorse and signs of some deadening anguish and shame over that momentary exaltation. . . . And you're sorry that the ephemeral beauty has faded so rapidly, so irretrievably, that it

flashed so deceptively and pointlessly before your eyes—
you're sorry, for you didn't even have time to fall in
love with her. . . .

But, even so, the night was better than the day! This
is what happened.

It was very late when I got back into the city. As I
approached the house I live in, it struck ten. I was
walking along the embankment; at that hour there was
no one around, for I live in a remote part of town. I
sang as I walked, for when I'm happy, I always hum
something—as does every happy, friendless man who has
no one with whom to share his happiness. Then suddenly
the most unexpected thing happened to me.

I saw a woman leaning against the railing along the
embankment. She appeared to be gazing attentively at
the murky water. She wore a ravishing little yellow hat
and an elegant black cape. "She must be young and dark-
haired," I decided. I don't think she heard my footsteps,
and she didn't even stir when I passed her, holding my
breath, my heart beating wildly. "Strange," I thought,
"she must be quite lost in thought——" Suddenly I
stopped dead. Stifled sobs reached my ears. Yes, that
was it—she was crying. Again I heard the girl trying
to catch her breath. Ah, God! My heart contracted with
pity, and shy though I am with women, I retraced my
steps and walked up to her. I'm sure I'd have exclaimed
"Madame!" had I not been so acutely aware that this
form of address has already been used so often in Russian novels with a high-society background. That was
all that stopped me. But while I was searching for an
alternative approach, the girl recovered, turned her head,
glanced at me, looked away, and darted off along the
embankment. I followed her. She must have realized, for
she turned her back to the water, crossed the street, and
went along the opposite sidewalk. I didn't dare follow
her across the street. My heart was quivering like that
of a bird held in a man's hand. Then something came to
my assistance.

I saw a man walking on the other side of the street,
not far from the girl. He wore a frockcoat, and seemed

to have reached an age of respectability, although there was nothing respectable about his gait. He was staggering and stumbling along, guiding himself by leaning against the walls. Now the girl was moving lightly and apprehensively, as girls do at night when they don't wish strange men to offer to see them home; the staggering gentleman never would have caught up with her if he hadn't changed his tactics (for which I thank my lucky stars).

But suddenly, without uttering a word, the man set off at a gallop. She darted ahead with quickened, fearful steps, but the swaying figure kept gaining on her. He came closer and closer, then he caught up with her. The girl let out a cry, and—I thank my lucky stars again for placing my excellent knobby walking stick in my right hand. In no time, I was on the opposite sidewalk; in no time, the uninvited gentleman made a practical appraisal of the situation, took into consideration the unanswerable argument in my hand, slowed down, and fell back. And only when he felt there was a safe distance between us did he voice his indignation in no uncertain terms. But his words hardly reached us.

"If," I said to the girl, "you will allow me to take your arm, that man won't dare annoy you again."

Silently she allowed me. Her hand was still trembling from fear and her earlier emotions. Ah, what blessings I wished at that moment upon the unwelcome gentleman! I squinted at her discreetly. She was terribly pretty. Her hair was dark, just as I'd guessed. Tears glistened on her black eyelashes, whether from her recent fright or from her sorrow, I didn't know, but a smile was already sparkling on her lips. She glanced at me out of the corner of her eye, blushed, and looked down.

"Now, you see, you shouldn't have spurned me like that. Nothing would've happened if I'd been at your side."

"But I didn't know you; I thought you too . . ."

"Do you feel you know me now?"

"A little. For instance, I know you're trembling. Tell me why."

"Ah, you've guessed right from the start!" I said,

delighted that she should turn out to be so clever—never a drawback in a woman, as long as she's pretty. "Yes, you've seen through me straight away. I'm afraid of women, and it's that fear that makes me tremble, just as it made you tremble a few moments ago when that gentleman frightened you. I'm frightened now, all right. It's like a dream, although I've never actually dreamed that I'd be talking like this to a woman."

"Really?"

"Yes. And if you feel my arm tremble, it's because it has never yet been held by a pretty hand like yours. I'm quite unused to being with women. In fact, I've never got used to them. I live all alone. I don't even know how to talk to women. For instance, I don't know if I haven't said something stupid to you. Please, tell me frankly—I promise I won't be offended."

"No, no, on the contrary. And since you want me to be frank, let me tell you that women like your sort of shyness; I'll even tell you that I like it too, and I won't ask you to leave me until we're at my doorstep."

"If you go on saying things like that," I said, out of breath with enthusiasm, "I'll lose my shyness and, along with it, my advantage. . . ."

"Advantage? Advantage to what end? Ah, now you've said something I don't like."

"I *am* sorry, it just slipped off my tongue. You can't really expect that, at such a moment, I shouldn't wish that . . ."

"What? Wish that I should like you?"

"Yes, that's it. But please, try to understand: I'm twenty-six already and I've never known anyone closely. So how can I be expected to be good at speaking to people? How can I say things well and to the point? Besides, isn't it better for you when everything is out in the open? For I don't know how to be silent when my heart is talking. Well, what's the difference? But believe me, I've never, never spoken to any woman. Never. I've never known one. I've only gone around dreaming that one day I might meet someone. If you only knew how many times I've fallen in love that way. . . ."

"But how's that, who did you fall in love with?"

"Why, no one in particular, just with the ideal woman, the one I'd dreamed of. I can dream up whole novels, you know. Oh, you really have no idea about me! Of course, as you can well imagine, I have come across two or three women in my time. But what sort of women were they? They were such housewives that— But now you'll laugh when I tell you that I planned for a long time to address some aristocratic lady in the street. When she was alone, of course. Talk to her shyly, respectfully, passionately; tell her that I was perishing in my loneliness; beseech her not to send me away; say that it was impossible for me to get to know any other woman; persuade her that it was even the *duty* of a woman not to spurn the timid approach of one so unhappy; convince her that, finally, all I wanted from her was a few understanding, sisterly words, and that she shouldn't just turn her back on me, but should believe what I told her—then she might laugh at me if she wished, so long as she said one or two words of hope, only two words, then, if she wished, we'd never meet again! . . . I see you're laughing. . . . Well, that's why I told you about it, after all."

"Don't be offended. I'm only laughing because you're your own worst enemy. If you'd tried you'd have succeeded, maybe even in the street. The simpler, the easier. . . . No decent woman, unless she was dismally stupid or happened to be very irritated about something at that particular moment, would have refused you the two words for which you begged with such humility. . . . Although, after all, she might very well have taken you for a madman. I was thinking of how I would have reacted, but then I have quite a good idea of what life is all about."

"Oh, thank you, thank you!" I cried. "You have no idea what you're doing for me!"

"All right, all right. But tell me, what made you think I was the type of woman with whom . . . well, who would be worthy of . . . your attention, your friendship? How did you know that I was not just another housewife, as you put it? What made you decide to speak to me?"

"What made me—why, you were alone, and that man was most indiscreet, and it's night time. . . . I couldn't have done anything else."

"No, no, before that, on the other sidewalk. Weren't you thinking of speaking to me?"

"On the other sidewalk? I really don't know what to say. I was happy today. I was walking along and singing. I went beyond the city limits. I'd never before experienced such happy moments. And you—please excuse me, I may have imagined it, but I thought you were crying, and I couldn't bear it. . . . My heart shrank. . . . Ah, God, why shouldn't I be entitled to grieve with you? Why is it a sin for me to feel brotherly compassion for your sorrow? . . . Excuse me, I said compassion. . . . Well, I don't see why it should offend you if I couldn't resist my impulse to come over and talk to you."

"Enough, don't talk of it any more." She lowered her head, and her fingers pressed my arm. "It's my fault for bringing it up, and I'm so pleased that it wasn't a mistake. . . . But we're almost at my place. I must turn here, into that street. It's only a few steps from here. Goodby now, and thank you very much!"

"But is it possible that we'll never meet again? Can we leave it like this?"

"But you said you were only after two words," the girl said, laughing, "and now you . . . However, who can tell, perhaps we'll meet again some day."

"I'll be waiting here tomorrow. Forgive me, I seem to be demanding things already."

"Yes, you're quite impatient, and you *are* almost demanding things——"

"Listen, listen to me," I interrupted her, "and forgive me if I say something wrong. You see, I can't help coming here tomorrow. I'm simply a dreamer who has little real life, and moments like this are so rare in my existence that I must repeat them again and again in my thoughts. You'll stay in my thoughts throughout the night—throughout a whole year. I'll be here without fail

tomorrow, in this very spot, at this very time—and I'll
be happy thinking of what happened today. Already this
spot is dear to me. I have two or three spots like this in
Petersburg. Once I even cried, like you. . . . Well, how
can I know? Perhaps a few minutes ago you too were
crying at the thought . . . Ah, forgive me, I'm forgetting
myself again. . . . I simply meant, perhaps you were once
especially happy here somehow. . . ."

"All right then," the girl said, "I suppose I'll be here
tomorrow night too. At ten. I see I can't stop you, and
I have to come here anyway. But don't think I've made
a date with you. I warn you: I have to be here for my
own reasons. So I may as well tell you now: I won't
mind if you're here too, because that may save me an
unpleasant incident like tonight's. But that's just incidental. To be brief, I'd be very pleased to see you . . .
to say a couple of words to you. But I don't want you
to think badly of me. You mustn't think that I make
dates so easily. I would never have agreed to meet you
again had it not been for . . . No, let it remain a secret!
Only, from now on, let's reach an agreement."

"An agreement? Just name it! I agree to anything in
advance!" I said with ardor. "I assure you, I'll be docile,
respectful . . . you know me."

"It's because I know you that I want you to come
tomorrow," the girl said, laughing. "And I know you
fully. But if you come, it must be on my terms. First—
and please do as I ask, for I'm being completely frank
about it—don't fall in love with me. You mustn't, believe
me. But I'd like us to be friends. Here, let's shake
hands on it. But, remember, no falling in love!"

"I swear!" I shouted, taking her hand.

"Stop, don't swear so readily. I know very well that you
can burst into flame in a second, like gunpowder—forgive
me for saying so. Ah, if you knew . . . I, too—I have
had no one with whom I could exchange a word, of
whom to ask advice. Where could I look for advisors?
Certainly not in the street. But you're an exception. I
know you as if we'd been friends for twenty years. Am
I right in thinking you won't let me down?"

"You'll see. Only I don't know how I'll keep myself alive, waiting for twenty-four hours."

"Sleep deeply. Good night, and remember I've put my trust in you. But you put it so well yourself: Does one really have to give an account of every feeling, even of brotherly compassion? You know, you put it so well that right away I decided to confide in you."

"For heaven's sake, what is it? What?"

"Tomorrow. Let it remain a secret for the moment. It's better for you that way; at least from a distance all this may resemble a romance. I may tell you tomorrow and I may not. I'll talk to you some more; we'll become better acquainted first."

"Well, I—I'll tell you everything about myself tomorrow! But it's as if a miracle were happening to me. Where am I? Oh, God! Tell me, are you glad you didn't get angry with me and chase me away at first, as another woman would have done? It took you two minutes to make me happy once and for all. Yes, happy. Who knows, perhaps you've made me accept myself, maybe you've resolved my doubts. Perhaps such moods come over me that . . . Well, I'll tell you everything tomorrow, you'll know all. . . ."

"Good, I accept; and you'll begin. . . ."

"Agreed."

"Good night."

"Good night."

We parted. I walked around all night. I couldn't make myself go home. I was so happy. . . . Tomorrow!

The Second Night

"So you survived after all," she said to me, laughing as she pressed my hands.

"I've been waiting for two hours. You can't imagine how I got through the day."

"I know, I know. . . . But let's talk business. Do you know why I really came? Certainly not to talk nonsense as we did last night. You know, from now on, we'll act more intelligently. I thought a lot about it last night."

"In what? More intelligently in what? I agree to whatever you say, but to be absolutely sincere, it seems to me I've never been cleverer than now in my whole life."

"Is that so? Well, in the first place, I'd like you to stop squeezing my hands like that, and in the second, I wish to inform you that today I've given quite a bit of thought to you."

"And what conclusions have you reached?"

"Conclusions? Well, I decided to start all over again because I concluded that I still knew nothing about you, that yesterday I acted like a child, a little girl—and I ended up blaming everything on my oversensitive heart. In other words, I ended up praising myself—the way we always end when we begin analyzing ourselves. Now, to correct that mistake, I've decided to find out every little thing about you. And since I have no other way of finding out, you'll just have to supply me with all the information. So, what manner of man are you? Quick, start telling me your story!"

"My story!" I said, becoming alarmed. "What makes you think I have a story to tell in the first place? In fact I don't have any——"

She laughed.

"But how could you live and have no story to tell?"

"So far I've lived without any stories at all. I've lived keeping to myself, as they say, which means that I've been completely alone. Alone, all alone—do you understand what that means?"

"What do you mean alone? You never saw anyone?"

"No, I saw people, of course. But still I was all alone."

"What then? You mean you never spoke to anyone?"

"Strictly speaking, I didn't."

"But who are you, anyway? Tell me! No, wait—I think I can guess. I'll bet you have a grandmother, as I do. Mine is blind, and she doesn't let me go anywhere—I almost forget how to talk. A couple of years ago, when I misbehaved, she felt she couldn't control me any longer, so she called me over to her and pinned my dress to hers with a safety pin. Sometimes we sit like that for days at a time, she knitting a sock despite her blindness and me, at her side, sewing or reading something aloud to her. So, I've been pinned to someone for two years, a rather strange situation, don't you think?"

"Ah, that's really awful! But I don't have a grand-mother."

"You haven't? Then how can you sit home all the time?"

"Listen, shall I tell you who I am?"

"Yes, of course."

"Shall I tell you exactly?"

"Yes, exactly."

"All right then, I'm a queer fish."

"So, you're a queer fish, are you? What sort of queer fish?" the girl said, exploding with laughter, as if she had been holding it in for a whole year. "Ah, you're really great fun to be with! Let's sit down on that bench over there. Nobody ever passes there, so you can tell me your story without being overheard. Go on now, I want to hear it! You can't make me believe you have nothing to tell; you're just being secretive. First of all, what's a queer fish?"

"A queer fish? A queer fish is a ridiculous man, a man unlike others," I said, infected by her childish laughter. "He's a sort of freak. Listen, do you know what a dreamer is, for instance?"

"A dreamer? Well, how could I *not* know what a dreamer is? I suppose I'm one myself. You can't imagine what things go through my head sometimes, as I sit next to my grandmother! I plunge into my dreams, and sometimes, when I really get going, I reach a point where I marry a Chinese prince. . . . Why, sometimes it's so nice to dream!" But then she added unsmilingly: "Well, not really! Especially when there are other things to think of."

"Wonderful! Since you've already been married to a Chinese potentate, you'll probably be able to understand me too. So listen . . . But wait, I don't even know your name."

"It's Nastenka."

"Nastenka. Is that all?"

"Is that all! Nothing satisfies you. You seem to be insatiable."

"Ah no, it satisfies me all right, it thoroughly satisfies me! You're a very nice girl to become Nastenka for me right away!"

"That's better! But go on, tell me about yourself."

"All right, Nastenka, listen to this ridiculous story then."

I installed myself on the bench next to her, assumed a grave, theatrical pose, and began, as if I were reading the script of a monologue.

"There are, my dear Nastenka, in case you don't know, some rather strange corners in Petersburg. It's as if the sun that warms the rest of the city never shines on them, and instead another sun, especially designed for them, supplies them with a different light. In those corners, Nastenka, a life goes on quite unlike the one seething around us, a life that is possible in some far-away dreamland but certainly not here in our over-serious time. That life is a mixture of something out of pure fantasy ardently idealistic, with, alas, something bleak and dull and ordinary, not to say outright vulgar."

"Brrr! . . . What an introduction! What am I to hear next?"

"You'll hear, Nastenka—I think I'll never get tired of calling you Nastenka—that dreamers live in those corners. A dreamer, if you want me to define him, is not a real human being but a sort of intermediary creature. He usually installs himself in some remote corner, shrinking even from the daylight. And once he's installed in that corner of his, he grows into it like a snail or at least like that curious thing which is at the same time an animal and a house—the tortoise. And why do you think he so loves his four bleak walls that are sooty, reek unspeakably of tobacco smoke, and are always daubed over with green paint? Why do you think this ridiculous creature, when some rare acquaintance comes to see him (ultimately he's bound to lose all his acquaintances anyway), looks so embarrassed and taken aback, as if he'd just committed a crime between those very walls, as if he'd been forging money or writing verses to be sent to a magazine with an anonymous letter explaining that the author of the piece is dead and that the sender considers it his sacred duty to see the poem published? Why do you think, Nastenka, that conversation between the two of them is so painful? Why can't the visitor laugh or say something amusing now? In other circumstances he is prone to laugh, say amusing things, and chat about the fair sex and other pleasant matters. Why does that acquaintance, probably a recent one, on his very first visit— for under such circumstances there cannot be more than one visit, as no friend returns for a second time—even assuming that he's exceptionally perceptive, why does he feel so awkward looking at the agonized face of his host, who, after desperate but futile efforts to comfort the hapless man who has blundered into his house on a friendly visit by making the conversation flow, giving it some sparkle, and showing that he too is fully aware of elegant ways and can talk about the fair sex, has become completely lost by then? And why, in the end, does the visitor suddenly remember that he has some terribly urgent matter to attend to, grab his hat and dart off, managing to free his hand from the warm pressure of his host's while the host tries by every means possible to show that he's sorry and is trying to redeem himself? Why does the departing visitor laugh as he closes the door behind him and promise himself never to return to the house of that queer fish, although deep down the queer fish really means well? Why, at the same time, is the visitor unable to refrain from comparing his host's face during his visit to a kitten perfidiously captured, manhandled, and scared by children—which kitten then, completely bewildered, hides under some chair in the darkness, and can't help bristling and spitting while he washes his offended little face with his front paws, and even after that, goes around for a long time looking with apprehension and hostility at the world and even at the titbits from the master's table saved for him by a compassionate housekeeper?"

"Now look here," Nastenka interrupted me. She had been listening with her eyes and her small mouth wide open. "I have no idea why it all happened nor why you should ask me to answer all those ridiculous questions. I'm sure of one thing only: that all this happened to you exactly as you have told me."

"You're right," I said with a straight face.

"Well, why don't you go on? I'm anxious to find out how it all ends."

"You'd like to find out, Nastenka, why the hero of the story—that is, me—was so perturbed and bewildered by the unexpected visit of a friend? You'd like to know why I became so flustered and turned so red when the door of my room was opened, why I was incapable of receiving my visitor properly, and why I was crushed so ignominiously under the weight of my embarrassment?"

"Well, yes, yes, that's just it! And then—you speak beautifully, but couldn't you please speak less beautifully? You sound as though you were reading aloud from a book."

"Nastenka," I said with ponderous gravity, hardly able to control my laughter, "I know I say things too beautifully; I'm terribly sorry, but I don't know how to say them otherwise. At this moment, Nastenka, I feel like the spirit of King Solomon that has been kept imprisoned for a thousand years in a jar under seven seals—and now all the seals have been removed. Now, Nastenka, that we have come together again after our long separation—for the fact is, I've known you a long time. You see, I've been looking for someone, and that's a sure sign that it must have been you I was looking for and that we were destined to meet. Now, thousands of valves have been opened in my head, and I cannot hold back the torrent of words or I'll burst. So, I must ask you to be a good girl and listen to me without interrupting. Otherwise, I won't tell you any more!"

"No, no, please go on! Keep talking, I won't say another word."

"So, I'll go on, Nastenka. There's a certain hour of the day, my dear, of which I'm particularly fond. It is the hour when practically all business, office hours, and all that sort of thing come to an end and people rush off home to dine, to have a little rest; and on their way, they think up ways to spend the evening ahead, the night, or whatever free time is left to them that day. At that hour, the hero of this story—for I hope you'll allow me, Nastenka, to go on telling it in the third person, it's really too embarrassing to say certain things in the first person—at that hour, my hero walks along among the others. But there's a strange, pleased expression on his pale, somewhat crumpled face. He watches with a certain pleasure as the red sunset slowly fades in the cold Petersburg sky. When I say he watches, I am wrong; he takes it in distractedly, like someone too tired to look or preoccupied with some more absorbing matter, so that he has only a passing awareness of what is going on around him. He's pleased, for he's through until tomorrow with business that bores him. He's like a schoolboy let out of school hurrying to play his favorite games or pull his favorite pranks. Look at him from the side, Nastenka, and you'll see right away that his happy feeling has already had a beneficial effect on his weak nerves and over-excitable imagination. Now he is plunged deep in thought. . . . Thinking of dinner? Of the approaching evening? What is he looking at like that? Isn't it at that dignified-looking gentleman who has just bowed so gracefully to the lady driving past in a glittering carriage drawn by fleet-footed steeds? Oh no, Nastenka, he has no time for such trifles now! Now he's rich in his *inner life*. And he has struck it rich suddenly—the last rays of the setting sun restored warmth to his heart and stirred up a whole stream of impressions. Now he hardly notices the street where, before, the tiniest detail would have struck him. The Goddess of Fantasy has already spun a golden web with her divine hand and has started unfolding before his eyes patterns of an imaginary, marvelous life; who knows, perhaps she has picked him up with her divine hand and transported him from the granite sidewalk he is still following to paradise. Just stop him now and ask him which streets he took to get here and where he is now. I'm sure he won't know, so he'll blush and invent some lies just for appearances' sake. That's why he started so violently, almost let out a cry, and looked around apprehensively when a nice old lady stopped him in the middle of the sidewalk and asked him to help her find her way. Now frowning angrily, he resumes his way, hardly aware of the grins on the faces of the people he passes, some of whom even stop to give him a second look; oblivious of the little girl who jumps quickly out of his path, bursts into loud giggles, and gapes indiscreetly at his absent smile and gesticulating arms. And already the same Goddess of Fantasy has managed to catch in flight the old lady who'd lost her way, the curious passers-by, the giggling little girl, the bargemen on their barges tied up along the Fontanka, and everything around the Fontanka Embankment—assuming that our hero happens to be walking there at the time. The goddess then playfully weaves everyone and everything into her canvas like flies in a spider's web. Now the queer fish carries these new acquisitions off to his den. He sits down at his table, and after his dinner is long over, he is still sitting there, reviving only when the dreamy and ever-sad Matryona removes the remains of the meal and brings him his pipe. Then he suddenly realizes that he's already dined, although dinner had completely escaped his attention. The room has grown dark. His heart feels empty and sad. His world of fancy silently and without a crackle collapses around him and evaporates without his being able to remember what he was dreaming about. But some dark feeling presses on his breast, making it heave faster; a new desire tickles and excites his fancy; and, almost without noticing it, he summons an array of new ghosts. The little room is dark. Loneliness and idleness excite the imagination. The gentle flame is lit, and fancies start perking like the water in the coffee pot around which Matryona is fussing in the kitchen. Then fancy becomes like a flame itself, flashing and flaring so that the book picked up at random drops out of the dreamer's hands before he has reached the third page. Now his imagination is again vibrating, and suddenly another world with a different life unrolls its enchanted horizons before his eyes. A new dream—new happiness! A new dose of refined, voluptuous poison! Ah, what's real life to him! To his perverted eye, your life, Nastenka, and mine are unbearably humdrum, slow, and sluggish. He feels we're discontented with our lot and tired of life. And indeed, at first glance, life is bound to appear cold, gloomy, and rather unfriendly. Ah, the poor creatures! the dreamer thinks—and no wonder. Just look at the magical phantoms who so charmingly, subtly, yet somehow casually fall into place in the panoramic, animated picture that shapes itself before him, a picture in which his own exalted person is always in the foreground. Look at all the different adventures he has there —the endless succession of blissful visions! Now perhaps you would like to ask what he's dreaming about. But why ask? He dreams of everything . . . of being a poet, at first unrecognized, later crowned; of friendship with Hoffmann the poet; of St. Bartholomew Night; of playing a heroic part in the storming of Kazan under Ivan the Terrible; of Diana Vernon, Clara Mowbray, Effie Deans, and other heroines of Sir Walter Scott; of Jan Hus facing the tribunal of prelates; of the rising of the dead in *Robert the Devil* (Remember the music? It has a smell of the churchyard about it, don't you think?); of the Battle of Berezina; of a poetry reading at the Countess Vorontsova-Dashkova's; of Danton; of Cleopatra *i suoi amanti*; of Pushkin's "Little House in Kolomna"; of having a little house of his own and being there on a wintry evening with his beloved listening to him with her eyes and mouth wide open, just as you're listening to me now, my dearest angel. . . .

"No, Nastenka, what can this voluptuous idler find in the life so dear to people like you and me? He thinks it a poor life, without realizing that for him too there may come a sad hour when, for a single day of that miserable life, he would give away all his years of fancy. And he would exchange his dreams neither for happiness, nor joy; at that grim hour of regret and unrelieved gloom he won't even care to choose. But until that perilous time comes, the dreamer can have no desires, for he has everything; he is above desire, he is surfeited, he is himself the artist creating his life at every hour, guided only by his own inspiration.

"And how effortlessly, how naturally the dreamer's world of fantasy springs up! It looks so real and not at all like a mirage! In fact, sometimes he almost believes that his dream life is no figment of the imagination, no self-deception, no delusion, but something real, actual, existing.

"Now tell me, Nastenka, why does he so often feel out of breath at those moments? Tell me, by what magic, by what uncanny chance, does his pulse quicken, do tears gush from his eyes and his pale cheeks flush, as his whole being fills with inexpressible delight? Why do sleepless nights flash by in a second, in inexhaustible gaiety and happiness? Then, when the rosy rays of dawn appear in the window and the uncertain light of our Petersburg morning fills the gloomy room, our exhausted dreamer throws himself on his bed and falls asleep with an aching feeling of rapture.

"Yes, Nastenka, he deceives himself and winds up by believing that he is moved by true, live passion, that there is substance—flesh and blood—to his fancies! And it is quite a deception! Just look at him and see for yourself. Can you believe, looking at him, Nastenka, that he doesn't even know the woman he loved so passionately in his sultry flights of fancy? Can you believe that he has only seen her in irresistibly voluptuous mirages and that he simply dreamed that passion? Is it really possible that they have never walked hand in hand during so many years, spurning the rest of the universe, merging their own two worlds and lives? Is it possible that at the late hour when they had to part, she didn't really lay her head, sobbing and miserable, on his chest, not hearing the wind that snatched tears from her black eyelashes? Would you believe it was all nothing but a dream—the wild, neglected garden with its path overgrown with moss, so lonely and desolate, along which they used to walk together so often, hoping, suffering, loving so tenderly and for so long? And that there was no strange, ancestral home where she had lived for so many dull, lonely years with her stern old husband, always silent and irritable, who frightened them, timid children that they were, children sadly and shyly hiding their love from each other? Ah, how afraid they were, how they languished, how pure and innocent was their love, and how wicked— it goes without saying, Nastenka—were the people around them! And did he never meet her later, far away from their native shore, under an alien, southern sky, in a divine, eternal city, at a glamorous ball, to the thunder of music, the whole affair taking place in a *palazzo* (it must be a *palazzo*) drowned in a sea of lights? . . . They are on a terrace wreathed in myrtle and roses . . . she recognizes him, tears off her mask and, whispering, "I am free now!" flings herself into his arms, trembling with rapture. . . . They hold each other tight, and in a moment they've forgotten their unhappiness, their separation, all their sufferings, the forbidding house, the old man, the bleak garden in their remote homeland, the bench where he kissed her for the last time, holding her in his desperate embrace from which she had to tear herself, leaving him with his suffering. . . .

"Ah, Nastenka, you must agree that anyone would feel awkward and embarrassed and would turn red like a boy who has just stuffed into his pocket an apple he's stolen from the next-door garden if some long-legged, healthy joker, an uninvited friend of his, opened his door and announced, as if nothing had happened: 'Hi chum! What do you know, I've just arrived from Pavlovsk!'

"It's unbearable. In dreamland the old count is dead and an inconceivable happiness is mine, and then this fellow arrives from Pavlovsk!"

My dramatic exclamations over, I fell dramatically silent. I remember that I wanted to force myself to laugh, for I felt that some hostile imp had installed himself inside me and was squeezing my throat, making my chin tremble and my eyes grow damp. I expected Nastenka, who had been listening with her intelligent, wide-open eyes fixed on me, to burst out in uncontrollable, childish laughter at any second, and I was already regretting having gone too far and told her things which had been weighing on my heart for a long time, things about which I could talk as smoothly as a book because I had long ago pronounced judgment on myself and couldn't help reading it out now and confessing without expecting to be understood. But to my great surprise, she remained silent for a while, then, pressing my hand slightly, asked me with a sort of timid understanding:

"Is that really how you've lived all this time?"

"All the time, Nastenka, and it looks as if I'll go on like that to the end."

"No," she said, looking worried, "that won't happen. That would be like me spending my whole life at my grandmother's side. Listen, I tell you it's not right to live like that."

"Ah, don't I know it, Nastenka!" I exclaimed, unable to control my emotions any longer. "At this moment, I see more clearly than ever before that I've wasted my best years. And the realization hurts me even more because it was God who sent you to me, my lovely angel, to make me see it. As I sit here next to you, it is already painful to think of the future, because there's nothing in it but a lonely, stale, useless existence. What could I dream of, now that I've been so happy with you in real life? Oh, bless you, my dearest girl, for not spurning me at first sight, for enabling me to say that I've lived at least two evenings in the course of my existence!"

"Ah no, no!" Nastenka said with emotion, tears sparkling in her eyes. "No, no more of that life! We shan't part like this! What's two evenings?"

"Ah, Nastenka, Nastenka! Do you realize that you have reconciled me with myself for a long time to come? Do you realize that now I'll never think quite as badly of myself as I sometimes have in the past? Do you know that perhaps I won't be unhappy any more over having committed a crime or a sin in my life, because now I realize that my whole life was nothing but a crime and a sin in itself? And don't imagine, please, that I'm exaggerating, Nastenka, for there are moments when I'm overcome by such anguish and despair that . . . In those moments, I feel that I'll never have a true life because I feel sure I've entirely lost touch with reality; because I feel damned; because, in the middle of my fancy-filled nights, I have moments of lucidity that are unbearable! In the meantime, I hear the din of the human crowd around me and see how people who are awake live, and I realize that their lives are not made to measure, that they don't shatter like dreams, like visions, that their lives are perpetually renewed, every hour in them different from the one before, whereas the timid daydream is horribly monotonous, a slave to the shadows, to ideas, to the first cloud that suddenly hides the sun and squeezes in anguish the heart of a true inhabitant of Petersburg who must have his sunshine—for what fancy is there that can do without sunshine? In the end, you feel that your much-vaunted, inexhaustible fantasy is growing tired, debilitated, exhausted, because you're bound to grow out of your old ideals; they're smashed to splinters and turn to dust, and if you have no other life, you have no choice but to keep rebuilding your dreams from the splinters and dust. But the heart longs for something different! And it is vain to dig in the ashes of your old fancies, trying to find even a tiny spark to fan into a new flame that will warm the chilled heart and bring back to life everything that can send the blood rushing wildly through the body, fill the eyes with tears— everything that can delude you so well!

"And shall I tell you, Nastenka, how far I've gone? Would you believe that I have taken to celebrating the anniversaries of my sensations, the anniversary of something that was delightful at one time, of something that actually never occurred. I am reduced to celebrating anniversaries because I no longer have anything with which to replace even those silly, flimsy dreams. For dreams, Nastenka, have to be renewed too. I like revisiting, at certain times, spots where I was once happy; I like to shape the present in the image of the irretrievable past. So I often roam like a sad, gloomy shadow, without need or aim, along Petersburg's streets and alleys. And what memories come to me! I may remember, for instance, that exactly one year ago, at this very hour, in this very street, I was walking along this very sidewalk, just as gloomy and lonely as now. And I may remember that although my dreams were sad and life was painful, somehow it was not as agonizing as it has become now; the black forebodings that have since taken hold of me weren't there yet; nor was there the gnawing, dreary feeling of guilt that now torments me day and night, never leaving me a moment's peace. And so I ask myself: 'Where are your dreams?' And I shake my head and mutter: 'How the years go by!' And I ask myself again: 'What have you done with those years? Where have you buried your best moments? Have you really lived? Look,' I say to myself, 'how cold it is becoming all over the world!' And more years will pass and behind them will creep grim isolation. Tottering senility will come hobbling, leaning on a crutch, and behind these will come unrelieved boredom and despair. The world of fancies will fade, dreams will wilt and die and fall like autumn leaves from the trees. . . . Ah, Nastenka, won't it be sad to be left alone, all, all alone, without even having anything to regret—nothing, but nothing; for everything I've lost is nothing but a stupid, round zero, nothing but a flimsy fancy?"

"Stop it, stop it. . . ." Nastenka brushed away a little tear. "It's all over now. Now there'll be the two of us. Now, whatever happens, we'll never part again. Listen, I'm only an ordinary girl. I've studied very little, although my grandmother did hire a teacher for me. But, believe me, I understand everything you've said because I felt the same way when Grandma pinned me to her dress. Of course, I can't express it as well as you because of my lack of education," she remarked shyly, apparently feeling that she ought to pay tribute to my pathetic monologue and high-flown style. "But I'm very glad that you've told me everything so frankly. Now I know you completely. And now I want to tell you my story, without holding anything back, then perhaps you'll give me your advice.

You are so intelligent—I want you to promise to give me advice."

"Ah, Nastenka, I've never been much of an advisor, especially an intelligent advisor, but since we're going to be together, I feel that my advice will be terribly clever and that each of us will have many, many intelligent suggestions to offer the other. Well, then, pretty Nastenka, let's see what advice I can give you. Come, tell me everything—I'm so happy, cheerful, daring, and clever that I'm sure I won't have to search for words."

"No!" Nastenka laughed. "It isn't clever advice I'm after, it's brotherly understanding from someone who, as it were, has loved me all my life."

"That suits me, Nastenka, suits me fine! As to loving, had I loved you for twenty years, I'm sure I couldn't possibly love you more than I do now."

"Give me your hand," Nastenka said.

I gave it to her.

"Here goes," she said.

"You already know half my story. You know I have an old grandmother——"

"If the other half is as short as the one I know . . ." I interjected, laughing.

"No, just keep quiet and listen. Don't interrupt me; it puts me off. Just listen.

"I have an old grandmother. I've lived with her ever since I was a very little girl, because my parents are dead. Grandma apparently was much better off before, for she keeps remembering better days. It was she who taught me French and later hired a teacher for me. I stopped taking lessons when I was fifteen—I'm seventeen now. When I was fifteen, I did something naughty. I won't go into what I did exactly, except to say that it wasn't much. Still, Grandma called me over to her that morning and said that since she was blind she couldn't very well watch me. Then she took a safety pin and pinned my dress to hers, saying that we were going to stay sitting like that forever, unless, of course, my behavior improved. Well, to make it short, at first it was impossible for me to move away from her; I had to

work, study, read—everything—sitting by my grandmother's side. Once I tried to trick her by persuading our
maid Fyokla to sit in for me. Grandma had fallen asleep
in her armchair. Fyokla is deaf, you see, and she took
my place while I ran out to the house of a girl, a friend
of mine who lived nearby. But it ended badly. Grandma
woke up and asked something, assuming that it was me.
Fyokla saw Grandma was trying to say something but,
of course, she couldn't hear what it was. So, not knowing
what else to do, she unfastened the pin and ran away."

This memory made Nastenka laugh so much that she
had to interrupt herself. I laughed too, but as soon as she
realized I was laughing, she stopped short and said:

"Now look here, you mustn't laugh at Grandma! I
laugh because I can't help it—she really is so funny. But
then, you see, I'm fond of her at the same time. Anyway,
I was in real trouble. She pinned me to her again, and I
wasn't even allowed to move.

"Ah, I forgot to tell you that my grandma owns the
house we live in. It's just a tiny wooden house with three
windows, and almost as old as she is. It also has an attic
room, and a new lodger came to live in the attic——"

"Therefore, I assume that there was a lodger before
him," I remarked.

"Of course there was—and he could keep quiet much
better than you can," Nastenka said. "True, he had difficulty moving his tongue at all, for he was a very, very
old man, quite mute, blind, and lame; in the end, living
became too much for him and he just died. So a new
lodger took his place, for we can't afford not to have a
lodger. That and Grandma's pension make up our entire
income. Now, the new lodger happened to be a young
man. He came from out of town. When Grandma told
him what the rent was, he didn't bargain, so she took
him and then asked me:

" 'Tell me, Nastenka, the new lodger is a young man,
isn't he?'

"I couldn't lie to her, so I said that although he wasn't
old, he wasn't so young either.

" 'Is he good-looking?' she asked me then.

"Again I didn't want to lie.

" 'Yes, Grandma, he's quite good-looking.'

" 'Ah, that's really too bad!' Grandma said, 'because I'm asking you all these questions so you won't keep staring at him. Ah, what times we live in,' she added. 'Think of it—just an insignificant lodger and he turns out to be handsome, too. Ah, what're we all coming to? You never saw such things happening in the good old days.'

"According to Grandma, everything was just wonderful in the good old days—she was younger in those days, and the sun shone brighter and was warmer, and milk didn't go bad as it does now! And while she goes on and on like that, I sit in silence and think to myself: 'It looks as if Grandma were trying to give me ideas, asking whether the lodger is handsome or not.' And then I got absorbed in counting the stitches in my knitting, and the lodger completely vanished from my mind.

"Then one morning the lodger came to inquire when they were going to paper his room as he'd been promised. And, Grandma being a great hand at chatting, they got into a conversation in no time, then she says to me: 'Nastenka, run and bring me the abacus from my bedroom.' I don't know why, but that made me turn red. I forgot all about the safety pin and jumped up to scamper into the other room. The movement yanked the pin and Grandma's armchair came rolling along on its casters. I don't know how I could have forgotten about that safety pin and neglected to unfasten it discreetly! And now, realizing that the lodger had found out about it, I stopped dead where I was and burst into tears. I felt so hopelessly ashamed and humiliated at that moment that I thought I'd never be able to face the world again.

" 'What are you waiting for?' Grandma kept shouting at me, but that only made me cry worse. And the lodger, seeing how embarrassed I was, muttered some excuse and rushed off.

"After that day, I felt like dying whenever I heard the slightest noise in the passage. The lodger's coming, I said to myself each time, and I'd quietly unfasten the pin. But it was never him.

"A couple of weeks passed, and the lodger sent us a note by Fyokla saying he had a lot of books, some French ones among them, and perhaps Grandmother would like him to send us some so that I might read to her to pass the time? Grandmother accepted gratefully after first inquiring whether they were decent, proper books. 'Because if they aren't,' she told me, 'I won't allow you to read them, for I don't want you to learn any wicked things from them, Nastenka.'

" 'But what sort of wicked things,' I asked her, 'could I learn from them, Grandma?'

" 'Well,' she said, 'they may describe young men seducing well-brought-up young girls, abducting them from their parents' homes under the pretext of wishing to marry them, then abandoning them to their fate and perdition. I have read many books like that,' Grandma told me, 'and they describe that sort of thing so well and so vividly that sometimes I used to read them on the sly throughout the night and into the morning. So mind, Nastenka,' she added, 'you stay away from books like that. Now what are the books he's sent us called?'

" 'They're all novels, Grandma, novels by Sir Walter Scott.'

" 'Walter Scott, you say? You'd better make sure there's no trick. See that he hasn't tried to slip some note in along with them, some love letter.'

" 'No, Grandma, there's no note . . . nothing.'

" 'Yes, but we'd better watch out!'

"So we started reading Walter Scott, and within a month or so, we were through almost half of it. Later he sent us some more books, including Pushkin; finally, I couldn't imagine how I could live without books, and I stopped dreaming about marrying that Chinese prince. . . .

"That was the situation when one day I bumped into our lodger on the stairs as I was going on some errand for Grandma. He stepped back, and I saw he'd turned red. But he laughed, said hello, inquired after Grandmother's health, and asked me:

" 'Have you read the books?'

" 'I have.'

" 'And which did you like best?'

" '*Ivanhoe,*' I said, 'and, of course, Pushkin.'

"And that was all that happened that time.

"A week later we again met on the stairs. This time Grandma hadn't sent me. I was going somewhere on an errand of my own. It was around two in the afternoon, and that happened to be the time at which the lodger usually came home.

" 'Hello,' he said.

" 'Hello,' I answered.

" 'Tell me,' he said, 'don't you get bored sitting all day with your grandmother like that?'

"Now when he asked that, I don't know why, but I became very embarrassed, and flushed. I felt humiliated because apparently even strangers were beginning to inquire about what was going on. I decided not to answer, just to turn away and leave, but I didn't have the strength.

" 'Please,' he said, 'forgive me for speaking to you like that. I have great respect for you, and believe me, your well-being means more to me even than it does to your grandmother. Don't you know any girls whom you could visit?'

"I explained to him that I had only one friend, called Mashenka, and that she'd moved to Pskov with her family, and I had no one left.

" 'Tell me,' he asked then, 'what would you say if I asked you to come to the theater with me?'

" 'The theater? But what about my grandmother?'

" 'Couldn't you manage it without her finding out?'

" 'No,' I said, 'I don't want to deceive my grandmother. Good-by.'

" 'Good-by then.'

"And that was all he said.

"But, after dinner, he came down to our rooms, sat down, and had a long talk with Grandma. He asked her whether she ever went out and whether she had any friends, then suddenly slipped in, as if in passing:

" 'I have tickets, a loge in fact, for tonight's performance of *The Barber of Seville*. Some friends of mine got them, but couldn't make it tonight, so I have the tickets——'

" '*The Barber of Seville*!' Grandmother exclaimed. 'Why, it must be the same *Barber* they used to put on in the good old days!'

" 'Yes, ma'am,' the lodger said, 'the very same!'

"And as he said that he gave me a look that made me go crimson and set my heart skipping in expectation.

" 'That's one opera that I really know,' Grandmother said. 'In fact, in my younger days, I myself sang Rosina in an amateur dramatic group.'

" 'Wouldn't you like to come with me tonight? I think it'd be a shame to waste the tickets.'

" 'Well, I don't see why we shouldn't go,' Grandma decided, 'especially as my Nastenka here has never been to the theater.'

"Ah, what a joy it was! We immediately started preparing, got dressed, and drove over to the Opera. Grandma, although she couldn't see a thing, still wanted to listen to the music. And, deep down, she was a kind old thing and very pleased that I should have such fun—we would never have gone anywhere without this opportunity.

"I won't describe my impressions of *The Barber of Seville*, but I'll tell you that all that evening the lodger kept looking at me so nicely and talking to me so eloquently that I realized that, by asking me earlier whether I'd come to the theater with him in secret, he'd only wanted to test me. Ah, it was such joy! So I went to bed incredibly proud and happy, and my heart beat so hard that I worked up a slight fever and raved about *The Barber of Seville* the rest of the night.

"I imagined, after that, that he'd come to see us often. But, on the contrary, he hardly ever came. He might come in once or twice a month, and only to invite us to the theater. In fact, we went twice more with him, I believe. But I was no longer happy on those occasions. I thought he was just sorry for me leading that sad life with my grandmother and that there was nothing else to it on his part. And, as time went by, strange moods started coming over me. I was unable to stay quiet, unable to take in what I was reading, unable to concentrate on my work; sometimes I burst out laughing just to irritate Grandmother, and sometimes I suddenly dissolved into tears. I grew very thin and was almost seriously ill. The opera season was over, and the lodger stopped coming at all. And when he did meet me—always on the stairs, of course—he bowed so unsmilingly that I felt sure he didn't even wish to talk to me; and after he had already left the house, I would still be standing in the middle of the stairs, red as a cherry, for when I saw him, the blood never failed to rush to my head.

"Now, let me tell the end of my story. Just a year ago, in May, the lodger came to tell my grandmother that his business in Petersburg was over and that he must now move to Moscow. When I heard that, I turned as pale as the tablecloth and went all limp in my chair. Grandma never noticed anything; the lodger just said goodnight and left.

"What was I to do? I racked my brains in despair, and finally, I decided. The day before he was to leave I decided to take a desperate step in the evening, after Grandma had gone to bed. And I did. I picked out some dresses and the necessary underwear, made a bundle out of them and, carrying it, went, half alive, half dead, upstairs to the lodger's room. Walking up that flight of stairs seemed to take a whole hour.

"When I opened his door, he turned his head and, seeing me, let out a cry. He must have taken me for a ghost, for I had turned white, and my legs were hardly able to carry me. He hurried to get me some water. My heart was beating so hard it hurt, and my head ached, and everything inside it went all blurry.

"When I came to, the first thing I did was put my bundle on his bed, sit down next to it myself, and let my tears pour in two rivers. I believe he understood everything right away. He stood there looking at me, and his expression was so wretched that my heart was torn by a terrible anguish.

" 'Nastenka,' he said at last, 'I want you to understand. I can do nothing. I'm poor; I haven't a thing to my name. I don't even have a decent job. So what would we live on if I married you?'

"We discussed it for a long time, in the end, I lost all control over myself and declared that I could no longer live with my grandmother, that I'd run away, that I'd had enough of being fastened to her with a safety pin, and that, whatever he might say, I was going to Moscow with him because I couldn't live without him. Shame, love, pride—everything—was seething within me at the same time, and fearing that he might refuse me, I collapsed on the bed almost in convulsions.

"He sat in complete silence for a few moments, then he got up and took my hand.

" 'Listen, my nice little Nastenka,' he said, and I saw that there were tears in his eyes, too. 'I swear to you that I'm certain I'd be happy with you if I were ever in a position to marry you. Listen: I have to go to Moscow, and I'll be staying there for exactly a year. I must go there to take care of my business. When I come back, if you still love me, I swear we'll be happy. But now I have no right to promise you anything. I'll say too, however, that if I can't make it in one year, I'll still come and find you later—that is, if you don't prefer someone else by then, because I cannot, I have no right to bind you to me by promises.'

"The next day he was gone. We'd agreed not to say a word to Grandma. He'd insisted upon that. Well, that's about all there is to my story. The year has gone by, and he's come back. Indeed, he's been here for three days already, and—and——"

"And what?" I cried, unable to stand it any longer.

"He hasn't come to see me," Nastenka said, and I felt that she was making a great effort, "he hasn't given a sign of life——"

She cut herself short, remained silent for a few seconds, then covering her face with her hands, burst into sobs that tore at my heart.

I hadn't expected such an ending.

"Nastenka," I ventured imploringly, "please, please don't cry. Maybe he simply hasn't come yet. . . ."

"No, no, he's here, he's here!" Nastenka cried. "I know it! We agreed that evening before he left. . . . After we'd said all the things I've already told you, we came out to take a walk on this embankment. It was ten o'clock. We sat down on the bench; I'd stopped crying. I loved the things he was saying to me. . . . He told me that as soon as he was back in town, if I still wanted him, we'd tell everything to Grandma. And now he's back in town—I know it for sure—but he still hasn't come to see me. . . ."

And she burst into tears again.

"But, my God, is there really nothing I can do for you?" I leaped up from the bench in complete despair. "Tell me, Nastenka, couldn't I go and see him or something?"

"Do you think that's possible?" she said, suddenly raising her head.

"No, of course not," I said, coming back to my senses. "You know what you should do? Write him a letter."

"No, I can't; that's impossible too," she said firmly, but this time she lowered her eyes.

"Why is it impossible? Why?" I insisted. "Do you know what letter you ought to write, Nastenka? There are letters and letters, you know. So please trust my judgment; I won't give you bad advice. Everything will turn out fine, I'm sure. You took the initiative in the first place, so why not now?"

"Impossible, impossible, it would look as if I were throwing myself at him——"

"But no, you're wrong, dear little Nastenka!" I interrupted her without trying to hide my smile. "You have the right to demand. He promised, after all, didn't he? And, from what I understand, he's an honest, considerate man, and I'm sure there's nothing dishonorable in his behavior." I continued, admiring the logic of my own reasoning and arguments more and more: "What did he do? He tied himself down by a promise. He declared that if he married anyone it would be you, while leaving you completely free to refuse him if your feelings changed. So it is quite natural that you make the first move. It's your right, your advantage over him, and you should do it even if, for instance, you decide to release him from his word."

"Tell me, how would you write to him?"

"What?"

"The letter, of course."

"Well, I'd start like this: 'Dear Sir——' "

"Must I really address him 'dear sir'?"

"Yes, it's indispensable. But after all, I think——"

"Well, go on!"

"I'd write like this:

" 'Dear Sir, Forgive me——' No, no apologies are necessary. The letter justifies itself. Write simply:

" 'I thought I would write to you first. Please forgive my impatience, but for a whole year I have lived on hope. Am I to blame, then, if I cannot stand even one day of doubt? Now that you are back in town, and may have had a change of heart, let me assure you by this letter that I have nothing to reproach you for, for I cannot command your love. So I will consider it simply as my fate.

" 'You are a decent and honorable man, and I am sure you will not laugh or be angry reading these impatient lines. You will keep in mind that they are written by a poor, lonely girl who has no one to advise her and who never could control her own heart. But forgive me for entertaining even a fleeting suspicion that you could hurt, even in thought, the girl who has loved you so much and who still loves you.' "

"Yes, yes, that's exactly what I had in mind!"

Nastenka was very enthusiastic and her eyes sparkled with joy.

"Ah, you have resolved my doubts! I think God Himself sent you to me! Thank you, thank you, thank you!"

"Thank me for what? For being sent by God?"

It was a delight to look at her pretty face, so happy now.

"Yes, thank you for being sent to me to begin with."

"Ah, Nastenka, since we feel grateful sometimes to people just for living with us, let me thank you for having met you, for making it possible for me to remember you as long as I live."

"Well, that will do for now. Listen, we agreed that when he came back, he'd let me know by leaving a letter for me with some friends of mine, nice, simple people who know nothing about this. Or, if he couldn't leave the letter, he'd come here to this bench, at ten in the evening, on the very day he returned to Petersburg. Now I know he's in town, but he hasn't kept our date or written the letter. I cannot possibly leave my grandmother in the morning, so couldn't you, please, take my letter to those friends I mentioned? They'll see that he gets it. And if there's an answer, bring it to me here tomorrow evening at ten."

"But what about the letter? You have to write it first; at best, you might get a reply the day after tomorrow."

"The letter . . ." Nastenka said, somewhat at a loss, "the letter . . . but . . ."

She didn't finish. She suddenly turned her face away from me, growing red as a red rose, and I felt her slipping a letter into my hand that, it turned out, had already been written and sealed. Something light, graceful, and familiar flashed through my mind.

"R-r-o-si-i-na . . ." I intoned.

"Rosina!" we sang together, and I was so moved and delighted that I felt terribly like putting my arms around her. She was blushing deeply and laughing, and tiny glistening tears hung on her black eyelashes.

"Enough, enough. Good-by now, good night!" she rattled. "You have the letter and the address. Good night, see you tomorrow!"

She pressed both my hands hard, nodded, and darted off. I remained standing there for a long time, following her with my eyes.

"See you tomorrow . . . tomorrow . . ." flashed in my head as she disappeared around a corner.

The Third Night

It has been a sad, drizzly day, without relief—just like my future senility. I am oppressed by strange thoughts and dark sensations; throngs of vague questions obsess me, but I have neither the strength nor the desire to cope with them. No, I cannot cope with it all!

We won't meet tonight. Last night, as we parted, clouds overcast the sky and a mist was rising. "Tomorrow will be a miserable day," I said. She didn't answer. She didn't want to shed doubt on a day that shone before her bright and sunny. She didn't want to cast a single cloud over it.

"If it rains tomorrow," she said, "I won't come."

I didn't think she'd notice that it was raining, but she must have, for she didn't come.

Last night was our third meeting, our third white night. . . .

Yes, joy and happiness do make a person beautiful. His heart overflows with love, and he seems to try to pour that love into the heart of a fellow creature. He wants everything to laugh and to sparkle. And his joy is so contagious! There was so much tenderness, so much friendliness, for me in her heart last night. She was so full of solicitude for me and tried so hard to make me feel happy. Ah, a happy woman is always so full of seductive charm, but I . . . I took it at its face value; I imagined that . . .

But how could I imagine anything of the sort. How could I be so blind, since I knew that all that had already been taken by someone else, that none of it could be for me; that even her niceness, her solicitude, her love—yes, her love for me—was nothing but happiness caused by a forthcoming meeting with another man, a wish on her part to impart a bit of that happiness to me. And when he didn't turn up, when we'd waited in vain, she frowned, lost her composure, looked afraid. Her movements and her words were no longer light or playful or gay. And, strangely, she doubled the attentions she showered on me, as if she wanted instinctively to give me something she was longing for herself, something she feared she wouldn't get. Nastenka had become so timid and fearful that I believe she grasped finally that I was in love with her and took pity on my poor love, for our own unhappiness makes us more sensitive to the unhappiness of others. When someone is unhappy, his sensitivity is not scattered; it becomes tense and concentrated.

I had come to meet her tense with emotion, hardly able to wait for the moment of meeting. I never expected to feel what I felt, nor that it would end the way it did. She was beaming. She expected an answer from him. The answer was to be himself; he would come running in answer to her call. She'd come a whole hour before me. At first, every word made her burst into happy laughter.

"Do you know why I'm so happy tonight?" she said. "Why I'm so pleased to see you? Why I like you so much?"

"Yes?" I said, beginning to shiver.

"I like you so much because you haven't fallen in love with me. Someone else in your position might have started pestering me, become full of self-pity, moaned—but not you, you're so nice!"

She suddenly pressed my hand so hard that I started and almost cried out. She laughed.

"Ah, you're such a wonderful friend," she said a moment later, seriously this time. "Yes, God sent you to me, really, I mean it. I can't imagine what would have become of me without you. You're so selfless, you've been so nice to me! When I'm married, we'll see a lot of each other, we'll be closer than brother and sister. I'll love you almost as much as I love him. . . ."

Somehow I felt awfully sad, yet something resembling laughter stirred somewhere deep down inside me.

"You're overwrought," I said. "You're afraid he won't come."

"Whatever are you talking about? If I weren't so

happy, your remarks and your lack of trust in me would make me cry. But it makes me think, after all . . . But I'll think later; in the meantime, I admit you're right. Yes, I'm not myself now, I'm all expectation, I feel a little too light. . . . But let's leave this conversation about feelings——"

At that second we heard steps and we saw a figure moving through the darkness. It was coming toward us. We both began to tremble. She just managed to suppress a cry. I let go of her hand and moved away discreetly. But it wasn't him.

"What are you afraid of? Why did you let go my hand?" She thrust her hand back into mine. "Well, what do you say, shall we meet him together? I want him to see how much we love each other."

"How much we love each other?" I repeated.

"Ah, Nastenka," I thought, "those words mean so many things! That sort of love sometimes freezes a heart and makes life seem unbearable. Your hand is cold—mine is burning. You're blind. There certainly are times when happy people are unbearable—but I could never be angry with you!"

But finally I couldn't stand it.

"Listen, Nastenka," I said tensely, "to how I got through this day."

"What? Tell me! Why haven't you said anything about it till now?"

"First I went to carry out all your errands. I went to see your friends, left your letter there, then . . . then I went back home and turned in."

"And that's all?" She laughed.

"Almost all . . ."

I made a great effort to control the idiotic tears that otherwise would have spurted from my eyes.

"Then I woke up. About an hour before I was to meet you. But I felt I hadn't slept at all. I didn't know what was happening to me. It was as if time had stopped and one sensation, one feeling would remain in me from then on; as if one minute was going to stretch out into eternity; as if life would stop and stand still for me. I was going to tell you all this as soon as we met. When I woke up, I was under the impression that some sweet melody, heard somewhere long ago and since forgotten, had come back to me now, that for all these years, I'd been searching for it, longing for it, but only now——"

"My God, what's this all about?" Nastenka interrupted me. "I don't understand a thing you're saying."

"I was trying, Nastenka, to make you understand the strange feeling——" I started in a pitiful voice in which there was still a note of hope, even if a very faint one.

"Stop it! That's enough, stop it," she repeated quickly.

It hadn't taken her long to guess, the sly girl! She suddenly became very talkative, gay, and full of jokes. Laughing, she took my arm, trying to make me laugh, too. Every awkward, embarrassed word of mine set off such long peals of silvery laughter that I was on the point of losing my temper. Then she became flirtatious.

"You see," she began, "I'm a bit offended with you for not falling in love with me. People don't always make sense, remember! But still, Mr. Unmovable, you can't avoid complimenting me for being so straightforward. Why, I tell you everything, however inane, that crosses my mind."

"Wait, I believe that's eleven striking," I said. The even booming had started in a distant clocktower. She stopped laughing, and counted.

"Yes, eleven," she said in a weak, hesitant voice.

I was sorry that I had alarmed her and had made her count the strokes. I cursed myself for my spitefulness. I felt miserable for her, and didn't know how to make up for my nastiness. I tried to cheer her up, to find good reasons for his failure to turn up, to argue, prove, plead. She was, of course, very easy to convince on that subject, only too delighted to clutch at any excuse for him that I could think up.

"It's really funny," I was saying heatedly, admiring the persuasive power of my own arguments, "your assurance that he'd be here led me to accept it as a fact and even lose my sense of time. Actually, he couldn't possibly have made it. Just think, he's hardly had time to receive the letter. Now suppose he couldn't come tonight and wrote a note to that effect. It couldn't get to your friends' before tomorrow, could it? I'll go and see first thing tomorrow morning and let you know right away. Now there are hundreds of other possibilities; for instance, he may not have been at home when the letter arrived, and maybe he hasn't read it to this very moment. . . . Anything could've happened."

"Yes, of course," Nastenka said, "that hadn't even occurred to me. Of course—anything could have happened."

Her tone was extremely cooperative, but I detected a jarring, discordant note in it, an echo of thoughts of a different kind.

"Here's what we'll do," she said. "You'll go there tomorrow as early as you can, and if there's something, you'll let me know immediately. You know where I live, of course." And she repeated her address.

Then she became breathtakingly tender and at the same time shy. . . . I thought she was attentively following what I was saying, but when I asked her some question, she said nothing, became embarrassed, and turned her head away from me. I looked into her eyes. That was it—she was crying.

"You mustn't, you mustn't! Ah, you're behaving like a child. You're just a baby!"

She tried to smile to control herself, but her chin was trembling and her bosom heaving.

"I've been thinking of you," she said after a moment's silence. "You've been so kind that I'd have to be made of stone not to be touched. And, you know, I compared the two of you and decided that you are the better of the two, although I love him more."

I didn't answer. She seemed to expect me to say something.

"Of course, I may still not understand him or know him perfectly," she said. "Come to think of it, I've always been afraid of him. He's always been so grave, so proud in a way. Of course, I know that it's only

the way he looks, that there's more tenderness in his
heart than in my own. . . . I remember how he looked at
me when—remember?—I came to his room with that
bundle. Still, I look up to him with respect, which may
mean we aren't equals, don't you think?"

"No, Nastenka, no, it simply means that you love him
more than anything in the world, and much more than
yourself."

"All right, let's assume you're right," naïve Nastenka
replied. "But shall I tell you what has just occurred to me?
All right. Only I won't talk about myself now but speak
in general, for this thought has recurred to me several
times. Tell me, why aren't we all like brothers? Why does
even the best person hold back something from another?
Why not say directly what we feel if we know that what
we entrust won't be scattered to the winds? As it is,
everyone looks much tougher than he really is, as if he
felt it'd be an insult to his feelings if he expressed them
too readily——"

"Ah, that's it exactly, Nastenka," I interrupted her,
doing more violence than ever to my own feelings, "and
it's due to many causes——"

"No, no!" she said heatedly. "Take you, for instance—
you're not like the rest. I don't quite know how to explain it . . . but I feel . . . yes, even now, you are
sacrificing something for my sake." She shyly cast a side-
long glance at me. "Forgive me for speaking to you like
this, but I'm a simple girl who hasn't seen much in this
world yet, and there are times when I can't talk." Her
voice trembled with some hidden emotion and, at the
same time, she tried to smile. "All I wanted to tell you
was that I'm grateful, that I too—I feel all that— Ah, may
God reward you with happiness! But what you told me
before about that dreamer of yours, that's untrue. I
mean, it has absolutely nothing to do with you. You're
recovering now; you're really a completely different person from the one you tried to pass yourself off as. If
you ever fall in love, may you be happy with her! And
I don't have to wish her anything, for I know she'll be

happy with you. I know it, for I'm a woman myself, and you must believe me. . . ."

She fell silent and squeezed my hand. I couldn't utter a word. Several minutes went by.

"Well, it doesn't look as though he's coming tonight," she said at last, lifting her head. "It's getting quite late."

"He'll be here tomorrow," I said in a firm, convincing voice.

"Yes," she said, growing suddenly cheerful, "I can see now that he'll come tomorrow. So good night, see you tomorrow. If it rains, I may not come. But the night after that I'll be here, without fail, whatever happens. You must be here too; I want to see you and tell you everything."

When we were saying good-by, she gave me her hand, looked at me brightly, and said:

"We'll always be together now, won't we?"

Oh, Nastenka, Nastenka! if you had any idea how lonely I feel!

When it struck nine I couldn't stand it in my room. I dressed and went out. I walked over to our spot and sat on our bench. Then I walked along her street, but I felt ashamed and, before I'd quite reached her house, turned back without even glancing at the windows. I returned home in a state of dejection such as I'd never known before. What gloomy, damp, depressing weather! If only it had been fine I'd have walked around her neighborhood all night.

But she'll tell me everything tomorrow.

Of course, there wasn't any letter today, but then, that's quite natural. They're together already.

The Fourth Night

My God, what a way for it all to finish! Ah, what an ending!

I got there by nine. She was already there, waiting. I caught sight of her when I was still at a distance. She was standing as she was the first time, leaning on the guard-rail of the embankment, and didn't hear me approach.

"Nastenka!" I called out to her, managing to overcome my anguish.

"Come here," she said. "Hurry!"

I looked at her without understanding.

"Well, let me have the letter! You have it, haven't you?" She clenched the railing with her hand.

"No, I have no letter," I said finally, "but haven't you seen him yet?"

She went terribly pale and stared at me. I had shattered her last hope.

"Well, good luck to him," she said in a gasping tone. "Good luck to him, if that's the way he feels about me."

She lowered her eyes, then tried to look up at me, but couldn't. For several moments more, she tried to get hold of herself, but she couldn't. She turned her head away, leaned on the rail, and dissolved into tears.

"Stop, stop . . ." was all I said. Looking at her, I hadn't the strength to say more—and anyway, what else was there to say?

"Don't try to make me feel better," she said, crying. "Don't mention him, don't tell me he'll come, don't persuade me he hasn't thrown me over so cruelly, so callously as he has. What did I do wrong? Could it be something I wrote in that ill-fated letter?"

At this point, sobs overwhelmed her. I couldn't bear to see her this way.

"Ah, how cruel and callous!" she said again. "And he never even bothered to write me a single line! If only he had answered that he didn't need me, that he rejected me. But no, he hasn't written a word during these three days! How easy it is for him to hurt and humiliate a poor girl whose only sin is to love him! Ah, how much I've been through in these three days! Ah, my God! My God! When I think that it was I who came to him in the first place, that I humbled myself before him, cried, begged him for a crumb of his love. . . . And after all that! . . . Listen," she said, turning her flashing dark eyes to me, "it can't be—it's not natural—one of us, you or I, has made a mistake! Maybe he never got my letter! Maybe he doesn't know a thing to this minute! How is it possible—please explain to me, for God's sake—for him to be so unspeakably rude to me? Not a single word! People show more pity than that for the lowest of creatures! Maybe he's heard something; maybe someone has told him some slander about me? What do you think?"

She shouted the last question at me.

"I'll go, Nastenka, and see him on your behalf tomorrow."

"Yes?"

"I'll tell him everything and ask him to explain."

"Yes? Yes?"

"Write him a letter. Don't say no. Wait! I'll force him to respect what you did. He'll be told everything, and if——"

"No, my dear, no, that's enough! No more about it; not one line, not one word, enough's enough! I don't know him. I don't love him any more. I'll forget him . . ."

She couldn't complete her sentence.

"Calm yourself, calm yourself, Nastenka! Here, sit down," I said, indicating the bench.

"But I *am* calm! Stop fussing! It's true. My tears will dry. You don't really think that I'd go and drown myself or something, do you?"

My heart was overflowing. I tried to speak but words wouldn't come.

"Tell me!" she said, catching hold of my hand, "you wouldn't have acted that way, would you? You wouldn't have hurled a shameful sneer at a girl who'd come to you herself; you wouldn't have made fun of her weak, tender heart. You'd have spared her. You'd have realized that she was lonely, unable to take care of herself, unable to prevent herself from falling in love with you, that she hadn't done anything wrong . . . that she hadn't done anything . . . Ah, my God, my God!"

"Nastenka!" I cried, completely overcome, "you're torturing me, Nastenka! You're tearing at my heart, you're killing me! I can't remain silent! I must tell you, at last, all that has accumulated inside me."

I got up from the bench as I said that. She took my hand, looking at me surprised.

"What's come over you?" she said.

"Nastenka, everything I'm going to tell you now is absurd, impossible, idiotic! I know that it can never happen, but I can't remain silent. So, in the name of your present suffering, I beg you to forgive me in advance!"

"Well, what is it?" She stopped crying and looked at me closely. There was a strange curiosity in her eyes.

"I know it cannot be, but I love you, Nastenka. That's what it is. Now you know everything." I shrugged hopelessly. "Now see if you can still talk to me the way you did before, if you can listen to what I'm going to say——"

"But what of it?" Nastenka interrupted me. "I've known all along that you loved me, but I thought that you just loved me simply—you know . . . Oh, good gracious!"

"It was simply at first, Nastenka, but now—now—I'm exactly in the position you were in, Nastenka, when you came to him with that bundle of yours. In fact, my plight is even more hopeless than yours was then, for he wasn't in love with anyone, but you are."

"What are you saying? You puzzle me altogether. But listen, why do you . . . I mean, how is it that . . . Ah, God, I don't know what I'm saying. But you . . ."

She became completely confused. Her cheeks were on fire; she lowered her eyes.

"Well, what am I to do, Nastenka, what? I'm to blame for having abused . . . but no, no, it's not my fault, really—I know it, I feel it—for my heart tells me I'm right. There's no way I can harm you or offend you! I was your friend before, and I'm your friend now. I haven't betrayed a thing. And now, Nastenka, the tears are running down my cheeks; let 'em run, they aren't hurting anyone. They'll dry, Nastenka. . . ."

"Oh come, sit down, sit down," she said, pulling me down on the bench. "Ah, dear God!"

"No, Nastenka, I won't sit down; I can't stay here. You shouldn't see me any more. I'll tell you all I have in my heart, then leave. I want only to tell you that you'd never have found out I love you. I'd have kept my secret.

I wouldn't have inflicted my selfishness upon you at such a moment. No! But I couldn't keep it to myself. It was you who brought it up; it's your fault, it's all your fault. You can't send me away."

"But no, of course not. I don't intend to send you away," Nastenka rattled off quickly, trying, the poor dear, to conceal her embarrassment.

"So you won't send me away? But I was going to run away from you anyway. I'll leave too, but first I must tell you everything because I could hardly bear it when you were talking and crying and so full of despair, because . . . well, because—let me say it, Nastenka—because you have been rejected, because your love has been spurned. I—I felt so much love for you, Nastenka, so much love . . . and I felt terribly bitter because I couldn't do anything for you, despite all that love . . . I felt I was being torn to pieces. I couldn't keep silent, I had to talk. I had to, Nastenka."

"Yes, yes, tell me, talk to me!" Nastenka said with an inexpressible gesture. "It must seem strange to you that I should say that, but go on, speak! I'll explain later; I'll explain everything!"

"You're sorry for me, Nastenka, you're simply sorry for me. Well, the way I look at it—what is lost is lost, what has been done cannot be undone. Isn't that so? Now you know everything, and that's the point of departure. All right then, that's fine, but listen to this: while you were sitting here crying, I thought—oh, please let me tell you what I thought—I thought—of course I'm well aware it cannot be, Nastenka—I thought that somehow or other, without it having anything to do with me . . . you didn't love him any more. . . . In that case, Nastenka—I thought of that yesterday and the day before—I would've behaved in such a way that you'd have come to love me. . . . For you said yourself that you'd almost fallen in love with me, Nastenka, you said so yourself! And what then? Nothing much. That's just about all I had to say! All I have left to describe is what it would have been like had you fallen in love with me. But there's not much I can say about that.

So listen, my friend Nastenka, for you're still my friend—
I am, of course, a simple man, poor and unimportant,
but that's not what matters (I keep straying from the
subject out of shyness, Nastenka); only—I'd have loved
you so much that even if you'd still gone on loving that
man, you'd still never have felt my love as an imposition
upon you. You'd only have heard a grateful, warm heart
beating by your side and felt its proximity every second. . . . Ah, Nastenka, Nastenka, what have you done
to me?"

"Stop, I don't want you to cry!" She got up quickly from
the bench. "Come, get up, come with me, and stop crying!
Stop it!" She dried my eyes with her handkerchief. "Come,
perhaps I'll tell you something. After all, he's abandoned
me, forgotten me, even though I still love him, for I
don't want to lie to you. . . . But tell me truly: if, for
instance, I did come to love you—that is, if I only—oh,
my dear, dear friend, when I think how I hurt you, when
I laughed at your love, pretending to congratulate you for
not falling in love with me— Ah, God, how could I have
failed to foresee . . . How stupid I was! But now I've made
up my mind—I'll tell you everything."

"You know what, Nastenka, I'll go away! I simply torment you when I'm near you. Now, because of me, you're
feeling guilty about making fun of me. But I don't want
to add to your sorrow. I am the guilty one, Nastenka,
but forgive me and farewell!"

"Wait, listen to me! Can't you wait?"

"Wait? Wait for what?"

"I do love him but I'll get over it. I'm bound to. In fact,
I'm already getting over it. I feel it. . . . One can never
tell, I might even overcome it today. Because I hate him—
he was making fun of me while you and I were crying
here together. Because you haven't pushed me away as
he has; because you love me, and he never loved me;
because, finally I myself—I love you. . . . Yes—I love
you—I love you the way you love me. Remember, I told
you that before; you heard me! Because you're a better
man than he is; you're more honorable; because he . . ."

Nastenka was so moved that she couldn't finish. She let

her head rest on my shoulder; from there it slipped onto my chest as she shed bitter tears. I tried to cheer her up, but she couldn't stop crying. She just kept pressing my hand and repeating between sobs:

"Wait, wait, I'll get over it in a moment. . . . Don't think these tears mean that . . . I just feel weak. . . ."

Finally she stopped crying and wiped away her tears. We resumed our walk. I would have spoken, but she wanted me to wait a bit longer. So we walked in silence. At last she mustered up her courage and spoke.

"You know," she began in a weak, quivering voice that nevertheless had something in it that immediately clutched at my heart, making it throb with a sweet pain, "you mustn't think I'm so fickle and irresponsible, that I'm so quick to forget and to betray. I've loved him for a whole year, and I swear to God that I've never, not once, been unfaithful to him. Not even in thought. But he's scorned that; he's made light of my feelings. Well, good luck to him! But he has also wounded me and slighted my love. No, I don't love him, for I can only love one who is generous, understanding, and kind, because I myself am like that—so he's unworthy of me. All right, I wish him all the best! It's better like this than finding out later that I had deluded myself, than discovering too late what sort of man he is. . . . Anyway, it's over! But come to think of it, my dear, maybe all my love for him was nothing but a delusion; maybe it began as a childish adventure; maybe it was caused by the wish to escape from under my grandmother's thumb; maybe I was destined to love a man other than him, a man who could feel for me, understand me, and . . . But let's leave that!" Nastenka was short of breath in her excitement. "All I want to say is that if, although I love—no, rather *loved*—him—although, you might say . . . If you think your love is great enough to displace my former love . . . If you will take pity on me and not leave me to face my destiny all alone without offering me consolation, support, and hope—if you're willing to love me always as you love me now, then I swear to you that my gratitude—I mean my love—will, in the end, be worthy of your love. . . . Here, will you take my hand now?"

"Nastenka!" I cried, choked with sobs, "Nastenka! Oh, Nastenka!"

"Enough, enough for now, that's definitely enough," she said, getting hold of herself. "Everything has been said now, hasn't it? Right? And you're happy and so am I. Not another word about it. Wait. Spare me. For heaven's sake talk of something else!"

"Right, Nastenka, enough! I'm happy now, I . . . So, Nastenka, let's talk of something else. Quickly. Yes, I'm ready. . . ."

We didn't know what to say. We laughed. We cried. We exchanged thousands of disconnected, meaningless words. We walked along a street, then suddenly turned and retraced our steps. Without any apparent reason, we crossed the street to the opposite sidewalk; we went to the embankment. . . . We were like a couple of children.

"I live all by myself now, Nastenka. But tomorrow . . . Of course, you know, I'm poor. I've only twelve hundred rubles, but it doesn't matter, for——"

"Of course not. And then my grandmother has a pension. So she won't be a liability. She must, of course, come and live with us."

"Certainly, of course she must live with us. The only snag is that Matryona——"

"Ah! And we have our Fyokla!"

"Matryona's kind. The only thing wrong with her is that she has absolutely no imagination. But it doesn't matter!"

"Never mind, they can live together. Anyway you're coming over to live with us tomorrow."

"What did you say? Come to your place? That's fine by me!"

"Yes, you must rent our top floor room. It's empty now. There was an old woman living there, but she's left, and I know Grandma wants to let it to a young man. I asked her, 'Why a young man?' and she said: 'I'm getting old, see, but don't you get it into your head, Nas-

tenka, that I'm trying to marry you off.' So I guessed
that that was the reason."

"Ah, Nastenka!"

We both laughed.

"All right, that's enough now," she said. "And, by the
way, where do you live? I've forgotten."

"Over there, by that bridge, in the Barashnikov House."

"The large house?"

"Yes, it's quite large."

"I know it. It's a nice house, but forget it anyway and
come and live with us. Quickly."

"I'll come tomorrow, Nastenka, no later than tomorrow. I'm somewhat late with my rent, but that'll be all
right. I'll be getting my pay soon."

"You know what? Perhaps I'll give private lessons.
First I'll learn something myself, then I'll teach it."

"It's all turned out wonderfully . . . and soon I'm due
for a bonus, Nastenka."

"Then, starting tomorrow, you'll be my lodger."

"Yes, and we'll go to see *The Barber of Seville*, for
they'll be putting it on again soon."

"Yes, yes, let's," Nastenka said, laughing, "and if
not *The Barber*, we'll go and see something else."

"All right, something else then. That would be better,
of course. I should have thought of it myself. . . ."

Talking that way, we walked as if in a drunken haze,
like walking through clouds, with no idea of what was
going on around us. We stopped, chatted without moving
from the spot, then set off walking again, God knows
where, as we laughed, cried, and laughed again. . . . Nastenka decided to return home, and I didn't dare detain
her; I accompanied her to her very door, but a quarter
of an hour later, we found ourselves back at our favorite bench. She sighed and a tear glistened in her eye
again; I became frightened, turned cold . . . But she immediately pressed my hand and pulled me along behind
her, and we again walked and chatted and talked. . . .

"It's time for me to go back home now," Nastenka declared finally. "Enough of this childish stuff!"

"All right, Nastenka, but I—I won't be able to go to sleep tonight, so I don't think I'll go home."

"I don't expect to sleep either. Nevertheless, I want you to see me to my door."

"Most certainly."

"But this time it must be for good."

"Yes, yes, of course."

"Do I have your promise? For I must get home in the end."

"I promise," I said, laughing.

"Then let's go."

"Let's go, Nastenka," I said. "And look at the sky: it will be a wonderful day tomorrow. What a blue sky! What a moon! Look at that yellow cloud about to veil the moon. Look at it! look at it—no, it has just missed the moon. Look at it—look!"

But Nastenka wasn't looking at the cloud. She stood still as a tree. Then, after a while, she pressed herself against me in a strange way. Her hand was trembling in mine. I looked at her. She pressed herself even closer to me.

At that moment, a young man was passing near-by. Suddenly he stopped and gave us a close, scutinizing look. Then he walked a few more steps. My heart throbbed.

"Nastenka," I said very softly, "who is it, Nastenka?"

"It's him!" she whispered, pressing herself even more closely to me. I could hardly keep my feet.

"Nastenka, Nastenka, is that you?" I heard a voice behind us, and the young man came toward us.

My God, that cry! The shiver that passed through her! She tore herself from my arm and rushed toward him. I stood staring at them. I was dead. But she hardly had time to seize his hand and fling herself into his arms before she turned her head and looked at me. Then, with the speed of lightning, she was by me, her arms were around my neck, and before I knew what had happened, I felt her passionate kiss. Still without uttering a word, she again rushed toward him, caught his hand, and hurried away with him.

For a long time I kept following them with my eyes ...
Finally they vanished from sight

The Morning

My nights were over. It was the morning after. The
weather was bad. It was raining. The rain beat a gloomy
tattoo on my window. It was dark inside my room and
bleak outside the windows. My head ached. Objects swam
before my eyes. Fever was sneaking along my limbs.

"There's a letter for you." Matryona's voice hovered
somewhere over me. "It has just come."

I jumped up.

"What letter? From whom?"

"How do I know who it's from? Look; maybe it says
inside who wrote it."

I opened it. It was from her. It said:

Please, please forgive me! I beg you on my knees. Forgive me! I deceived both you and myself. It was a
dream, a mirage. I feel terrible about you now. Forgive
me, forgive me!

Don't be too hard on me, for what I feel for you
hasn't changed. I told you I loved you—well, I do love
you, and it's even more than love. Oh God, if only it
were possible to love both of you at the same time! Ah,
if only you could be him!

"Oh, if only he could be you." The thought flashed
through my head. I remembered your very words, Nastenka. The letter continued:

God only knows what I wouldn't do for you! I know
that you feel sad and depressed. I have hurt you. But,
as you know, we won't resent for long a wound inflicted
by those we love, and you do love me!

Thank you! Yes, thank you for that love! It lingers
now in my memory like a sweet dream that remains
long after awakening. I will always remember the moment when you opened your heart to me so fraternally
and when you so nobly accepted the gift of my heart—

wounded as it was—to love and cherish it, and heal its wounds. . . .If you forgive me, my memory of you will be ennobled by gratitude that will never fade. I shall cherish that memory, be faithful to it always, never betray it, never betray my heart—it is too constant for that. Only yesterday it went back to the one to whom it belongs forever.

We'll meet again. You'll come to see us. You won't abandon us. You'll always be my friend and my brother. And when we meet, you'll give me your hand, won't you? You'll give it to me because you love me as much as ever.

Please love me, and don't abandon me, because I love you so much at this moment, because I'm worthy of your love, because I'll earn it. . . . oh, my dear, dear friend!

I'm marrying him next week. He came back to me full of love. He hadn't forgotten me. . . . You won't be angry with me for writing this about him, will you? I want to come and see you with him. You'll like him, won't you?

So forgive, remember, and go on loving

your Nastenka

I read and reread that letter. I was on the verge of tears. At last it fell from my hands, and I covered my face.

"Here, look at that!" Matryona said.

"What is it, old woman?"

"Why, I've swept all them cobwebs from the ceiling so now you can marry any time and, while you're at it, invite a houseful of guests."

I looked at Matryona. She was still vigorous. She was a very young *old woman,* but I suddenly visualized her all wrinkled and shrunk, an invalid. And I don't know why, but my whole room suddenly aged the way an old woman ages. The walls and the ceilings peeled, everything faded, cobwebs multiplied. . . . And when I looked out of the window, I don't know why, but the house opposite turned dimmer too, the plaster on its columns fell off, the cornices became all grimy and full of cracks, and the walls, which used to be dark yellow, turned grayish.

A ray of sun that for a second had broken through a

rain cloud disappeared behind it again, and everything darkened once more. Or was it just my sad and barren future that flashed before me? Did I see myself exactly the way I am now, fifteen years later, having aged in this very room, just as lonely, still living with Matryona, who hasn't grown any more intelligent in all these years?

I remember the hurt inflicted upon me, Nastenka! But I never sent a dark cloud to sail over your clear, serene sky. I never reproached you, never made you sad or gave you a secret guilty feeling. I never trampled any of the tender flowers that you entwined in your black curls when you walked to the altar with him. Oh, never, never! So may the sky lie cloudless over you, and your smile be bright and carefree; be blessed for the moment of bliss and happiness you gave to another heart, a lonely and a grateful one.

My God, a moment of bliss. Why, isn't that enough for a whole lifetime?

From: *The House of the Dead*

❦

BAKLUSHKIN'S STORY

I've never met a man with more charm than Baklushkin. He didn't let anyone push him around or poke his nose into his affairs, and as a consequence, he had a few clashes with other prisoners, in which he showed he knew how to take care of himself. But he never held a grudge for long, and I believe everyone liked him. Wherever he went, people seemed pleased to see him. Even outside the penal settlement he was known as the most amusing of the convicts, a man whose cheerfulness never deserted him.

He was a tall fellow, around thirty, with a bold, open, rather handsome face with a wart on it. Sometimes he twisted that face of his into the most extraordinary expressions that made us all roar with laughter. He was always ready with a joke, and since the killjoys knew he wouldn't take it, they never dared call him a useless empty-head to his face. He was very lively and full of fire.

I got to know him soon after my arrival here. He told me he had been a noncom in the army and once had even been noticed and praised by some very high ranking officers, a fact of which he was proud to that day. When we met, he immediately started asking me all sorts of questions about Petersburg, where he had been stationed at one time. He apparently had even read some books.

It turned out, though, that Baklushkin hadn't stayed

62

very long in the capital. He'd got into trouble there, and had been transferred to the garrison battalion at R——, retaining, however, his rank as a noncom.

"And from there I landed here," Baklushkin said.

"What happened?"

"What happened? It happened that I fell in love. So it was love that brought me here."

"I didn't know they sent people here for that."

"Well, maybe it was also because I happened to kill one of the local Germans with an old pistol. But do you really think it's right to send a man here for killing a German?"

"But what happened? Tell me. It sounds interesting."

"It's a very funny story."

"Well, so much the better; go ahead and tell me."

"All right."

And then I heard a story that, although it wasn't really so funny, was an unusual murder story.

"Here's what happened," Baklushkin began. "When I got to R——, I found it was a nice, large town, although there were really too many Germans. Well, I was young and cocky, and had managed to get on good terms with my superiors, so I spent most of my time swaggering around the place with my cap over one eye, winking at the German *fräuleins*. And what do you know, I took a fancy to one of them. Luise was her name. She and her aunt worked as laundresses, and the clothes they washed were the cleanest I'd ever seen. The aunt was old and stuck up, and they lived quite well, I'd say. At first I just walked up and down in front of her windows, but later I became really friendly with her. That Luise, she even spoke good Russian, except for her '*r*s'—she couldn't manage those. She was such a nice, pretty thing; I'd never seen anyone like her before. At first I tried, you know. I tried this way and that, but she always said to me:

" 'No, Sasha, I can't let you. I want to keep it and be a wife worthy of you.' And she cuddled up to me and laughed, and that laugh of hers sounded so nice.

"Yes, she was purer than any I'd ever seen, and it was she herself who put the idea of marrying into my head.

And how could I not want to marry her? Just think of it! Well, I was already preparing to put in a request to my colonel for permission to get married.

"Then I realized something had happened. Luise didn't turn up at our usual meeting place. She wasn't there again the next day and the day after. I sent her a letter, but there was no answer to that either. I couldn't understand what was going on. If she'd wanted to lead me on, she'd have managed to keep our dates and to answer the letter. But she didn't know how to lie, so she simply broke it off, just like that. 'It must be that aunt of hers,' I said to myself. You see, I'd never been to their house, although the aunt knew what was going on between us; we always met outside, sort of on the quiet.

"So I went walking all around town like a crazy man, then I went back and wrote another letter to Luise, warning her that if she didn't show up next time, I'd come to the house, aunt or no aunt. That did it. She got scared and came. She cried. There's a German by the name of Schultz, she said, a watchmaker, some distant cousin of theirs, and he's rich and quite old already, and now he suddenly wants to marry her—to make her happy, he says, and also not to be without a wife in his old age. And, she added, it turns out he's loved her for a long time, but has never told her.

" 'So you see, Sasha,' she said, 'that's how it is. He's rich, and it looks to me like great luck, and I don't believe that you, Sasha, would want to deprive me of my happiness. . . .'

"She was crying, and she put her arms around me. 'Ah,' I said to myself, 'what she's saying makes good sense. Why should she marry a soldier, even though I am a noncom?'

" 'Well, good-by then, Luise,' I said. 'Why should I deprive you of your happiness? Best of luck to you. But tell me,' I added, 'is he good-looking at least?'

" 'Oh no,' she said, 'he's no youngster, and you should see the nose he's got!' And she even laughed herself.

"So I walked away from her, thinking, 'Well, what can I do about it? It just isn't my fate, I guess.' Still, the next day I went along the street where she'd told me he had his watch store.

"I looked inside through the shop window, and there was a German sitting there working away on a watch. He was around forty-five, his nose was hooked, and his eyes bulged out, he wore a tail-coat and stand-up collar, and looked mighty important. I spat, and really felt like breaking his window for him, but I said to myself, 'What the hell! It's all over anyway, and that's all there is to it.' So I went back to the barracks, as it was beginning to get dark, lay on my cot, and believe it or not, burst out crying. . . .

"Well, one day passed, then another, and a third, without my seeing Luise. Then I heard from another old laundress who did some work for Luise that the German had found out all about our love, and that was what had made him decide to marry Luise in a hurry. Otherwise the laundress said, he might have waited for another couple of years. And now he'd made Luise swear she'd never see me again—for he was still free to change his mind, so he had both Luise and her aunt under his thumb. She told me also that he'd invited them both to have coffee with him on Sunday and that another relative of his would be there, an old man who used to be a shopkeeper, but was now completely broke and was a watchman in some basement or other.

"Now when I found out that they wanted to settle the whole matter the next Sunday, and without consulting me, I got mad. I couldn't control myself any longer. All the next day, which was a Friday, and all of Saturday, I couldn't think of anything else. I think I could've eaten that German then.

"I still had no idea what would happen Sunday morning. But, after church parade, I put on my overcoat and went over to the German's place. I expected to find them all there, but I swear I hadn't the slightest idea why I was going or what I meant to tell the German. Still, somehow I slipped my pistol into my coat pocket. I'd had that lousy old pistol with its old-fashioned trigger for a hell of a long time. In fact, I used to fire it when I was a boy. I didn't even think it'd go off anymore. I loaded it, however, telling myself that if they tried to be rude and throw me out of there, I'd bring out the pistol and scare the daylights out of 'em.

"I walked over to the German's place. There was no one in the store; they were all in the back room. And aside from them, there was no one around—no servants, not a soul. Anyway, he only had one German woman working for him, and she cooked for him, too. I crossed the store and saw that the door leading to the inside room was locked. It was an old door, and it was fastened with a hook. I stopped by it and listened. My heart was beating like crazy as I stood there listening. They were jabbering in German among themselves.

"So I gave the door a terrific kick, and it flew open. The table was set and there was a large coffee pot perking over an alcohol heater on it. There were cookies on a plate and a tray with a decanter of vodka, herring, salami, and another bottle of some stuff—wine or something. Luise and her aunt, in their Sunday best, were sitting on a sofa. Next to them, on a straight chair, was the German bridegroom, all carefully combed and wearing his frockcoat and his stand-up collar. A bit to one side, also in a straight chair, sat the other German. He was really an old man, fat and white-haired; and he said nothing. As I broke into the room, Luise went all white; her aunt jumped up, then let herself slide back onto the sofa again.

"The German frowned. He looked very angry as he came toward me.

" 'Vat ees eet,' he said, 'do you vish?'

"I felt kind of stupid, not knowing what to say, and then my rage got the better of me.

" 'You ask me what I want!' I said to him. 'What kind of manners is that? I've come to visit you, so you'd better offer me some vodka.'

"The German gave it some thought, then said:

" 'Goot, you seet down.'

"I sat down.

" 'How about that vodka?'

" 'Here's votka, helb yourzelv, blease.'

" 'Come on,' I said, 'I want some decent vodka. And you'd better get me some.'

"As you can see, I was working myself up and getting really nasty.

" 'Dis ees goot votka.'

"It made me even more furious him treating me so offhand, and what made it worse was that Luise never took her eyes off me. I downed the glass, then I said to him:

" 'Why are you being so rude, German? I've come here to be pals with you, so why don't you treat me like a pal?'

" 'I cannot pe your bal pecause you're chust an enlisted man.'

"That made me really wild.

" 'Ah, you damned, sausage-eating kraut, you lousy scarecrow! You've no idea what I can do to you if the fancy takes me. Would you like me, for instance, to shoot you with a pistol?'

"I got out that old pistol of mine and put the muzzle against his head. When they saw that, the others were neither dead nor alive. They were afraid to make a sound. The old man shivered like a leaf in the fall. He couldn't utter a word, and his face turned ashen.

"The German was kind of taken aback at first, but he got hold of himself and said to me:

" 'I'm not afraid ov you, und I request you stop dis choke pecause I'm not scared ov you ad all.'

" 'Oh no?' I said. 'You're lying—you're scared to death.'

"And I saw that he didn't dare move his head away from my pistol; he just sat there like a lump.

" 'No,' he repeated, 'I'm not afraid, und you'll nefer do id.'

" 'What makes you so sure?'

" 'Pecause idz strickly forbitten to do deese tings, und zey bunish you fery zeverely for it. Dat's vy I tink you don't do it.'

"Damn that stupid German son of a bitch! If he hadn't pushed me so far, he'd still be alive today. The whole matter was in that argument now.

" 'So you don't think I'll do it?'

" 'No, you veel not.'

" 'No?'

" 'I said no, und you nefer dare——'

" 'All right, take that, you liverwurst.' And I let him have it. He rolled off his chair and all the others shouted. . . .

I slipped the pistol into my pocket and got out of there, but fast. Then, as I passed by the gate of the barracks, I tossed the pistol into the nettles.

"I went to my room, threw myself down on my cot, and waited for them to come for me. An hour passed, then another, and still no one came . . .

"I stayed there until it started to get dark, and I got so blue and sick inside that I couldn't stand it any more, so I went out. I had to see Luise if it was the last thing I did. I passed by the watchmaker's shop and I noticed that there were plenty of people around and some cops, too. Then I ran to the old laundress and asked her to call Luise. I didn't have to wait long. In a little while I see Luise running toward me.

"Ah, you should've seen how she threw herself at me, flung her arms round my neck, and cried and kept repeating, 'It's all my fault, Sasha; I shouldn't have listened to my auntie in the first place.' She also told me that after what happened in the morning, her aunt was so scared that she'd gone to bed sick and had said she wasn't going to tell anyone a thing and that Luise should keep her mouth shut too and let the police do what they liked.

" 'No one saw us going out,' Luise told me, 'for he'd sent away the woman who worked for him because she'd have scratched his eyes out if she'd found out he was about to get married.' He had made the coffee and prepared the snacks himself, and as for that relative, he hadn't spoken a word—he'd just grabbed his hat, and was the first to leave. 'And,' Luise added, 'I'm sure he'll keep his mouth shut too.'

"And that's just what happened. For two weeks no one bothered me. It looked as if they never even suspected

I'd had anything to do with it. And, believe it or not, it was in those two weeks that I found out what happiness really is. I saw Luise every day, and she got terribly fond of me too.

" 'I'll follow you wherever they send you,' she told me, crying. 'I'll leave everything and come with you.'

"I couldn't stand it. That girl really did something to me inside. . . .

"Well, after two weeks, they took me in. The old man and the aunt talked it over and decided to inform on me. . . ."

AKULKA'S HUSBAND

It was late at night, twelve or so. I had dozed off, then suddenly awakened. A dim night-light glimmered faintly in the ward. Almost everyone was sleeping. Even Ustyantsev was asleep. It was hard for him to breathe, and in the silence, I could hear phlegm gurgling in his throat with every breath. In the passage outside, the heavy footfalls of the relief guard resounded. A rifle butt clanged against the floor. The door of the ward opened; a corporal came in, trying to walk quietly, and checked over the sick prisoners. A minute later, the ward was locked again, a new sentry was posted at the door, and the patrol marched off. Then all was quiet again. Only then did I notice that a few beds from me, on my left, two men were awake, whispering to each other. Sometimes in prison wards two men will lie side by side for days, even months, without exchanging a word, then suddenly, swayed by the stillness of the night, one of them will start laying bare his past to his neighbor.

They must have been talking for quite a while. I'd missed the beginning, and even now I couldn't make out their words distinctly. Little by little, however, I got into it, and what they were saying began to make sense. Unable to sleep, I listened.

One of them was speaking heatedly. He'd propped himself up in his bed and was craning his neck toward the other. He seemed excited and agitated, obviously bent on getting his story out. His gloomy, indifferent listener sat up in bed, constantly stuffed snuff into his nose, and now and then grunted sympathetically—out of politeness, I felt, rather than real interest. He was a soldier from the penal battalion called Cherevin, a man of fifty or so, sullen, finicky, a squabbler, and a conceited fool.

The speaker, Shishkov, was a civilian prisoner, still young, around thirty, who worked in the prison tailor shop. Until then I had never paid much attention to him and, even after that night, I never really felt like getting to know him better. He was shallow and impulsive, often sullen, gloomy, and unfriendly. Sometimes he didn't say a thing for weeks on end; then suddenly, he got involved in something. He'd get excited, go around gossiping and spreading all sorts of rumors. Then he'd get beaten up and relapse into silence. He was a cowardly, pitiful fellow, thin and rather small, and the others treated him rather contemptuously. His eyes usually had a restless quality about them, but occasionally they were stilled by a dull dreaminess. Sometimes he talked with considerable ardor, gesticulating wildly, then suddenly interrupted himself or abruptly changed the subject, and plunging into something altogether different, completely forgot what it was he had started to say. He had many arguments with other prisoners, during which he never failed to accuse his opponent of having done him some wrong at one time or another that had nothing to do with the matter at hand. He'd make these reproaches emotionally, almost tearfully. He enjoyed playing the balalaika and could play it rather well. On holidays, he even danced occasionally, and he danced well when he was pushed into it. It was really quite easy to make him do things. Not that he was so amenable, but he wanted to be "one of the gang" and would do anything to be accepted.

For a while, I couldn't make heads nor tails of what he was saying. At first, he seemed to be holding back from

his real subject and getting involved in irrelevancies.
Maybe he suspected that Cherevin did not really care to
hear his story, yet wanted to convince himself that his
audience was lapping up every word. Probably he'd have
been quite miserable if he'd failed to do so.

"So he'd come to the market place," Shishkov was saying, "and everyone would start bowing and scraping to him
—he was the rich man, no doubt about it."

"Did you say he was a merchant?"

"Sure he was. And, I'm telling you, there weren't many
like him. The rest—a bunch of beggars, the lot of 'em,
see? The women had to fetch water from the river and
haul it up the steep bank for their vegetable patches.
They ran themselves ragged but, come fall, there wasn't
even enough for cabbage soup anyhow. Real misery. But
he—he'd leased a piece of land, hired three hands, and
then he had his own beehives and sold the honey. He had
cattle too, so everyone respected him plenty. He was
pretty old, seventy, I'd say, white-haired, big-boned, heavy
set, like. As I said, when he turned up in the market
place in his foxskin coat, everybody bowed and scraped
to him. They felt his importance, all right. 'Good day to
you, Ankudim Trofimych, sir!' they would say. 'Good
day,' he'd answer, 'to you too.' He never turned up his nose
at a person. 'God keep you,' they'd say, 'Ankudim Trofimych!' 'And you, how's business?' he'd ask. 'As usual—
as white as soot. And you, sir?' 'I'm getting along too, and
still smoking up heaven with my sins.' 'May you continue
like that for a long time, sir.' As I said, he never turned
his nose up at anyone, and his every word was as good as
a silver ruble. He was a Bible reader, sort of literate,
always reading something godly. He'd sit his old woman
down in front of him and say, 'Listen, Wife, try to
understand. . . .' and he'd start talking away. As a matter
of fact, his old woman wasn't all that old—she was his
second. He married her because he wanted kids—the
first hadn't had any. From her, Maria she was called,
he got two children—Vasya, the little one, who was
born when Ankudim was all of sixty. He was still a kid.

Then there was Akulka, the girl. She was eighteen, see."

"And she's your wife, right?"

"Wait a minute! First there was that Filka Morozov, who caused all that mess. 'Let's,' Filka says to Ankudim, 'divide everything up. I want the whole four hundred rubles that's coming to me. What d'you take me for—your hired hand or something? I don't want to stay in the business with you and I don't want any part of your Akulka either. Now that my parents are dead, I'm going on a binge, see,' he says to Ankudim. 'I'll drink every kopek they left me, then I'll hire myself out as a substitute for someone who's been drafted, and in ten years I'll be back here as a fieldmarshal.' So Ankudim paid up, every penny, because, you see, he and Filka Morozov's old man had been business partners. And as he handed Filka the money, he says to him: 'You, Filka,' he says, 'are a lost man.' 'We'll see whether I'm lost or not,' Filka says to him just like that, 'but with you, you gray-beard, I'd wind up eating my soup with an awl. To save an extra kopek,' he says, 'you'd collect every piece of garbage and put it in your stew. You make me sick,' he says, 'I can't stand all this saving. You save and save and you never get anything out of it. I'm a man with a strong character,' Filka says. 'And as for your Akulka, I won't marry her whatever you do. Anyway,' he says, 'I've already slept with her.' 'What are you saying!' Ankudim said, and he started to shake with anger. 'How dare you come and tell me, her father, that you've disgraced her, you filthy, fat-headed adder, you lousy fishbelly. . . .' I got the story from Filka himself.

" 'Not me nor anyone,' Filka said then, 'I'll see to it that nobody marries her—not even Mikita—because she's been disgraced. We've been sleeping together since the fall, and now I wouldn't touch her for a hundred rubles. Try'—he dared Ankudim—'offer me a hundred rubles; I won't go through with it.'

"Filka went on a binge after that, and he was so wild that the whole town rang and the earth itself moaned. With all that money, he soon had a whole bunch hanging around him, and in three months he'd spent it all.

'When I'm through this lot,' he said, 'I'll sell the house, I'll sell everything, drink that money too and then join the army or turn tramp.' So he was drunk from morning till night, driving around in a cart drawn by a pair of horses with bells on their harness. And you should've seen—the girls loved him something terrific! He was such a fine accordion player!"

"So he'd been carrying on with Akulka even before that?"

"Wait, don't get ahead. I'd also buried my father around that time, and my mother was working for Ankudim, making gingerbread; that's how we lived. It wasn't much of a life, that's for sure. We also had a little lot behind the woods, and we used to sow corn on it, but after my father died, we got rid of it, because I went on a spree too, and after that I even beat my mother to get money out of her . . ."

"It's not right to beat your mother; it's a terrible sin."

"What do you want, friend? I was drunk from morning till night. We still had our house. It was old and rotten, but it was still ours. But it was bare and empty inside—you could've chased a rabbit around in it. So we sat there with nothing to chew on for days on end, and my mother nagged me all the time. But I didn't care. At that time, I hung around with Filka Morozov from morning till night. 'You must play your guitar for me,' he'd say, 'and dance if I tell you to. And I'll lie down and toss money at you, because I'm the richest guy around here.' Oh, the things he came up with! Just the same, there was one thing he didn't do—receive stolen goods. 'I'm an honest man and no thief,' he always said, 'so if you want to do something for me, let's go and smear Akulka's gate with pitch, because I don't want Mikita to marry her. That's more important than money to me now.' You see, old Ankudim had had his eye on Mikita for Akulka for a long time—even before all this happened—for Mikita was an oldster like himself, a merchant too and a widower, who went around in glasses. When old Mikita heard all those rumors about Akulka, he started hedging. 'It would be a great disgrace for me, Ankudim,' he said, 'and besides, I don't

think I'll marry after all at my age. Well, we smeared
Akulka's gate with pitch and she got whipped something
terrible for it and her mother'd shout: 'I'll kill you! There's
no room for the likes of you on this earth.' And her
father'd explain that in the old days, under the patriarchs,
he'd have burned her at the stake himself, but he's not
allowed to do it now because the world's gone to pot.
Sometimes, even from the street, you could hear Akulka
bawling as they thrashed her. And Filka kept chanting
all over the market place: 'Who wants a dame?/Just
come to me;/I've one of some fame,/and there's no
fee./She drinks and wears clean underwear;/she's a good
one—that I'll swear.'

"One day around that time, I met Akulka. She was carrying buckets, and I shouted at her: 'Good morning,
madam, to you./The sky is bright and blue./That's a fine
shawl on your head./Who was the last man in your bed?'
She just looked at me. Her eyes were big, for she'd grown
all skinny. As she was looking at me, her mother, who
thought she was fooling around, shouted from their
window, 'What're you up to this time, you shameless
hussy? Get back in the house this minute!' And so she
gave Akulka another whipping. In fact, she beat her for a
whole hour, hollering all the time: 'I'll beat you to death
—you're no longer a daughter of mine.' "

"She was kinda whorish, I gather?"

"Wait, just listen to this. I was hanging around with
Filka, remember? My mother comes to me one morning
when I'm still in bed and says, 'Huh, you still in bed,
you scum?' And she starts nagging me. 'You'd better get
married,' she says. 'How about Akulka, now? They'd be
glad to have even you, and they'll fork out three hundred
in cash alone.' 'But,' I says, 'she's been disgraced before the
whole world.' 'You stupid fool,' she comes back at me,
'don't you know that marriage'll cover everything and it'll
be all to your advantage, for she'll feel guilty toward you
as long as she lives? And we could use that money,' she
says. 'I've already had a word with her mother about it,
and she sounded very eager, too.' So I says to my ma:
'Twenty rubles on the table, and I'll marry her.' And

after that, believe it or not, I never sobered up till the day of my marriage. And all that time, Filka Morozov, he kept threatening me: 'I'll break every bone in your body, you Akulka's husband, you! And I'll sleep with your wife whenever I fancy.' 'You're lying, you dog's carrion!' I says, so he let me have it—shamed me before the whole street. I went running home and told my ma: 'I won't marry her unless you give me fifty, and I want 'em right now!' "

"And they let her marry you?" Cherevin asked.

"Let *her* marry *me? Why* not? *We* weren't the ones who were disgraced, were we? My pa only went broke toward the end of his life, and that was due to a fire. Before that, we were maybe even better off than them. Ankudim said to me, 'You're just a penniless bum,' and I told him, 'It looks like your gate hasn't been smeared with pitch enough yet.' 'No need for you to be so clever,' he said. 'First prove she's been disgraced if you can. People just wag their tongues, and there's no way of stopping them. That's all there is to it. Here's the door,' he said, 'take it instead of Akulka. But then, I want the money back you got from me in advance.' So I talked it over with Filka and sent a fellow to tell him I'd make him look stupid yet. Then I really got dead drunk and stayed that way till the wedding day. My head only began to clear a bit in the church. And when we got back from church, my Uncle Mitrofan said to me, 'It's not an honorable deal, but it's signed and sealed now.' Old Ankudim got drunk too. He sat there and cried, and I could see the tears glistening in his whiskers. Now, I'll tell you what I did. I'd got me a whip even before the wedding, and I decided I'd have fun with Akulka and teach her a lesson, because I'd been tricked into marriage. That way, I thought, people would at least see that I hadn't really been made a fool of . . ."

"I don't blame you for that. It was right that she should know her place in the future——"

"Shut up and listen. In my part of the country, when the newlyweds come back from church, they're locked in a room by themselves right away, while the others go on drinking. So they locked me in with Akulka, and I looked at her sitting there all white, not a drop of blood in her face, scared like, see. Even her hair was like flax, almost white, you know, and her eyes were very big. . . . Later, she was like a mute around the house, never saying much, real strange. I had that whip ready by the bed. But then, believe it or not, it turned out that she wasn't guilty of the things they'd said about her, after all."

"How's that possible?"

"I'm telling you, she was completely innocent! So why did she have to go through all that misery? And why did Filka Morozov go around telling all those lies about her and disgracing her in the eyes of the world?"

"Yes, I'll say——"

"So I got out of the bed and down on my knees before her. I clasped my hands like I was praying, you know, and I said to her: 'Forgive me, dear Akulka, fool that I am, for believing all the things people said. Forgive me, I beg you, for I know I behaved like a dirty dog.' And she just sat there in front of me, looked at me, put her hands on my shoulders, and laughed, tears pouring out of her eyes; she cried and laughed and cried. . . .

"When I went out of that room to join the others, I said to myself: 'Just wait till I lay my hands on that bastard Filka Morozov. There's no room for him in this world now.' Her parents didn't know what to do with themselves. The mother, howling away, almost kissed her daughter's feet, and the old man said, 'If we'd had any idea, my dearest daughter, we'd have found you a better husband than this!' And when, on the first Sunday after the wedding, we went to church, I wore an astrakhan cap, a coat of fine cloth, and corduroy trousers, and she had on a brand new rabbit-fur coat, and a silk kerchief. We were quite a couple, and everyone was looking at us; and, if I do say so myself, we didn't look bad at all."

"So everything turned out all right in the end."

"You listen, and I'll tell you how it turned out. After the wedding, although I was still drunk, I managed to get away from my guests and went running around shouting: 'Show me where that no good son of a bitch Filka Morozov is, I'll teach the bastard!' I shouted that all over the market place. I was very drunk, I must say, and I was finally collared near the Vlasovs' house; it took three men to get me back home. And all over town, the girls whispered, 'What d'you know, Akulka was honest, after all.' One day I met Filka, and he said to me, in front of people: 'Why don't you sell your wife? You'd make enough to keep yourself drunk. We used to have a soldier round here,' he said. 'Yashka was his name. That Yashka married specially for that; he never once slept with his wife, but he managed to stay drunk all the time.' 'You're a dirty swine,' I told him. 'And you,' he says, 'are a damn fool. Why, you were cockeyed drunk on your wedding day,' he sneered, 'how could you possibly understand what was what?' So I returned home hollering, 'Hey, they married me while I was drunk!' My ma was there, and she tried to calm me down. 'You must have your ears stuffed with gold, ma, you'd better send Akulka in here!' And I started pushing Akulka around and hitting her; I went on like that for two hours, till I was too tired to stand up myself. She couldn't get out of bed for three weeks after that."

"To be sure," Cherevin remarked ponderously "if you don't beat 'em, they just . . . But did you catch her with a man?"

"No, I didn't," Shishkov said with an apparent effort, after a pause. "But the whole thing made me sore. They teased the hell out of me. Particularly Filka. He was the worst of the lot. 'Your wife,' he said, 'is so virtuous, men should take their wives to watch her and copy her—she's kind and noble and everything; but you seem to forget that you yourself used to smear her gate with pitch.' I was drunk when he said that. Suddenly he grabbed me by my hair, and pulled my head down. 'Dance!' he shouted: 'dance, you Akulka's husband, you! I'll lead you by the hair, and you'll dance to amuse me.' 'Son of a bitch!' I shouted at him, and he says, 'I'm coming to your place with some friends of mine. I'm going to give your wife a whipping while you watch—I'll beat her till I've had my fill.' After that, I was scared to leave the house. 'Now, he'll come and disgrace me,' I kept thinking. And that's why I started beating her...."

"That kind of beating is no good! Wagging a whip doesn't stop wagging tongues. It's all right to punish, but after that a man must be nice to his wife. She's his wife, after all, isn't she?"

Shishkov remained silent for a while.

"I was sore," he began again, "and then I got into the habit. Sometimes I'd beat her from morning till night for not getting up quick enough or not walking fast enough. She sat by the window and said nothing, and she cried and cried till I felt sort of sorry for her—but I still beat her. My mother kept nagging me about her. 'You low bully,' Ma would say, 'you carrion!' 'Keep out of it, or I'll kill her,' I'd yell. 'Don't say a word, any of you, now it was you who tricked me into this marriage!' At first old Ankudim tried to stop me. 'You aren't so tough,' he told me, 'I'll find a way to cope with you.' But he soon gave up. Then his wife came over, and she really groveled and cried. 'I've come to beg you,' she whimpered, 'calm down, dear boy. You know yourself that our daughter was slandered by wicked tongues.' And she cried and cried. But I just looked her up and down. 'I don't even want to listen to you,' I said. 'As far as the lot of you are concerned, I'll do as I please, because I don't have to control myself any more. And Filka Morozov,' I added, 'is my pal and I'm his best friend....' "

"So you two went on a binge again?"

"What're you talking about? I couldn't even get close to him. He'd drunk everything away and hired himself out to a shopkeeper to take the place of his oldest son in the army. And, let me tell you, in my part of the country, when a man hires himself out to replace a rich son in the army, everyone in that house has to lie down at his feet until the army gets him out of the way. He gets his money down the day he agrees to go, but, while he's waiting—and sometimes he waits six months—he can live in his 'employer's' house. He can make them put up with so much that they're better off taking the ikons out, so the saints don't see what goes on. It's like this: 'I'm

taking your son's place in the army, so I'm your bene-
factor, and you'd better respect me, or I won't go through
with it.' So Filka is having one hell of a time at the shopkeeper's: he sleeps with the daughter, pulls the father
around the house by his beard every day after dinner,
and does just about anything that comes into his head.
He ordered a steam bath every day and demanded to
be carried to the bath house by the women and have vodka
added to the water too. Sometimes he'd come home from a
drinking bout, stop in the street, and summon his shopkeeper. 'I don't want to go into your yard through the
gate; I want you to have the fence taken down right
here.' And that's where he went in. Finally his time came,
and they sobered him up and drove him off to hand him
over to the army. People poured out into the street:
'Hey,' they buzzed, 'Filka Morozov's being turned over
to the army!' And Filka bowed to everyone. It so happened that my Akulka was coming from our cabbage
patch just at the moment when they were driving Filka
past our gate. 'Stop!' Filka shouted. Then he jumped down
from the cart and threw himself at her feet. 'Ah,' Filka
says to her, 'I've loved you for two whole years, and now
they're taking me away to the army. Forgive me, you
honest daughter of an honest father, for I'm a low son
of a bitch and I'm guilty before you!' And he got up and
bowed to the the ground before her. Akulka looked scared
at first but then she bowed back to him. 'And you forgive me too,' she said, "for I bear no malice toward you
in my heart.' I went after her into the house—'What did
you say to him, you bitch?' And she, believe it or not,
she looked at me, just like that. 'Now,' she said, 'I love
him more than all the world put together.' "

"You don't say!"

"I never said another word to her till the end of the day.
Then, in the evening, 'Akulka,' I said to her, straight out,
'I'm going to kill you now.' I couldn't sleep that night, so
I got up to draw myself a glass of kvass and I saw it
was beginning to get light already. I went back in the
house. 'Akulka,' I said, 'get ready to drive out to the
field.' My ma knew I'd been intending to drive over there

for some time, so she said: 'That's right, you'd better go. The laborer's been laid up with a pain in his stomach for three days now, and it's harvest time.' I said nothing, just harnessed the horse. There's a pine forest stretching for maybe ten miles all around our village, and we had to drive through it to get to our field. We drove about three miles into that forest, then I stopped the horse. 'Get out of the wagon, Akulka,' I said, 'your end has come.' She stared at me. She looked scared, standing there in front of me and saying nothing. 'I'm fed up with you,' I said. 'Say your prayers.' I grabbed her by the hair, quickly like. She had two long, thick braids, and I wound them round my hand. I held her tight between my knees from behind, got my knife out, pulled her head back, and slid the blade across her throat . . . Then she let out a cry, and the blood spurted out all over the place. . . . I threw away the knife, put my arms around her, and lay down on the ground; I was screaming and bellowing like a bull. So I yelled and she yelled too. She was shivering all over and pushed me away, and tried to slip out of my embrace; meanwhile, her blood kept spurting, and I got it all over me, my hands, my face—it kept streaming and streaming . . . so I let go of her. I got so scared I left the horse and cart there and just ran and ran like a madman. I slipped through our backyard and shut myself in the bath house, which is old and never used. I hid myself under a bench and sat there till night."

"And what about Akulka?"

"Akulka? Looks like she got up after I left and tried to get home too. They found her later about a hundred yards from the spot."

"So you hadn't cut deep enough then?"

"Yes. . . ." Shishkov stopped for a moment.

"There's a special vein, there, you know," Cherevin commented. "If you don't manage to cut through it on the first slash, a man will keep kicking, and no matter how much blood he loses, he won't die."

"But she did die. They found her there in the evening—dead. The police came looking for me, and found me in the

bath house that same night. . . . This is my fourth
year here," he added after a pause.

"Yes, to be sure, if we don't beat 'em, no good will come
of it," Cherevin observed with detachment, slowly and
deliberately helping himself to some snuff. "But then, I
must say, lad, you're something of a fool. I also surprised my wife with a man. So I called her into the barn
and folded the bridle in two. 'Who was it you swore to
be true to? Who was it—I'm asking you?' And I beat her
with that bridle for, I'd say, an hour and a half. She
screamed. 'Forgive me,' she yelled, 'I'll wash your feet
now and drink the water too.' Ovdotya, her name was."

IN THE HOSPITAL

(Punishment and Punishers)

I'll speak here of punishment and of those who were en-
trusted with this interesting duty, because it was only
in the hospital that I acquired a clear understanding of
these matters. Until then, all I had known about it was
hearsay.

All the prisoners from the surrounding area, whether
military or civilian, were sent to our two wards after they
had suffered corporal punishment.

During those early days, when I still drank in everything that went on around me with such fascination, all
these strange happenings, all these men who had been
punished or were awaiting punishment, naturally made a
deep impression upon me. I felt agitated, troubled, frightened. I remember that I suddenly began impatiently in-
vestigating every detail of this aspect of prison life, which
was quite new to me. I listened to what the other prisoners said, to their stories connected with punishment; I
questioned them, too. I tried hard to understand. Among
other things, I wanted to find out the various gradations
of sentence and punishment—all the shades of punishment, and the prisoners' attitude toward them. I tried to
picture to myself the states of mind of prisoners going

out to be punished. I have already said that it was rare
to find a man who remained cool before punishment, even
among those who had repeatedly been beaten. Generally,
the condemned man suffers an acute, but purely physical, fear—an inevitable reflex that utterly crushes a man's
spirit. Later, too, during my prison years, I couldn't help
watching prisoners who stayed in the hospital until their
backs were healed, then were discharged to face the
balance of the strokes coming to them. It was always the
attending physician who decided whether or not the
punishment was to be divided into two parts. If the sentence called for more strokes than the prisoner could
stand at one time, then they dealt them out to him in two
or even three parts, depending on what the doctor said
during the punishment itself—whether the prisoner was
able to continue running the gauntlet or whether it would
endanger his life. Usually five hundred, a thousand or even
fifteen hundred strokes were meted out in one session,
but if the sentence called for two or three thousand blows,
then they divided it into two or even three sessions.
Those who, their backs healed, were leaving the hospital
to take the second installment of their punishment were
usually very sullen, morose, and silent the day before and
on the actual day of their discharge. I noted in them a
certain dullness of mind, a strange absent-mindedness. A
man in this position is reluctant to talk; he mostly remains silent, and what's more, the other prisoners never
address him and avoid mentioning what is in store for
him. No unnecessary word, no comfort—they try to take
as little notice of him as possible. This, of course, is
better for him.

There are exceptions. Orlov, for instance. After the
first installment of his punishment, all he wanted was for
his back to heal quickly so that he could be discharged
from the hospital for the second beating, then leave under
convoy for his final place of imprisonment—and escape
on the way there. But then, it was this aim that kept
him going, and God knows what went on in his mind. His
was a passionate nature, tenacious of life. He was pleased
and excited in the hospital, although he tried to conceal

it, because he had never expected to come out from the first half of his punishment alive; he had been sure that his time to die had come. Even during his trial, he had heard rumors about the way sentences were carried out, and he had prepared himself for death then. But, having come through the first half, he recovered some hope. He was half dead when they brought him into the hospital —I'd never seen such welts. But he was cheerful and hopeful that he would live, pleased because the rumors had proved false and he had come out alive from under the sticks. Now, after his long imprisonment before his trial, he started to dream again of the forthcoming journey, of escape, of freedom, of fields and forests. Two days after he was pronounced fit to undergo the second half of his punishment, he was brought back to the hospital to die on the same cot. The balance of the strokes had proved too much for him.

And yet, the very prisoners who looked so miserable during the days and nights preceding their punishment took their beatings manfully, even the most fainthearted of them. I hardly ever heard any of them, including those most dreadfully beaten, moan, even during their first night. In general, these simple people know how to bear pain. I asked many questions about the pain itself. I wanted to find out just how intense it was, what it could be compared with. I really don't know why I was so concerned about it. I only remember that it wasn't idle curiosity. As I said before, I was agitated, shaken. But no matter whom I asked, I never obtained an answer that satisfied me. "Burns like fire," was all I could get out of them; "it burns," and that was all. In those early days, as I got to know M——better, I asked him about it, too.

"It hurts terribly," he told me. "Burns. It's like my back was roasting over the hottest fire." They all said the same thing, almost word for word.

Incidentally, I made one strange observation at that time. I can't vouch for its authenticity, but it was strongly supported by the unanimous opinion of the prisoners: the birch, if you're given a large number of strokes, is the worst of all the punishments practiced. This may seem absurd and impossible at first sight, but a man may not survive four or five hundred strokes of it and almost certainly not more than five hundred. Even the strongest man could not endure a thousand strokes at one time, although five hundred with a stick can be borne without the slightest risk to one's life. Even a man of mediocre constitution can take a thousand blows with a stick, and a healthy man of medium strength can survive two thousand. All the prisoners agreed that the birch was worse than the stick.

"The birch smarts more," they said. "It's worse."

Certainly the birch causes greater suffering than the stick. It is harder to bear, acts more violently upon the nerves, exacerbates them more, and gives you a greater shock.

I don't know how it is today, but in the not-too-distant past, there were distinguished people to whom beating some victim afforded feelings similar to those of the Marquis de Sade and the Marquise de Brinvilliers. I think that there is something in these sensations that, in these people, make the heart stop in agonizing delight. There are people like tigers who long for a taste of blood. Anyone who has once experienced this power, this unlimited control over the body, blood, and spirit of a man like himself, a fellow creature, his brother in Christ—anyone who has experienced the power to inflict supreme humiliation upon another being, created like himself in the image of God, is bound to be ruled by his emotions. Tyranny is a habit; it grows upon us and, in the long run, turns into a disease. I say that the most decent man in the world can, through habit, become as brutish and coarse as a wild beast. Blood and power intoxicate, callousness and vice develop; the most abnormal things become first acceptable, then sweet to the mind and heart. The human being, the member of society, is drowned forever in the tyrant, and it is practically impossible for him to regain human dignity, repentance, and regeneration. One such instance—the realization that such arbitrary power can be exercised—can infect all society; such power is seductive. A society

which can watch this happen with equanimity must itself be basically infected.

Thus, the power given to one man to inflict corporal
punishment upon another is a social sore; it is perhaps
the surest way of nipping the civic spirit in the bud. It
will inevitably lead to the disintegration of society.

Society abhors a flogger. But gentlemen-whippers are
far from being abhorred. The latter opinion has been
disputed, but only in books, and abstractly at that. And
not all those who have disputed it have managed to suppress their own need to tyrannize. Every manufacturer,
every business man, must feel a sort of peevish pleasure
in the realization that the worker and all his family are
sometimes entirely dependent upon him. That is certainly
so, for one generation does not so easily tear itself away
from what it has inherited; a man does not deny so
quickly what is in his blood, what he has drunk in, one
might say, with his mother's milk. Such sudden reversals
do not occur. To recognize one's guilt and the sins of
one's fathers is a small part of it, a very small part; one
must rid oneself of the habit altogether. And that cannot be done so quickly.

I have mentioned floggers. There are traces of the
whipper in almost every man. But then, the bestial side
does not develop equally in all men. If the beast in a man
overpowers all his other sides, he becomes horrible, monstrous.

There are two kinds of floggers: the volunteers, and
those who are forced into it. Of course, the volunteers
are worse, from every point of view, than the others;
yet people abhor the latter, displaying terror, revulsion,
and an unaccountable, almost superstitious fear of them.
Why this horror for the one and such indifference, bordering on approval, of the other?

I have known the most incredible instances where people—even good, honest, respected people—could not bear
it if the victim undergoing punishment did not cry out
under the birch, cringe, and beg for mercy. Men being
punished are supposed to cry out and beg for mercy. It
is considered the decent thing to do and quite essential.

1862

Once when the victim refused to cry out, the flogger, a man whom I knew and who, in other respects, could even be considered kindly, took it as a personal offense. At first he had intended to make the punishment a light one. But when the usual cries for mercy were not forthcoming, he grew furious and ordered fifty extra lashes, seeking both cries and begging—and he had his way.

"What could I do—the man was so insolent," he said quite seriously in answer to my questions.

The ordinary flogger, the man who has been ordered to do his job, is just another prisoner. Instead of being deported to Siberia, he is retained in a central penitentiary to serve as flogger. First he has to learn his trade from an experienced colleague. Then, when he has learned, he is kept permanently in one prison, where he keeps to himself, has his own room, and even does his own housekeeping, although he is almost always under guard. Of course, a man is not a machine; although he beats another man because he has to, he sometimes becomes emotionally involved. Nevertheless, he hardly ever feels personal hatred for his victim, even though he may derive a certain pleasure from his work. His self-esteem is heightened by his agility in administering his blows, by his mastery of his trade, by his desire to show off before his audience. He does his best for art's sake. Besides, he knows very well that he is a total outcast, that everywhere he goes he will be met by superstitious fear—and it is impossible to assert that this has no influence upon him, that it doesn't push him toward further violence and exacerbate his bestial inclinations. Even the children know that "he has disowned father and mother." Strangely enough, every flogger I have ever known was intelligent, clever, and sensible, with an extraordinary amount of self-respect and even pride. Did they develop this pride to counteract the general scorn? Was it strengthened by their awareness of the fear they inspire in their victims and their feeling of mastery over them? I can't say. Perhaps the ceremoniousness and theatricality of their appearance before the public contribute to the development of a certain haughtiness in them.

I used to know a flogger, and was able to observe him closely. He was a fellow of about forty, of medium height, lean and muscular, with a pleasant, intelligent face and curly hair. He was always very dignified and composed and, outwardly at least, conducted himself like a gentleman. When I spoke to him he always answered briefly, to the point, even amiably, but with a sort of haughty amiability, as if he felt somewhat superior. I detected a certain respect for him in the way the officers on duty talked to him in my presence. He sensed this, and in talking to an officer, deliberately doubled his politeness, his terseness, his air of self-esteem. The more amiable the officer's tone, the more unbending he became and, although he in no way departed from the most refined politeness, I'm sure that he considered himself immeasurably above the officer. It was written all over his face.

Sometimes, on very hot summer days, he was sent, under guard and armed with a long, thin pole, to round up the town's stray dogs. There were an incredible number of dogs in that town that belonged to no one and multiplied with extraordinary rapidity. In hot weather, they were a menace, and by order of the authorities, the executioner was sent to exterminate them. But even this degrading job did not seem to degrade him. He walked through the streets of the town, accompanied by his weary guard, with such dignity, it had to be seen to be believed. The mere sight of him frightened the women and children, and he calmly, even patronizingly, met the gaze of everyone he encountered.

However, floggers have an easy life. They have money, they eat very well, they get vodka. They get the money from bribes. The civilian prisoner sentenced to corporal punishment always gives the flogger something, even if it is his last kopek. And of an affluent prisoner, the flogger himself demands money, fixing the sum according to the man's reputed means. It can be as high as thirty rubles and more. There may be quite a bit of bargaining with the very well-off.

Of course, the flogger cannot make the punishment too obviously mild—he'd answer for it with his own back. Nevertheless, for a certain sum, he promises the victim not to beat him very painfully. Almost everyone agrees to his price, for if they don't, he can make the punishment really savage. He will sometimes demand a considerable sum from a poor prisoner. The man's relatives go to him and bargain with him most respectfully, and God pity the victim if they don't satisfy him. On these occasions, the superstitious fear he inspires is a great asset.

All sorts of legends circulate about floggers. Prisoners themselves have assured me that they can kill a man with a single blow. Yet, when has this contention ever been tested? But, after all, it could be so. The prisoners were certainly convinced of it, and a flogger himself assured me that he could do it. I have also been told that he can strike a prisoner on the back with a full swing in such a way that not even a tiny welt will be raised by the blow, and the prisoner will not feel the slightest pain. But there are already far too many stories about these tricks and subtleties.

Be that as it may, even when an executioner takes a bribe to beat a man lightly, he still delivers the first blow with his full strength. This is a tradition. The subsequent blows he softens, especially if he has been paid beforehand. But whether he has been paid or not, the first blow is his own. I'm sure I don't know why there is such a custom. Is it so that the victim will be prepared for the subsequent blows, on the theory that after such a heavy blow the light ones won't seem so terrible? Or is it simply a desire to show the victim who is master, to instill fear in him, to stun him from the start, to make him see whom he has to deal with, to show the flogger's actual power? In any case, prior to the beating, the flogger is in a state of excitement; he has a sense of his own power, feels himself the lord and master. At that moment he is an actor; he fills the public with wonder and terror, and it is with a feeling of pleasure that he

shouts to his victim before the first blow: "Lo͟
now! I'll scorch you!"—the sinister words usually u͟

It's hard to imagine to what an extent a man's nature
can be corrupted.

tes from Underground

ख़ुर्ग

Part One

The Mousehole*

I

I'm a sick man . . . a mean man. There's nothing attractive about me. I think there's something wrong with my liver. But, actually, I don't understand a damn thing about my sickness; I'm not even too sure what it is that's ailing me. I'm not under treatment and never have been, although I have great respect for medicine and doctors. Moreover, I'm morbidly superstitious—enough, at least, to respect medicine. With my education I shouldn't be superstitious, but I am just the same. No, I'd say I refuse medical help simply out of contrariness. I don't expect you to understand that, but it's so. Of course, I can't explain whom I'm trying to fool this way. I'm fully aware that I can't spite the doctors by refusing their help. I know very well that I'm harming myself and no one else. But still, it's out of spite that I refuse to ask

---

* It goes without saying that both these *Notes* and their author are fictitious. Nevertheless, people like the author of these notes may, and indeed must, exist in our society, if we think of the circumstances under which that society has been formed. It has been my wish to show the public a character of the recent past more clearly than is usually shown. He belongs to the generation that is now rounding out its days. In the excerpt entitled "The Mousehole," this man introduces himself and presents his views, trying to explain why he has appeared, and could not help but appear, in our midst. The next excerpt consists of this man's actual "notes," relating to certain events in his life.

FYODOR DOSTOYEVSKY

for the doctors' help. So my liver hurts? Good, let it hurt even more!

I've been living like this for a long time, twenty years or so. I'm forty now. I used to be in government service, but I'm not any more. I was a nasty official. I was rude and enjoyed being rude. Why, since I took no bribes, I had to make up for it somehow. (That's a poor attempt at wit, but I won't delete it now. I wrote it thinking it'd sound very sharp. But now I realize that it's nothing but vulgar showing off, so I'll let it stand if only for that reason.)

When petitioners came up to my desk for information, I snarled at them and felt indescribably happy whenever I managed to make one of them feel miserable. Being petitioners, they were a meek lot. One, however, wasn't. He was an officer, and I had a special loathing for him. He just wouldn't be subdued. He had a special way of letting his saber rattle. Disgusting. For eighteen months I waged war with him about that saber. I won out in the end, and he stopped the thing from rattling. All this, however, happened when I was still young. But shall I tell you what it was really all about? Well, the real snag, the most repulsive aspect of my nastiness, was that, even when I was at my liverish worst, I was constantly aware that I was not really wicked nor even embittered, that I was simply chasing pigeons, you might say, and thus passing the time. And so I might be frothing at the mouth, but if you had brought me a doll to play with or had offered me a nice cup of tea with sugar, chances are I would have calmed down. I'd even have been deeply touched, although, angry at myself, I would be certain to gnash my teeth later and be unable to sleep for several months. But that's the way it was.

I was lying just now when I said I used to be a nasty official. And I lied out of spite. I was having fun at the expense of the petitioners and that officer, but deep down, I could never be really nasty. I was always aware of many elements in me that were just the opposite of wicked. I felt that they'd been swarming inside me all my life, trying to break out, but I had refused to let them. They tormented me, they drove me into shame and convulsions, and I was fed up with them. Ah, how fed up I was with them! Doesn't it seem to you as if I were trying to justify myself, to ask for your forgiveness? I'm sure you must think that. . . . Well, believe me, I don't care if you do think so.

I couldn't manage to make myself nasty or, for that matter, friendly, crooked or honest, a hero or an insect. Now I'm living out my life in a corner, trying to console myself with the stupid, useless excuse that an intelligent man cannot turn himself into anything, that only a fool can make anything he wants out of himself. It's true that an intelligent man of the nineteenth century is bound to be a spineless creature, while the man of character, the man of action, is, in most cases, of limited intelligence. This is my conviction at the age of forty. I'm forty now, and forty years is a whole life—forty is deep old age. It's indecent, vulgar, and immoral to live beyond forty! Who lives beyond forty? Answer me honestly. Or let me tell you then: fools and good-for-nothings. I'll repeat that to the face of any of those venerable patriarchs, those respected grayheads, for the whole world to hear. And I have a right to say it, for I'll live to be sixty! I'll live to be seventy! I'll live to be eighty! . . . Wait, give me a chance to catch my breath. . . .

Do you think I'm trying to make you laugh? Then you've got me wrong again. I'm not at all the cheerful fellow you think I am, or you may think I am. But if you're irritated by all my babble (I feel you must be by now) and feel like asking me who the hell I am after all, I'll have to answer that I'm a collegiate assessor. I entered the service to have something to eat (and for that only). And so, when a distant relative died, leaving me six thousand rubles, I immediately resigned and installed myself in my corner here. I had lived here even before that, but now I've really settled down. My room is miserable and ugly, on the outskirts of the city. The maid here is a peasant woman, nasty out of sheer stupidity;

moreover, there's always a bad smell about her. They tell
me that the Petersburg climate is bad for me and that,
with my miserable income, it's a very expensive place to
live. I know all that myself. I know it better than all my
would-be advisers. But I'm going to stay in Petersburg!
I won't leave! I won't leave because . . .

Ah, it's really all the same whether I go or stay.

Now then, what does a decent man like to talk about
most? Himself, of course. So I'll talk about myself.

II

Now I want to tell you, ladies and gentlemen, whether
you like it or not, why I couldn't even become an insect.
I must first solemnly declare that I tried many times to
become one. But even that was beyond me. I swear that
too great a lucidity is a disease, a true, full-fledged disease. For everyday needs, the average person's awareness
is more than sufficient, and it is about a half or a quarter of
that of the unhappy nineteenth century intellectual, particularly if he's unfortunate enough to live in Petersburg,
the most abstract and premeditated city on earth (there
are premeditated and unpremeditated cities). The extent of consciousness at the disposal of what may be
termed the spontaneous people and the men of action
is sufficient. I bet you think I say that just to take a crack
at men of action, and that this kind of showing off is
just as much in poor taste as the saber rattling of that
officer I mentioned. But I ask you, who on earth goes
around showing off his sickness, and even glorying in it?

On second thought though, I'd say that everyone does.
People do pride themselves on their infirmities and I,
probably, more than anyone. So don't let's argue about
it—I admit my contention was inane. But I still say that
not only too much lucidity, but any amount of it at all
is a disease. That's where I stand. But let's leave that for
a moment too. Now tell me this: why, just when I was
most capable of being conscious of every refinement of
the "good and the beautiful," as they used to put it once

upon a time, were there moments when I lost my awareness of it, and did such ugly things—things that everyone
does probably, but that I did precisely at moments when
I was most aware that they shouldn't be done.

The more conscious I was of "the good and the beautiful," the deeper I sank into the mud, and the more
likely I was to remain mired in it. But what struck me
was the feeling I had that, in my case, it wasn't accidental,
that it was intended to be that way, as if that were my
normal state rather than a sickness or depravity; so that
finally I lost all desire to fight my depravity. In the end,
I almost believed (perhaps I even *did* believe) that it
actually *was* my normal state.

But, in the beginning, what agonies I went through
in this inner struggle! I didn't believe that there were
others who went through all that, so I've kept it a secret
all my life. I was ashamed (perhaps, even now, I am still
ashamed). I reached a point where I felt a secret, un-
healthy, base little pleasure in creeping back into my hole
after some disgusting night in Petersburg and forcing myself to think that I had again done something filthy, that
what was done couldn't be undone. And I inwardly gnawed
at myself for it, tore at myself and ate myself away,
until the bitterness turned into some shameful, accursed
sweetishness and, finally, into a great, unquestionable
pleasure. Yes, yes, definitely a pleasure! I mean it! And
that's why I started out on this subject: I wanted to find
out whether others experience this sort of pleasure too.
I'll explain it to you: I derived pleasure precisely from
the blinding realization of my degradation; because I felt
I was already up against the wall; that it was horrible
but couldn't be otherwise; that there was no way out and
it was no longer possible to make myself into a different
person; that even if there were still enough time and
faith left to become different, I wouldn't want to change
myself; and that, even if I wanted to, I still wouldn't have
done anything about it, because, actually, there wasn't
anything to change into. Finally, the most important point
is that there's a set of fundamental laws to which heightened consciousness is subject so that there's no changing

oneself or, for that matter, doing anything about it. Thus, as a result of heightened consciousness, a man feels that it's all right if he's bad as long as he knows it—as though that were any consolation. But enough. . . . Ah, what a lot of words! And what have I explained? What's the explanation for this pleasure? But I'll make myself clear! I'll go through with it! That's why I've taken up my pen.

I, for instance, am horribly sensitive. I'm suspicious and easily offended, like a dwarf or a hunchback. But I believe there have been moments when I'd have liked to have my face slapped. I say that in all seriousness— I'd have derived pleasure from this too. Naturally it would be the pleasure of despair. But then, it is in despair that we find the most acute pleasure, especially when we are aware of the hopelessness of the situation. And when one's face is slapped—why, one is bound to be crushed by one's awareness of the pulp into which one has been ground. But the main point is that, whichever way you look at it, I was always guilty in the first place, and what is most vexing is that I was guilty without guilt, by virtue of the laws of nature. Thus, to start with, I'm guilty of being more intelligent than all those around me. (I've always felt that and, believe me, it's weighed on my conscience sometimes. All my life, I have never been able to look people straight in the eye—I always feel a need to avert my face.) And then, I'm also guilty because, even if there had been any forgiveness in me, it would only have increased my torment, because I would have been conscious of its uselessness. I surely would have been unable to do anything with my forgiveness: I wouldn't have been able to forgive because the offender would simply have been obeying the laws of nature in slapping me, and it makes no sense to forgive the laws of nature—but neither could I have forgotten it, because it is humiliating, after all. Finally, even if I hadn't wanted to be forgiving at all, but on the contrary, had wished to avenge myself on the offender, I couldn't have done it, for the chances are I'd never have dared to do anything about it even if there had been something I could do. Why wouldn't I have dared? Well, I'd especially like to say a few words about that.

III

Now let's see how things are with people who are capable of revenge and, in general, of taking care of themselves. When the desire for revenge takes possession of them, they are drained for a time of every other feeling but this desire for revenge. Such a gentleman just rushes straight ahead, horns lowered, like a furious bull, and nothing stops him until he comes up against a stone wall. (Speaking of walls, it must be noted that spontaneous people and men of action have a sincere respect for them. For these people a wall is not the challenge that it is for people like you and me who think and therefore do nothing; it is not an excuse to turn back, an excuse in which one of our kind doesn't really believe—although he always welcomes it. No, their respect is perfectly sincere. A wall has a calming effect upon them; it is as though it solved a moral issue—it is something final and, perhaps, even mystical. . . . But we'll come back to walls later.)

In my view, such a spontaneous man—the real, normal man—is the fulfillment of the wishes of his tender mother, Nature, who so lovingly created him on this earth. I envy that man. I'm bilious with envy. He's stupid, I won't dispute that, but then, maybe a normal man is supposed to be stupid; what makes you think he isn't? Perhaps that's the great beauty of it. And what makes me even more inclined to suspect this is that if we take the antithesis of a normal man, the man of heightened consciousness, who is a test-tube product rather than a child of nature (this is almost mysticism, my friends, but I have a feeling that it is so), we find that this test-tube man is so subdued by his antithesis that he views himself —heightened consciousness and all—as a mouse rather than a man. So, even if he's a mouse with a heightened consciousness, he's still nothing but a mouse, whereas the other is a man. So there. And, what's more, he regards himself as a mouse; no one asks him to do so. This is a very important point.

Now let's look at this mouse in action. Let's assume it has been humiliated (it is constantly being humiliated) and that it wishes to avenge itself. It's possible too that there's even more spite accumulated in it than in *l'homme de la nature et de la vérité*. The nauseating, despicable, petty desire to repay the offender in kind may squeak more disgustingly in the mouse than in the natural man who, because of his innate stupidity, considers revenge as merely justice, whereas the mouse, with its heightened consciousness, is bound to deny the justice of it. Now we come to the act of revenge itself. In addition to being disgraced in the first place, the poor mouse manages to mire itself in more mud as a result of its questions and doubts. And each question brings up so many more unanswered questions that a fatal pool of sticky muck is formed, consisting of the mouse's doubts and torments as well as of the gobs of spit aimed at it by the practical men of action, who stand around like judges and dictators and laugh lustily at it till their throats are sore. Of course, the only thing left for it to do is to shrug its puny shoulders and, affecting a scornful smile, scurry off ignominiously to its mousehole. And there, in its repulsive, evil-smelling nest, the downtrodden, ridiculed mouse plunges immediately into a cold, poisonous, and —most important—never-ending hatred. For forty years, it will remember the humiliation in all its ignominious details, each time adding some new point, more abject still, endlessly taunting and tormenting itself. Although ashamed of its own thoughts, the mouse will remember everything, go over it again and again, then think up possible additional humiliations. It may even try to avenge itself, but then it will do so in spurts, pettily, from behind the stove, anonymously, doubting that its vengeance is right, that it will succeed, and feeling that, as a result, it will hurt itself a hundred times more than it will hurt the one against whom its revenge is directed, who probably won't even feel enough of an itch to scratch himself.

Then, on its deathbed, the mouse will remember it all again, plus all the accumulated interest and . . .

But it is precisely this cold, sickening mixture of hope and despair; this deliberate retreat to a tomb under the floor for all these years; this artificially induced hopelessness, of which I'm still not fully convinced; this poison of thwarted desires turned inward; this feverish hesitation; the final resolutions followed a minute later by regrets—all this is the gist of the strange pleasure I've mentioned. This pleasure is so subtle, so evasive, that even slightly limited people, or people who simply have strong nerves, won't understand the first thing about it.

"It may also be difficult to understand for those who've never been slapped around," you may add with a self-satisfied grin.

Thus you may politely suggest that I'm talking like an expert because I've been slapped. I bet that's just what you think. But let me reassure you, ladies and gentlemen: I don't care in the least what you may think, but I haven't really been slapped. But that's enough on this subject that seems to interest you so much.

I'll continue calmly about people with strong nerves who can't understand the somewhat more subtle aspects of pleasure. Although, under other circumstances, these people may roar like furious bulls and this may add immensely to their prestige, they capitulate at once before the impossible, that is, a stone wall. What stone wall? Why, the laws of nature, of course; the conclusions of the natural sciences, of mathematics. When they are through proving to you that you descend from the monkey, it will do you no good to screw up your nose—you'll just have to take it. Trust them to prove to you that a single drop of your own fat is bound to be dearer to you, when you come down to it, than a hundred thousand human lives and that this conclusion is an answer to all this talk about virtue and duty, and other ravings and superstitions. So just take it for what it is—there's nothing else you can do; it's like two and two make four. That's arithmetic. Just try and disprove it!

"Wait a minute," they'll call out to you, "why pro-

test? Two and two do make four. Nature doesn't ask
your advice. She isn't interested in your preferences or
whether or not you approve of her laws. You must accept nature as she is with all the consequences that that
implies. So a wall is a wall, etc., etc. . . ."

But, good Lord, what do I care about the laws of nature and arithmetic if I have my reasons for disliking
them, including the one about two and two making four!
Of course, I won't be able to breach this wall with my
head if I'm not strong enough. But I don't have to accept a stone wall just because it's there and I don't
have the strength to breach it.

As if such a wall could really leave me resigned and
bring me peace of mind because it's the same as twice two
makes four! How stupid can one get? Isn't it much better
to recognize the stone walls and the impossibilities for
what they are and refuse to accept them if surrendering
makes one too sick? Isn't it better, resorting to irrefuta-
ble logical constructions, to arrive at the most revolting
conclusions on the eternal theme that you too, somehow,
share the responsibility for the stone wall, although it's
obvious that you're not at all to blame for it; and then,
to sink voluptuously into inertia, gnashing your teeth in
impotent rage, unable to find someone on whom to vent
your rage and hatred, and losing hope of ever finding anyone; feeling that you've been short-changed, cheated, deceived, that everything is a mess in which it is impossible to tell what's what, but that despite this impossibil-
ity and deception, it still hurts you, and the less you can
understand, the more it hurts.

IV

"Ha!" you may object sarcastically, "this way you'll
soon find pleasure in a toothache."

"Well," I'd answer, "there's pleasure in a toothache too."

Once I suffered from a toothache for a whole month,
and I can tell you there's pleasure in it. In this instance,
of course, people don't rage in silence. They moan. But

they are no ordinary moans; they're malicious, and in this maliciousness lies the point. It's this moaning that expresses the pleasure of the sufferer, for if he didn't enjoy it, he wouldn't moan. This is a good example of what I mean, so I'll dwell on it for a while. To start with, these moans express all the humiliating pointlessness of the pain, a pain that obeys certain laws of nature about which you don't give a damn, for you're the one who must suffer, and nature can't feel a thing. Thus, these moans indicate that, although there's no enemy, the pain is there; that you, together with your dentist, are completely at the mercy of your teeth; that if it pleases someone, your toothache will stop, and if it doesn't, it may go on for another three months; and that, finally, if you refuse to resign yourself and go on protesting, all you can do to relieve your feelings is to give yourself a whipping or pound the stone wall with your fists. There's definitely nothing else you can do.

So it is these horrible insults and humiliations, inflicted on us by God knows whom, that generate a pleasure that sometimes reaches the highest degree of voluptuousness. Please, ladies and gentlemen, listen carefully some time to the moans of a nineteenth century intellectual suffering from a toothache. Listen on the second or third day of pain, when he is no longer moaning the way he did on the first day, that is, simply because his tooth ached. His moaning is quite unlike the moaning of a peasant, for he has been affected by education and by European civilization. He moans like a man who, as they say nowadays, "has been uprooted from the soil and lost contact with the people." His moans soon become strident and perverse, and they continue day and night. He certainly knows that he's not helping himself by moaning like that. No one knows better than he that he's tormenting and irritating himself and others for nothing; that his audience, and this includes his family, for whom he's trying so hard, is listening to him with disgust; that they don't believe he's sincere in the least and realize that he could moan differently, more simply, without all these trills and flourishes; and that he's putting it all on out of sheer spite and viciousness.

Well, there's voluptuous pleasure in all this degradation and in the realization of it.

I'm disturbing you? Breaking your heart? Keeping everyone awake? All right, stay awake then, feel every second that my teeth ache. To you, I'm no longer the hero I tried to appear at first, but simply a despicable little man. So be it. I'm very glad you've managed to see through me. It makes you uncomfortable to listen to my cowardly moaning? Well, be uncomfortable. I'll produce one of those moaning flourishes in a minute, then you can tell me how you feel. . . .

You still don't understand what I have in mind? Well, then it looks as if you have to grow up and develop your comprehension so that you can grasp all the twists of this voluptuousness. That makes you laugh? I'm very happy it does. Of course my jokes are in poor taste, inappropriate, and confused; they reveal my lack of security. But that is because I have no respect for myself. After all, how can a man with my lucidity of perception respect himself?

V

How can one, after all, have the slightest respect for a man who tries to find pleasure in the feeling of humiliation itself? I'm not saying that out of any mawkish sense of repentance. In general, I couldn't stand saying "Sorry, Papa, I'll never do it again."

And it wasn't at all because I was incapable of saying it. On the contrary, perhaps it was just because I was only too prone to say it. And you should've seen under what circumstances too! I'd get myself blamed, almost purposely, for something with which I'd had nothing to do even in thought or dream. That's what was most disgusting. But, even so, I was always deeply moved, repented my wickedness, and cried; in this, of course, I was deceiving myself, although I never did so deliberately.

It was my heart that let me down here. In this case, I can't even blame the laws of nature, although those laws have oppressed me all my life. It makes me sick to remember all this, but then I was sick at the time too. It took me only a minute or so to recognize that it was all a pack of lies; all that repentance, those emotional outbursts and promises of reform—nothing but pretentious, nauseating lies. I was furious. And if you ask me now why I tortured and tormented myself like that, I'll tell you: I was bored just sitting with my arms folded, so I went in for all those tricks. Believe me, it's true. Just watch yourself carefully and you'll understand that that's the way it works. I made up whole stories about myself and put myself through all sorts of adventures to satisfy, at any price, my need to live. How many times did I convince myself that I was offended, just like that, for no reason at all. And although I knew that I had nothing to be offended about, that I was putting it all on, I'd put myself into such a state that in the end I'd really feel terribly offended. I was so strongly tempted to play tricks of this sort that, in the end, I lost all restraint.

Once, or rather twice, I tried to make myself fall in love. And, believe me, ladies and gentlemen, I certainly suffered! Deep down, of course, I couldn't quite believe in my suffering and felt like laughing. But it was suffering nevertheless—the real stuff, with jealousy, violence, and all the trimmings.

And all that out of sheer boredom, ladies and gentlemen, sheer boredom. I was crushed by inertia. And what would the natural, logical fruit of heightened consciousness be if not inertia, by which I mean consciously sitting with folded arms! I mentioned that before. And I repeat again and again: spontaneous people and men of action can act precisely because they are limited and stupid. How shall I explain? Let me put it this way: because of their limitations, these people mistake the nearest secondary causes for primary ones. This way they become convinced faster and more easily than others that they have found an incontrovertible reason for acting, and they have no further qualms about acting, which, of course, is the important thing. Obviously, in order to act, one must be fully satisfied and free of all misgivings beforehand. But take me: how can I ever be sure? Where will I find the primary reason for action, the justification for it? Where am I to look for it? I exercise my power of reasoning, and in my case, every time I think I have found a primary cause I see another cause that seems to be truly primary, and so on and so forth, indefinitely. This is the very essence of consciousness and thought. It must be another natural law. And what happens in the end? The same thing over again.

Remember when I spoke of vengeance (I bet you didn't follow me too well)? It is said that a man avenges himself because he thinks it is the just thing to do. This implies that he has found the primary reason, the basis for his action, which, in this case, is Justice. This gives him foolproof peace of mind, so he avenges himself without qualms, efficiently, certain throughout that he's acting fairly and honestly.

But I can't see any justice or virtue in vengeance, so if I indulge in it, it is only out of spite and anger. Anger, of course, overcomes all hesitations and can thus replace the primary reason precisely because it is no reason at all. But what can I do if I don't even have anger (that's where I started from, remember)? In me, anger disintegrates chemically like everything else, because of those damned laws of nature. As I think, the anger vanishes, the reasons for it evaporate, the responsible person is never found, the insult becomes an insult no longer but a stroke of fate, just like a toothache, for which no one can be held responsible. And so I find that all I can do is take another whack at the stone wall, then shrug the whole thing off because of my failure to find the primary cause of the evil.

And, if I did try to follow my feeling blindly without thinking about primary causes, if I managed to keep my consciousness out of it, even temporarily, if I did make myself hate or love just to avoid sitting with folded arms —then, within forty-eight hours at the most, I'd loathe myself for deliberately sinking into self-deception. And everything would burst like a soap bubble and end in inertia.

You know, ladies and gentlemen, probably the only reason why I think I'm an intelligent man is that in all my life I've never managed to start or finish anything. I know, I know, I'm just a chatterbox, a harmless, boring chatterbox like all my kind. But how can I help it if it is the inescapable fate of every intelligent man to chatter, like filling an empty glass from an empty bottle?

VI

If only my doing nothing were due to laziness! How I'd respect myself then! Yes, respect, because I would know that I could be lazy at least, that I had at least one definite feature in me, something positive, something I could be sure of. To the question "Who is he?" people would answer, "A lazy man." It would be wonderful to hear that. It would imply that I could be clearly characterized, that there was something to be said about me. "A lazy man." Why, it's a calling, a vocation, a career, ladies and gentlemen! Don't laugh, it's the truth. I'd be a member of the foremost club in the land, and my full-time occupation would be constant respect for myself. I once knew a gentleman who, all his life, was proud of being a connoisseur of Château Lafitte. He considered it a great virtue and never had any misgivings about it. He died with a conscience that was not merely clear but jubilant. And he was absolutely right. If I'd had a choice, I'd have chosen for myself the career of a lazy man, a glutton—but one who would have been, at the same time, a supporter of "the good and the beautiful." How would you have liked that? I dreamt of it for a long time. "The good and the beautiful" sticks in my throat today, when I'm forty, but it didn't always. At one time I'd immediately have found some appropriate activity for myself, such as drinking to "the good and the beautiful." At every opportunity I'd have allowed a tear to roll down my cheek and fall into my glass, and I'd have raised my glass and emptied it to "the good and the beautiful." Then I'd have turned everything under the sun into goodness and beauty. I'd have uncovered it in the most unmistakable piece of rubbish. Tears would have oozed out of me like drops squeezed out of a sponge. An artist paints a picture of s——. All right, let's immediately drink to the health of that artist, because I'm a lover of everything that's "good and beautiful." Some author writes something that will be to everybody's liking, so let me drink to everyone's health, because I stand for "the good and the beautiful"!

And for this, I'd have demanded respect and have gone for anyone who grudged it to me.

So I'd have lived without worrying and died gloriously. What could be more delightful? And think what a belly, what a triple chin I'd have grown myself, and what a ruddy nose! Everyone who came across me would've said:

"There's a man for you! There's no doubt about him being a real, positive person, at least!"

And, say what you like, it's pleasant to hear such remarks in our negative century, ladies and gentlemen.

VII

But these are just golden dreams. Who was it that first said that man does nasty things only because he doesn't know where his real interests lie, that if he were enlightened about his true interests, he would immediately stop acting like a pig and become kind and noble? Being enlightened, the argument goes on, and seeing where his real advantage lay, he would realize that it was in acting virtuously. And, since it is well established that a man will not act deliberately against his own interests, it follows that he would have no choice but to become good. Oh, the innocence of it! Since when, in these past thousands of years, has man acted exclusively out of self-interest? What about the millions of facts that show that men, deliberately and in full knowledge of what their real interests were, spurned them and rushed in a different direction? They did so at their own risk without anyone advising them, refusing to follow the safe, well-trodden path and searching for another path, a difficult one, an unreasonable one, stubbornly working their way along it in the darkness. Doesn't this suggest that stubbornness and willfulness were stronger in these people than their interests?

Interest! What interest? Can you define exactly what is in the interest of a human being? And suppose the interest of a man is not only consistent with but even demands something harmful rather than advantageous? Of course, if such an instance *is* possible, then the whole rule is nothing but dust. Now, you tell me—is such an instance possible? You may laugh if you wish, but I want you to answer me this: is there an accurate scale of human advantages? Aren't there any advantages that are omitted, that cannot possibly be included in any such scale? As far as I can make out, you've based your scale of advantages on statistical averages and scientific formulas thought up by economists. And since your scale consists of such advantages as happiness, prosperity, freedom, security, and all that, a man who deliberately disregarded that scale would be branded by you—and by me too, as a matter of fact—as an obscurantist and as utterly insane. But what is really remarkable is that all of your statisticians, sages, and humanitarians, when listing human advantages, insist on leaving out one of them. They never even allow for it, thus invalidating all their calculations. One would think it would be easy just to add it to the list. But that's where the trouble lies—it doesn't fit into any scale or chart.

You see, ladies and gentlemen, I have a friend—of course, he's your friend, too, and, in fact, everyone's friend. When he's about to do something, this friend explains pompously and in detail how he must act in accordance with the precepts of justice and reason. Moreover, he becomes passionate as he expostulates upon human interests; heaps scorn on the shortsighted fools who don't know what virtue is or what's good for them. Then, exactly fifteen minutes later, without any apparent external cause, but prompted by something inside him that is stronger than every consideration of interest, he pirouettes and starts saying exactly the opposite of what he was saying before; that is, he discredits the laws of logic and his own advantage; in short, he attacks everything. . . .

Now, since my friend is a composite type, he cannot be dismissed as an odd individual. So perhaps there is something that every man values above the highest individual advantage, or (not to be illogical) there may exist a human advantage that is the most advantageous (and it is precisely the one that is so consistently left out), which is also more important than the others and for the sake of which a man, if need be, will go against reason, honor, security, and prosperity—in short, against all the beautiful and useful things—just to attain it, the most advantageous advantage of the lot, the one which is the dearest to him.

"So," you may interrupt me, "it's an advantage all the same."

Wait a minute. Let me make myself clear. It's not a question of words. The remarkable thing about this advantage is that it makes a shambles of all the classifications and tables drawn up by humanitarians for the happiness of mankind. It crowds them out, as it were. But before I name this advantage, let me go on record and declare that all these lovely systems, all these theories that explain to man what is to his true advantage so that, to achieve it, he will forthwith become good and noble—all these are, in my opinion, nothing but sterile exercises in logic. Yes, that's all there is to it. For instance, propounding the theory of human regeneration through the pursuit of self-interest is, in my opinion, almost like . . . well, like saying with H.T. Buckle that man mellows under the influence of civilization and becomes less bloodthirsty and less prone to war. He appears to be following logical reasoning in arriving at that conclusion. But men love abstract reasoning and neat systematization so much that they think nothing of distorting the truth, closing their eyes and ears to contrary evidence

to preserve their logical constructions. I'd say the example I've taken here is really too glaring. You have
only to look around you and you'll see blood being
spilled, and in the most playful way, just as if it were
champagne. Look at the United States, that indissoluble
union, plunged into civil war! Look at the Schleswig-
Holstein farce . . . And what is it in us that is mellowed
by civilization? All it does, I'd say, is to develop in man

a capacity to feel a greater variety of sensations. And
nothing, absolutely nothing else. And through this development, man will yet learn how to enjoy bloodshed.
Why, it has already happened. Have you noticed, for instance, that the most refined, bloodthirsty tyrants, compared to whom the Attilas and Stenka Razins are mere
choirboys, are often exquisitely civilized? In fact, if they
are not overly conspicuous, it is because there are too
many of them and they have become too familiar to us.
Civilization has made man, if not always more bloodthirsty, at least more viciously, more horribly bloodthirsty. In the past, he saw justice in bloodshed and
slaughtered without any pangs of conscience those he felt
had to be slaughtered. Today, though we consider bloodshed terrible, we still practice it—and on a much larger
scale than ever before. It was said that Cleopatra—
please forgive me this example from ancient history—
enjoyed sticking golden pins into the breasts of her
slaves, delighting in their screams and writhings. You
may object that this happened in relatively barbarous
times; or you may say that even now we live in barbarous
times (also relatively), that pins are still stuck into
people, that even today, although man has learned to be
more discerning than in ancient times, he has yet to
learn how to follow his reason.

Nevertheless, there's no doubt in your mind that he will
learn as soon as he's rid of certain bad old habits and
when common sense and science have completely re-
educated human nature and directed it along the proper
channels. You seem certain that man himself will give
up erring *of his own free will* and will stop opposing his
will to his interests. You say, moreover, that science

itself will teach man (although I say it's a luxury) that he
has neither will nor whim—never had, as a matter of fact
—that he is something like a piano key or an organ stop;
that, on the other hand, there are natural laws in the
universe, and whatever happens to him happens outside
his will, as it were, by itself, in accordance with the laws
of nature. Therefore, all there is left to do is to discover
these laws and man will no longer be responsible for his
acts. Life will be really easy for him then. All human
acts will be listed in something like logarithm tables, say
up to the number 108,000, and transferred to a timetable. Or, better still, catalogues will appear, designed to
help us in the way our dictionaries and encyclopedias do.
They will carry detailed calculations and exact fore-
casts of everything to come, so that no adventure and
no action will remain possible in this world.

Then—it is still you talking—new economic relations
will arise, relations ready-made and calculated in advance
with mathematical precision, so that all possible questions instantaneously disappear because they receive all
the possible answers. Then the utopian palace of crystal
will be erected; then . . . well, then, those will be the days
of bliss.

Of course, you can't guarantee (it's me speaking now)
that it won't be deadly boring (for what will there be to
do when everything is predetermined by timetables?) But,
on the other hand, everything will be planned very reasonably.

But then, one might do anything out of boredom.
Golden pins are stuck into people out of boredom. But
that's nothing. What's really bad (this is me speaking
again) is that the golden pins will be welcomed then.
The trouble with man is that he's stupid. Phenomenally
stupid. That is, even if he's not really stupid, he's so ungrateful that another creature as ungrateful cannot be
found. I, for one, wouldn't be the least surprised if, in
that future age of reason, there suddenly appeared a
gentleman with an ungrateful, or shall we say, retrogres-
sive smirk, who, arms akimbo, would say:

"What do you say, folks, let's send all this reason to

hell, just to get all these logarithm tables out from under our feet and go back to our own stupid ways."

That isn't so annoying in itself; what's bad is that this gentleman would be sure to find followers. That's the way man is made.

And the explanation for it is so simple that there hardly seems to be any need for it—namely, that a man, always and everywhere, prefers to act in the way he feels like acting and not in the way his reason and interest tell him, for it is very possible for a man to feel like acting against his interests and, in some instances, I say that he *positively* wants to act that way—but that's my personal opinion.

So one's own free, unrestrained choice, one's own whim, be it the wildest, one's own fancy, sometimes worked up to a frenzy—that is the most advantageous advantage that cannot be fitted into any table or scale and that causes every system and every theory to crumble into dust on contact. And where did these sages pick up the notion that man must have something that they feel is a normal and virtuous set of wishes; what makes them think that man's will must be reasonable and in accordance with his own interests? All man actually needs is *independent* will, at all costs and whatever the consequences.

Speaking of will, I'm damned if I——

VIII

"Ha-ha-ha! Strictly speaking there's no such thing as will!" you may interrupt me, guffawing. "Today, science has already succeeded in dissecting a man sufficiently to be able to tell that what we know as desire and free will are nothing but——"

Hold on, hold on a moment! I was coming to that myself. I admit I was even frightened about it. I was about to say that will depended on hell knows what and perhaps we should thank God for that, but then I remembered about science, and that stopped me short.

And it was at that point that you spoke up. Now, suppose one day they really find a formula at the root of all our wishes and whims that will tell us what they depend on, what laws they are subject to, how they develop, what they are aiming at in such and such a case, and so on and so forth—that is, a real mathematical equation? Well, chances are that man will then cease to feel desire. Almost surely. What joy will he get out of functioning according to a timetable? Furthermore, he'll change from a man into an organ stop or something like that, for what is a man without will, wishes, and desires, if not an organ stop?

Let's examine the probabilities then—whether or not it's likely to happen. Now, what do *you* say?

"Hm . . ." you say, "our wishes are mostly misguided because of a mistaken evaluation of what's in our interest. If we sometimes desire something that doesn't make sense, it is because, in our stupidity, we believe that it's the easiest way to attain a supposed advantage. But once all this has been explained to us and worked out on a sheet of paper (which is very possible, because it is contemptible and meaningless to maintain that there may exist laws of nature which man will never penetrate), such desires will simply cease to exist. For when desire merges with reason, then we will reason instead of desiring. It will be impossible to retain reason and desire something senseless, that is, harmful. And once all our desires and all our reasoning can be computed (for the day is bound to come when we'll understand what actually governs what we now describe as our free will), then we may really have some sort of tables to guide our desires like everything else. So, if a man sticks out his tongue at someone, it is because he cannot *not* stick it out and has to stick it out holding his head exactly at the angle he does. So what *freedom* is there left in him, especially if he's a learned man, a diploma-holding scientist? Why, he can plot his life thirty years in advance. Anyway, if it comes to that, we've no choice but to accept. We must keep repeating to ourselves that, at no time and in no place, will nature ever ask for our permission; that we must accept it as it is and not as we paint it in our imaginations; that if we're moving toward graphs, timetables, and even test tubes, well, we'll just have to take it all—including, of course, the test tube! And if we do not wish to accept, nature itself will——"

Yes, yes, I know, I know . . . But there's a snag here, as far as I'm concerned. You must excuse me, ladies and gentlemen, if I get entangled in my own thoughts. You must make allowances for the fact that I've spent all the forty years of my life in a mousehole under the floor. So allow me to indulge my fancy.

I will admit that reason is a good thing. No argument about that. But reason is only reason, and it only satisfies man's rational requirements. Desire, on the other hand, is the manifestation of life itself—of all of life—and it encompasses everything from reason down to scratching oneself. And although, when we're guided by our desires, life may often turn into a messy affair, it's still life and not a series of extractions of square roots.

I, for instance, instinctively want to live, to exercise all the aspects of life in me and not only reason, which amounts to perhaps one-twentieth of the whole.

And what does reason know? It knows only what it has had time to learn. Many things will always remain unknown to it. That must be said even if there's nothing encouraging in it.

Now, human nature is just the opposite. It acts as an entity, using everything it has, conscious and unconscious, and even if it deceives us, it lives. I suspect, ladies and gentlemen, that you're looking at me with pity, wondering how I can fail to understand that an enlightened, cultured man, such as the man of the future, could not deliberately wish to harm himself. It's sheer mathematics to you. I agree, it is mathematics. But let me repeat to you for the hundredth time that there is one instance when a man can wish upon himself, in full awareness, something harmful, stupid, and even completely idiotic. He will do it in order to *establish his right* to wish for the most idiotic things and not to be obliged to have only sensible wishes. But what if a quite absurd whim, my friends, turns out to

be the most advantageous thing on earth for us, as sometimes happens? Specifically, it may be more advantageous
to us than any other advantages, even when it most
obviously harms us and goes against all the sensible
conclusions of our reason about our interest—because,
whatever else, it leaves us our most important, most
treasured possession: our individuality.

Some people concede, for instance, that desire may
be the thing man treasures most. Desire, of course, can, if
it wishes, agree with reason, especially if one uses it
sparingly, never going too far. Then desire is quite useful,
even praiseworthy.

But in reality, desire usually stubbornly disagrees with
reason . . . and . . . and . . . let me tell you that this too
is useful and praiseworthy.

Let's assume, ladies and gentlemen, that man isn't stupid. (For, indeed, if we say he is stupid, whom will we
be able to call intelligent?) But even if he isn't stupid,
he is still monstrously ungrateful. Phenomenally so! I
would even say that the best definition of man is: ungrateful biped. But this is still not his main defect. His
main defect is his chronic perversity, an affliction from
which he has suffered throughout his history, from the
Flood through the Schleswig-Holstein crisis. Perversity
and, therefore, lack of common sense, since it is well
known that perversity is due to a lack of good sense.
Just have a look at the history of mankind and tell me
what you see there. You find it grand? Maybe so. The
Colossus of Rhodes is impressive enough to have
prompted Mr. Anayevsky to say that some consider it a
work of man and others consider it a creation of nature.
You find it colorful? Yes, I suppose there's plenty of
color in human history. Think of all the military dress
uniforms and the formal civilian outfits. This seems quite
impressive in itself. And if we think of all the uniforms
worn on semi-official occasions, there's so much color
that any historian would be dazzled by it. You find it
monotonous? Yes, you have a good point there. They
fight and fight and fight; they are fighting now, they fought

before, and they'll fight in the future. Yes, I must agree
that it's a bit too monotonous.

So you see, you can say anything about world history
—anything and everything that the most morbid imagination can think up. Except one thing, that is. It cannot be
said that world history is reasonable. The word sticks in
one's throat. And here's what happens all the time: good
and reasonable men, sages and humanitarians, try to live
constantly good and sensible lives, serving, so to speak,
as human torches to light the path for their neighbors, to
prove to them that it can be done. And what comes of it?
Sure enough, these lovers of mankind sooner or later give
up, some in the midst of a scandal, and often quite an
unseemly one too.

Now, let me ask you something: what can one expect
from man, considering he's such a strange creature? You
can shower upon him all earthly blessings, drown him in
happiness so that there'll be nothing to be seen but the
bubbles rising to the surface of his bliss, give him such
economic security that he won't have anything to do but
sleep, nibble at cakes, and worry about keeping world
history flowing—and even then, out of sheer spite and ingratitude, man will play a dirty trick on you. He'll even
risk his cake for the sake of the most glaring stupidity,
for the most economically unsound nonsense, just to in-
ject into all the soundness and sense surrounding him
some of his own disastrous, lethal fancies. What he wants
to preserve is precisely his noxious fancies and vulgar
trivialities, if only to assure himself that men are still men
(as if that were so important) and not piano keys simply
responding to the laws of nature. Man is somehow averse
to the idea of being unable to desire unless this desire
happens to figure on his timetable at that moment.

But even if man was nothing but a piano key, even if
this could be demonstrated to him mathematically—even
then, he wouldn't come to his senses but would pull some
trick out of sheer ingratitude, just to make his point.
And if he didn't have them on hand, he would devise
the means of destruction, chaos, and all kinds of suffering
to get his way. For instance, he'd swear loud enough for

the whole world to hear—swearing is man's prerogative, setting him apart from the other animals—and maybe his swearing alone would get him what he wanted, that is, it'd prove to him that he's a man and not a piano key.

Now, you may say that this too can be calculated in advance and entered on the timetable—chaos, swearing, and all—and that the very possibility of such a calculation would prevent it, so that sanity would prevail. Oh no! In that case man would go insane on purpose, just to be immune from reason.

I believe this is so and I'm prepared to vouch for it, because it seems to me that the meaning of man's life consists in proving to himself every minute that he's a man and not a piano key. And man will keep proving it and paying for it with his own skin; he will turn into a troglodyte if need be. And, since this is so, I cannot help rejoicing that things are still the way they are and that, for the time being, nobody knows worth a damn what determines our desires.

Now you scream that no one intends to deprive me of my free will, that they're only trying to arrange things so that my will coincides with what is in my own interest, the laws of nature, and arithmetic.

Ah, ladies and gentlemen, don't talk to me of free will when it comes to timetables and arithmetic, when everything will be deducible from twice two makes four! There's no need for free will to find that twice two is four. That's not what I call free will!

IX

Of course I'm joking, my friends, and I realize my jokes are weak. Still, everything can't be just laughed off. Perhaps I'm joking through clenched teeth. You see, I'm haunted by certain questions, and perhaps you'll allow me to ask them.

Now, you, for instance—you want to cure man of his bad old habits and reshape his will according to the requirements of science and common sense. But what makes you think that man either can or *should* be changed in this way? What leads you to the conclusion that it is absolutely necessary to change man's desires? How do you know that these corrections will actually be to man's advantage? And, if you'll allow me to speak quite openly, what makes you so sure that abstention from acting contrary to one's interests, as determined by reason and arithmetic, is always to one's advantage and that this applies to mankind as a whole?

So far, these are nothing but assumptions on your part. I'll grant you that they conform to the laws of logic. But are they in accordance with human law? In case you think I'm crazy, let me explain. I agree that man is a creative animal, doomed to strive consciously toward a goal, engaged in full-time engineering, as it were, busy building himself roads that lead *somewhere—never mind where*. And perhaps if he feels like straying now and then, it is just because he is *doomed* to build this road; even the man of action, however stupid he may be, must realize from time to time that his road always goes *somewhere* and that the main thing is not *where* it goes but keeping the well-meaning babe at his engineering chores, thus saving him from the deadly snares of idleness, which, as is well known, is the mother of all vice. There's no disputing that man likes creating and building roads. But why does he also like chaos and disorder even into his old age? Explain that if you can! But wait, I myself would like to say a few words on this particular subject. I wonder if he doesn't like chaos and destruction so much just because he's instinctively afraid of reaching the goal he's working for? How do you know, perhaps he likes his objective only from a distance; perhaps he only likes to contemplate it and not to live in it, preferring to leave it, when it comes down to it, to animals such as ants, sheep, and such. Of course, ants are different. They have a wonderful everlasting piece of engineering on which to work—the anthill.

The worthy ants began with their anthill and will most likely end with it, which is greatly to the credit of their single-mindedness and perseverance. But man is frivolous and unaccountable and perhaps, like a chess player, he enjoys the achieving rather than the goal itself.

And who can tell, perhaps the purpose of man's life on earth consists precisely in this uninterrupted striving after a goal. That is to say, the purpose is life itself and not the goal which, of course, must be nothing but twice two makes four. And twice two, ladies and gentlemen, is no longer life but the beginning of death. At least, man has always feared this twice two makes four, and it's what I'm afraid of now.

Let's assume that man does nothing but search for this twice two, that he crosses oceans and sacrifices his life in this quest, while, all the time, he is really afraid of finding that it does make four. He feels that once he has discovered it, he'll have nothing left for which to search. The workers, at least, when they receive their money at the end of the week, go to a tavern and then, perhaps, land in a police station, so there's something to keep them busy. But otherwise, what is a man to do with himself when he achieves one of his objectives? In any case, there is a visible awkwardness in him every time he does. He loves the achieving, but does not particularly enjoy what he achieves. Funny, isn't it? Yes, man is a comical animal, and there's obviously a joke in all this. Still, I say that twice two is an unbearable notion, an arrogant imposition. This twice two image stands there, hands in pockets, in the middle of your road, and spits in your direction. Nevertheless, I'm willing to agree that twice-two-makes-four is a thing of beauty. But, if we're going to praise everything like that, then I say that twice-two-makes-five is also a delightful little item now and then.

And what makes you so cocksure, so positive that only the normal and the positive, that is, only what promotes man's welfare, is to his advantage? Can't reason also be wrong about what's an advantage? Why can't man like things other than his well-being? Maybe he likes suffering just as much. Maybe suffering is just as much to his advantage as well-being. In fact, man adores suffering. Passionately. It's a fact. For this, there's no need even to go to world history. Just ask yourself, if you've had any kind of experience of life. And, personally, I even feel that it's shameful to like just well-being by itself. Right or wrong, it's very pleasant to break something from time to time.

Actually, I'm not advocating suffering any more than well-being. What I'm for is whim, and I want the right to use it whenever I want to.

I know, for instance, that suffering is inadmissible in light stage plays. In the utopian crystal palace, it'd be inconceivable, for suffering means doubt and denial, and what kind of crystal palace would that be, if people had doubts about it? Nevertheless, I'm certain that man will never give up true suffering, that is, chaos and destruction. Why, suffering is the only cause of consciousness. And, although I declared at the beginning that consciousness is man's greatest plague, I know that he likes it and won't exchange it for any advantage. Consciousness, for instance, is of a much higher order than twice two. After twice two, we'll of course have nothing left either to do or to find out. All that'll be left for us will be to block off our five senses and plunge into contemplation. With consciousness we have nothing much to do either, but we can at least lacerate ourselves from time to time, which does liven us up a bit. It may go against progress, but it's better than nothing.

X

So, you believe in an indestructible crystal palace in which you won't be able to stick out your tongue or blow raspberries even if you cover your mouth with your hand. But I'm afraid of such a palace precisely because it's indestructible and because I won't ever be allowed to stick my tongue out at it.

Try to understand: if, instead of that palace, there were nothing but a chicken house, and if I had to crawl into it to get out of the rain, I wouldn't call it a palace just out of gratitude, because it kept me dry. You may laugh and say that for that purpose it makes no difference whether

it is a chicken coop or a palace. I'd agree with you if
the only purpose of life was keeping from getting wet.

But suppose I decided that keeping dry is not the only
reason for living and that, while we're at it, we'd better
try and live in palaces? That's my wish and my choice.
You'll change it only when you manage to change my
preferences. By all means, do so if you can. But, in the
meantime, allow me to distinguish between the chicken
coop and the palace.

Let's assume now that the crystal palace is nothing but
a pipe dream, that the laws of nature don't provide for it,
that I dreamed it up, in my stupidity, influenced by
certain old, irrational habits of thought that are common
among my generation.

But I really don't give a damn whether the laws of
nature provide for it or not. And what difference would
it make, since it exists in my wish? Or, rather, it exists as
long as my wishes exist.

Are you laughing again? Go ahead, laugh, but I still
won't say that my belly is full when I'm hungry; I still
won't content myself with a compromise, with an infinitely recurring zero just because it is allowed to recur
by some law, just because it's there. I don't accept as the
crowning of my dreams a big building for the poor, with
apartments leased for one thousand years and a dentist's
sign outside in case of emergency.

But I'm prepared to follow you as soon as you have
eradicated my desires, destroyed my ideals, and replaced
them by something better. And if you ask why you should
be bothered with me, I can say the same to you. I'm
serious about the whole thing, but if you don't want to
waste your time and attention on me, my heart won't be
broken. I have my hole under the floor, remember?

And, in the meantime, I'll go on living and desiring,
and may my right arm wither if I contribute a single
brick to that apartment building of yours! Disregard what
I said before about rejecting the crystal palace because
I wouldn't be allowed to stick my tongue out at it. I said
that not because I love sticking out my tongue, but because I have yet to see a building of yours at which one

could refrain from sticking out one's tongue. On the contrary, I'd be willing to have my tongue cut out in sheer gratitude if it could be arranged that I would never again feel like sticking it out. But what can I do if that cannot be arranged and I'm invited to accept, in the meantime, cheap apartments? Why have I been provided with all these desires? Was it only to reach the conclusion that they're nothing but a big swindle? Is that the goal of everything? I don't believe it.

But, after all I've said now, shall I tell you something? I'm sure that mousehole dwellers like me should be kept out of the way. Their kind may spend forty years sitting under the floor somewhere, but once they escape, once they emerge from there, they'll talk and talk and talk; they'll talk your head off without stopping.

XI

And so, in the end, ladies and gentlemen, it's best to do nothing at all! Conscious inertia is the best! A toast to my hole under the floor! And, though I said that I was green with envy of the normal man, I still wouldn't take his place under present circumstances—although I'll go on envying him. No, no, my hole is better, whatever you may say! There, at least, it's possible—ah, there I go, lying again! I'm lying because I know, like twice-two-makes four, that it's not the mousehole that's better, but something quite different—something I long for, but cannot find. To hell with the mousehole!

I'd feel better if I could only believe something of what I've written down here. But I swear I can't believe a single word of it. That is, I believe it in a way, but at the same time, I feel I'm lying like a son of a bitch.

"Then why have you written all this?" you may ask me.

Well, I wish I could stick you into a mousehole for forty years or so with nothing to do, and at the end of that time I'd like to see what kind of state you'd be in. Do you think it's permissible to leave a man alone for forty years without anything to do?

"And what you're doing now—don't you think it's despicable?" you may say, perhaps shrugging contemptuously. "You say you're longing to live, and you try to solve the problems of life with tangled logic. And you're so insistent, so arrogant, and at the same time, so afraid. You talk all sorts of rot, and yet you're pleased with it. You're insulting and yet, fearing the consequences, you keep apologizing. You try to convince us that you fear nothing, but we find you cringing. You tell us that you're raging and talking through clenched teeth, but all the time you're trying to be funny and make us laugh. You're aware that your jokes are not very funny, but you seem to find some literary merit in them. It's possible that you have had to suffer, but you don't seem to have any respect for your own suffering. There is some truth in you, all right, but there's no humility; and it is out of the pettiest vanity that you drag forth your truth, to exhibit it, to offer it for sale, to disgrace it. You really have something to say, but you hide your final words, out of fear, because you really have no courage, only the impertinence of a coward. You were bragging about your consciousness, yet you can't grasp anything clearly because, though your head is quite lucid, your heart is murky as a result of debauchery, and real consciousness is impossible without a pure heart. And you're so indiscreet, so pushy, and such a show-off! Ah, you tell nothing but lies, lies, and more lies. . . ."

Of course, I've invented all your words myself. They too come from my hole. I've been listening to your words through a crack for forty years, while sitting in my hole under the floor. That was all I had to do. So, by now, I know them by heart, and it's no wonder I've been able to set them down like this, in literary form.

But are you really so credulous as to imagine that I'll have all this published for you to read? And there's another puzzle I'd like to solve: Why on earth do I keep calling you "ladies and gentlemen" and addressing you as if you were really my readers? The sort of confessions I'm about to make here don't get printed, nor does one give them to other people to read. I, at least, don't have sufficient determination to do so, nor do I feel there's any need for it. But, you see, I've taken a fancy into my head, and I want to realize it at any cost.

What I mean is that there are things in every man's past that he won't admit except to his most intimate friends. There are other things that he won't admit even to his friends but only to himself—and only in strictest confidence. But there are things, too, that a man won't dare to admit even to himself, and every decent man has quite an accumulation of such things. In fact, the more decent he is, the greater the accumulation he's bound to have. I have only recently dared to explore some of my past adventures which, until then, I had avoided with peculiar anxiety. But now that I have made myself remember them and have even dared to write them down, I want to make a test to see whether it is possible to be completely frank and unafraid of the whole truth. I would like to note here Heine's remark to the effect that sincere autobiographies are almost impossible and that a man is bound to lie about himself. In his view, Rousseau must have lied about himself deliberately and out of sheer vanity in his *Confessions*. I'm sure Heine is right. I realize that it is sometimes possible to pin full-fledged crimes on ourselves out of vanity. I can see that, all right. But Heine was passing judgment on a man confessing publicly. Now, in my case, I'm writing this just for myself, for even if I do address myself to imaginary readers, I do it only because it makes it easier for me to write. It's just a matter of form, nothing else, for as I said before, I'll never have any readers.

I don't want to let considerations of literary composition get in my way. I won't bother with planning and arranging; I'll note down whatever comes to my mind.

Now, of course, you may feel you've caught me and ask me why, if I really don't expect to have any readers, I bother to record all these explanations about writing without a plan, jotting down whatever comes to mind, and so on. What's the point of all these excuses and apologies then?

My answer is—well, that's the way it is.

There's a whole psychological explanation to it. Maybe it's because I'm a coward. Possibly, too, if I imagine an audience, my behavior will be more seemly while I'm writing this down. There may be thousands of reasons.

Then there's something else. Why, one may ask, do I want to write at all? If it's not for the public, couldn't I just reminisce in my head, without putting things down on paper? That's a good question, but I feel that writing will lend dignity to it. There's something impressive about the written word; it is more conducive to self-examination, and my confession will have more style. It is possible, too, that the very process of writing things down will relieve me somewhat. Today, for instance, I'm particularly oppressed by an old memory. It came back to me clearly a few days ago and, since then, it's been like an exasperating tune that I can't get out of my head. But I must get rid of it. I have hundreds of such memories, and from time to time, one of them detaches itself from the mass and starts tormenting me. I feel that if I write it down, I'll get rid of it. Why not try?

Finally, I'm bored with constantly doing nothing. Writing things down is a bit like work and I've heard people say that work makes people good and honest! So there may be a chance for me too, after all.

It's snowing today. A wet, yellow, murky snow is coming down. Yesterday it snowed too. And a few days ago, also. I believe that it was this wet snow that made me think of the incident I can't get out of my head. So this is a story connected with wet snow.

PART TWO

Brought to Mind by a Fall of Wet Snow

When my passionate, ardent plea,
From a wilderness of sea,
Rescued your poor soul at last;
Plunged in anguish and torment,

You wrung your hands in sad lament,
Damning your ignoble past;
Then with memories lashing, gory,
Making sleeping conscience fret,
You poured forth the awful story,
Of your life before we met.
Filled with shame that would not fade,
Covering your weeping face,
Bitter tears in wild cascade
Marked your infinite disgrace . . .
    etc., etc., etc.

FROM THE POETRY OF N. A. NEKRASOV

I

I was twenty-four, but even then I led the gloomy, disorganized, solitary existence of a recluse. I stayed away from people, avoided even speaking to them, and kept more and more to my hole. At the office, I avoided looking at anyone; I realized that the others regarded me as eccentric and even—so, at least, I felt—viewed me with a sort of disgust. Why, I wondered sometimes, did no one else feel that he was inspiring disgust in others? There was a clerk there with a repulsive, pockmarked face—in fact, he was quite sinister-looking. I wouldn't have had the courage to even show such a mug to anyone. Another clerk's clothes were so dirty that he smelled. But neither clerk seemed in the least perturbed by his face, his clothes, or by—I don't know—any mental quirk he may have had. It didn't occur to either fellow that he might inspire loathing. And even if it had, neither of them would have given a damn—unless the loathing came from their superiors. Now, it is absolutely clear to me that, because of an infinite vanity that caused me to set myself impossible standards, I regarded myself with furious disapproval, bordering on loathing, then ascribed my own feelings to everyone I came across. I hated my face. I found it odious and even suspected that there was something slimy in its expression, so, on arriving at the office, I always tried to assume a casual air and a dignified expression, so I wouldn't be suspected of cringing.

"Let my face be plain," I thought, "as long as it's dignified, expressive, and above all, incredibly intelligent."

I was painfully aware, however, that my facial expression could not possibly convey all these qualities. And worse yet—while I'd have settled for anything, as long as it looked intelligent, I found my face positively stupid. I'd even have accepted a depraved expression if, at the same time, everyone had agreed that I had a *terribly intelligent* face.

I, of course, loathed and despised everyone in my office, although I was afraid of them at the same time. At times, I even considered them above me. I kept shifting from one extreme to the other for no apparent reason: one day I'd despise them, the next I'd feel they were my betters.

A civilized, self-respecting man cannot be vain without setting unattainably high standards for himself and despising himself at certain moments. But, when I came across anyone, whether I admired or despised him, I always lowered my eyes first. I even tested myself to see whether I could withstand the look of this or that person, but I was always the first to yield. This tormented me and drove me mad with rage. I also had a morbid fear of appearing ridiculous, so I slavishly adhered to all the external conventions. I stuck enthusiastically to the ordinary and abhorred all signs of eccentricity in me.

But what chance did I have? I was painfully sensitive and complex, as a man of this age should be. The others, of course, were stupid and resembled one another like a flock of sheep. Perhaps I was the only one in the office to feel that I was a coward and a slave. I felt that because I was more highly developed than the others. But then it was not simply a feeling—I really was a coward and a slave. I say this without any shame. Every self-respecting man today must be a coward and a slave. That is now his normal state. I'm deeply convinced of it. That's how he's made. As a matter of fact, it's not only true of our

age and isn't due to any particular set of circumstances—
it goes for all times: a self-respecting man is bound to be
a coward and a slave. This is a natural law governing
every self-respecting man. Even if he manages once in a
while to show a little courage, there's no need for him to
be smug about it, for he's sure to lie down under the
next blow. It is the age-old solution, the only way out.
Only asses make a show of courage, and even then, only
until they come up against the wall. But why bother about
them anyway, since they are of no importance.

Another thing worried me then: I was unlike everyone
else, and everyone else was unlike me.

"I'm all alone while there are a lot of them," I mused.
This goes to show that I was still just a boy.

Sometimes I went from one extreme to the other in my
behavior. Sometimes I simply couldn't stand going to the
office; I would return home from it completely sick and
broken. Then, suddenly, I would go through a phase of
cynical indifference (with me, everything happened in
phases); I would laugh at my own finicky intolerance,
teasing myself for my romantic notions. One day I'd
refuse to talk to my colleagues at all; then, suddenly, I'd
be talking their heads off and even seeking their friendship. All my disgust would just vanish for no apparent
reason. But possibly I'd never really felt it in the first
place and had simply been affecting something I'd picked
up out of books. At one time I became really friendly with
my co-workers; I began visiting them at their homes,
played cards with them, drank vodka in their company,
talked with them about promotions . . . But allow
me to make a disgression at this point.

In general, we Russians have never had the sort of
stupid, starry-eyed romantics the Germans and especially
the French have—people who would never learn any
better even if the ground opened up under their feet or if
the whole of France were to perish on its barricades. Even
then they wouldn't have the decency to change; they'd
sing their starry-eyed songs going to their graves. This is
because they are fools. Russia, as is well known, has no
fools; this is what distinguishes us from other lands. Hence,

we have no starry-eyed natures, at least in an undiluted state. All our "affirmative" writers and critics, seeking to create paragons of efficiency, such as Kostanzhoglo and Uncle Peter Ivanitch,* because they imagine that they represent our ideal, have slighted our romantics, confusing them with the starry-eyed Germans and Frenchmen. In fact, our romantics are just the opposite of the starry-eyed Europeans, and no European yardstick can measure them. (I hope you'll allow me to use the word "romantic," which is a good, old, respectable word familiar to everyone.) The hallmark of our romantics is their desire to understand everything, *to see, to see everything, and often to see it incomparably more clearly than do our most practical minds;* never to take anyone or anything for granted, but neither to reject them out of hand; to examine everything; to take everything into account; to be diplomatic with everyone; never to lose sight of the useful, practical goal (rent-free housing, pensions, decorations); to keep an eye on this goal through all the exaltations and slim volumes of lyric verse, while preserving, to their dying hour, their allegiance to "the sublime and the beautiful," and while they are at it, preserving themselves like jewels wrapped in cotton wool —again in the name of "the sublime and the beautiful."

So, as you can see, our romantic is a man of impressive breadth of vision and, at the same time, a rogue. Believe me, I'm speaking from experience. Of course, all this only applies if the romantic in question is intelligent. But what am I saying! A romantic is, of course, always intelligent. I only wanted to note that, although we have had stupid romantics, they don't count, because, in their prime, they turned into Germans and, to assure their jewel-like preservation, settled in some place like Weimar or the Black Forest.

I, for instance, sincerely loathed my office work, and if I didn't spit in anyone's eye, it was only because I couldn't afford to—I was paid to sit there. The fact is, however, that in the final analysis, I didn't spit. Our romantic

* "Positive" characters from Gogol and Goncharov——A.R.M.

would sooner go out of his mind (which rarely happens, however) than spit, unless he has some other career in reserve. Anyway, they never throw him out unless it's to move him to a lunatic asylum in extreme cases of insanity, when he claims to be the king of Spain or something like that.

But then, only pale, puny people go crazy, while many, many romantics reach exalted positions later in life. What admirable versatility they have! What receptivity to the most incompatible feelings! This thought has always cheered me. This accounts for the number of people with a "broad outlook" among us, people who never lose their ideals even in the depths of degradation. And, although they wouldn't raise their little fingers to achieve their ideals, although they are arrant thieves and sharpers, the mere thought of those ideals brings tears to their eyes, and deep down somewhere, they are frightfully honest. Yes, sir, in our midst, the most incorrigible rogue can be perfectly and even heroically honest without ever ceasing to be a rogue. Why, again and again, we see our romantics turn out to be such shady dealers (I use this term lovingly), displaying such a grasp of reality and such practical agility, that the authorities and the public can only stand by clicking their tongues and gaping at them in surprise.

Yes, their versatility is really extraordinary. And one wonders what they may turn to in the future. Really sterling stuff, our romantics! And I'm not saying that out of jingoism either. But you must think I'm pulling your leg again. On the other hand, you may think I really believe what I'm saying. Either way, ladies and gentlemen, your opinion greatly honors and pleases me.

And now, forgive this digression; let's get on with the story.

It goes without saying that my friendship with my office colleagues never lasted long. In no time I fell out with them, and being young and inexperienced, I even stopped saying good morning to them and cut them dead. Actually, I went that far only once. But, in general, I was alone almost all the time.

At home I mostly read. I had to drown out the clamor in me, and reading was the only available way. Reading, of course, was helpful; it stirred, delighted, and tormented me. Now and then, however, I grew terribly tired of it. I became restless and plunged, not into real debauchery, but into murky, sordid, petty dissipation. My petty passions stabbed and burned me, because I was already on edge. I suffered hysterical outbursts of tears and convulsions. Aside from my reading, I had nothing to turn to, for there was nothing in my surroundings that I could look up to or that attracted me. I was sick of everything and longed to contradict and oppose. So I abandoned myself to dissipation. But I haven't brought this up to justify myself at all—no, that's a lie. I was trying to justify myself, all right. I note that for myself, ladies and gentlemen. I've promised myself that I won't lie here.

I indulged in vice at night, stealthily, fearfully, sordidly; the feeling of shame was always present, and in the most unspeakable moments, it was like damnation itself. Even then I carried this hole in the floor in my heart. I was terribly afraid to be seen and recognized. And I went to the lowest haunts.

Once, passing by a tavern, I saw some men fighting with billiard cues through a lighted window. One of them was tossed out of the window. At another time a scene like that would have made me sick, but this time I envied that ejected gentleman so much that I entered the tavern and stepped into the billiard room, thinking: "Maybe I could pick a fight too and be thrown out of the window."

As a matter of fact, I wasn't drunk—that's how far despair can drive a man. But nothing came of it. I couldn't even manage to be tossed out of a window, and I left without picking a fight.

An officer who happened to be there put me in my place immediately. I was standing by the billiard table, inadvertently blocking the officer's way. He grabbed me by the shoulders and, without a word, picked me up and, setting me down a bit further away, passed by as if I didn't exist. I could've forgiven anything, including a beating, but that was too much—to be brushed aside without being noticed!

I don't know what I wouldn't have given at that moment for a real quarrel, a decent one, something more *literary,* if you know what I mean. I'd been treated as one treats a fly. The officer was a husky six-footer, and I'm very small and thin. But it was still within my power to start trouble. All I had to do was make the smallest protest and I'd have gone through the window. But I changed my mind and decided to merge, full of rage, into the background.

I left the tavern ashamed and troubled and returned home.

The following night, I went out to satisfy my petty vices; I moved even more furtively, was shier, sadder, more abject than before—but I went.

Don't think, however, that I backed down before that officer out of cowardice. I've never been a coward at heart, although I've constantly acted like a coward when the chips were down. No, wait, don't laugh, I can explain—I have an explanation for everything, you may rest assured of that.

Oh, if only that officer had been a duelist! But he obviously was one of those who prefer to put their point across with a billiard cue (a species long extinct today) or by complaining to the authorities, like Gogol's Lieutenant Pirogov. People like him won't fight duels with the likes of me. And, in general, they consider dueling as some inconceivable, free-thinking, French institution. But they feel no compunction about bullying people. Especially if they happen to be husky six-footers.

So I backed out, not through cowardice, but through my boundless vanity. I was not taken aback by his size, nor by fear of physical punishment, nor because I might be flung out of the window. I'm quite sure that I had sufficient physical courage. It was moral courage that I lacked. I was afraid that not one of them, from the insolent lounge attendant to the miserable, pimply, evil-smelling government clerk hanging around there in his grubby shirt, would have understood me and that they just would

have laughed at me when I spoke up in literary language
—which I'd have had to use, because when it comes to a
point d'honneur (not to be confused with honor), one
had no choice but to use literary language. No word for a
point d'honneur exists in the vernacular. And I was sure
(practical instinct, notwithstanding all the romanticism)
that they'd have split their sides laughing and that the
officer wouldn't have given me an innocent beating, but
would've kicked me around the billiard table and only
later might have taken pity on me and flung me out the
window. Of course, this miserable little incident couldn't
end like that as far as I was concerned. Later, I often
passed that officer in the street, and I observed him very
carefully. I'm not sure, though, that *he* recognized me.
Judging by certain signs, he didn't. But I . . . I looked at
him with hatred and anger, and I went on like that for
. . . several years. My anger grew stronger as the years
went by. First, I started to gather information about the
officer. It was a lot of trouble, for I didn't know anyone.
But once someone called him by his last name from a
distance as I was following him. So I learned his name.
Another time, I trailed him to the house where he was
billeted and, for a quarter, found out from his super-
intendent which floor he lived on, whether he lived alone,
and all the things one can find out from superintendents.

One morning, although I'd never gone in for literature
before, I took it into my head to caricature this officer in
a short story. I wrote it with exaltation. I exposed him,
even slandered him. I changed his name in such a way
that it could be guessed immediately. Later, however, on
further thought, I invented a less obvious alias for him
and sent the story to the *National Journal*. But at that
time, exposés weren't in vogue yet, and my manuscript
was rejected. I was very disappointed. There were moments when fury almost choked me. Finally, I decided to
challenge him to a duel. I wrote him a beautiful letter
pleading with him to apologize to me. And, in case he
failed to comply, my letter hinted quite obviously at the
possibility of a duel. The letter was written in such a way
that, if the officer had had any idea of the "sublime and

the beautiful," he'd have rushed to my place, thrown himself on my neck, and offered me his undying friendship. Ah, wouldn't that have been nice! Can you imagine how we'd have lived after that! Some of his dignity would've washed off onto me, and he would have gained from my superior education and sensitivity. Ah, the consequences could have been so pleasant.

Note that two years had elapsed since his insults, so that my challenge was terribly out of date. But, thank God (I still, to this day, thank Him with tears in my eyes), I never sent that letter. I get gooseflesh at the mere thought of what would've happened if I had sent it.

And then, suddenly—suddenly I got my revenge in the simplest way. Through a real stroke of genius. Sometimes, on holidays, I went for a walk between three and four along the sunny side of Nevsky Avenue. Actually it was more torture, humiliation, and bilious irritation than a stroll, but apparently that was what I needed. I scurried along like a mouse in a most undignified way, skipping out of the path of important gentlemen, guards officers, and ladies. My heart vibrated convulsively and I felt hot all down my back at the mere thought of the sorry sight offered to the world by my scurrying, puny, seedy figure. I constantly tortured myself with the humiliating thought, which turned into a physical feeling, that, to the world, I was nothing but a dirty, pestiferous fly—more intelligent, sensitive and noble than the lot of them, of course—but nonetheless a fly that everybody scorned. Why I was willing to suffer such humiliation just for a stroll along Nevsky Avenue, I don't know; but something drew me there, and I went at every opportunity.

At that time I was beginning to experience waves of the pleasure I mentioned earlier. After the incident with the officer, I was even more drawn to Nevsky Avenue, which was where I most often saw and admired him. He went there too, mostly on holidays. And, although he scurried out of the way of high dignitaries and generals, as I did, he literally walked over people like me and even people who were quite a bit better, marching straight at them as if there were nothing but an empty space ahead of him, and never budging an inch off his course. I'd watch him coming at me, fascinated by my own hatred, and—skip aside at the last moment. I was exasperated, because even there in the street, I couldn't feel I was on an equal footing with him.

I woke up nights thinking about it. "Why must I always get out of his way?" I ranted in a hysterical rage. "Why always me rather than him? There's no law saying that that's the way it should be. Why can't it be fair, as it is when polite people meet—one moves aside a little and so does the other, and they pass respecting each other's dignity."

But that wasn't the case here. I kept stepping aside without his even noticing it. And then I got the most amazing idea.

"What would happen," I thought, "if I didn't move aside—didn't budge, even if it meant pushing him? What would come of it?"

This bold idea took hold of me. I had no peace. I kept thinking of it; it drove me out onto Nevsky Avenue again and again, to visualize more clearly how I'd do it when I decided to go through with it. I was in a state of elation. The idea seemed to grow more and more sensible and practical.

"Of course, I won't really shove him," I thought, mellowed in advance by happiness. "I just won't get out of his way, I'll butt into him—oh, not too hard; just bump him with my shoulder, well within the bounds of decent conduct. That way I'll push him as much as he pushes me."

My mind was now made up. But the preparations took a long time. In the first place, I had to look decent for the collision. I had to decide what I'd wear on that occasion.

"In case of a public scandal, I ought to be well dressed, for the public around there is very refined—princes, countesses, the whole literary world. Good clothes impress people and might put us on an equal footing in the eyes of society."

With this in mind, I asked for an advance on my pay and bought myself a pair of black gloves and a presentable hat at Churkin's. I decided that black gloves were both more dignified and in better taste than the butter-colored ones that I'd contemplated buying at first.

"Too loud," I decided. "It'd look as if I was trying to attract attention."

I already had a fine shirt with a pair of nice bone cuff links. What held me back was my overcoat. Mine was warm, but it was quilted and had a raccoon collar, which, of course, is unthinkably common. I had to change that collar at all costs and get myself a beaver one like the officer's. I started looking around for one in the stores, and after some hesitation, decided to buy one of those cheap German beavers which, although they wear very badly and acquire a mangy look in no time, look impressive when new; I only needed it for this one occasion anyway. I inquired about the price. Still quite expensive. After weighty deliberation, I decided to try to borrow from Anton Antonych, the head clerk in my office, a meek but serious and responsible man who never lent money but to whom I'd been specially recommended by a very important person who'd got me my job in the first place. I went through agonies. I felt it would be a disgrace to borrow money from Anton Antonych. I thought it monstrous. I even spent two or three sleepless nights thinking about it. Indeed, during that time I didn't sleep much anyway, as I was in a feverish state, with my heart either beating like mad or sinking altogether.

Anton Antonych was at first surprised, then frowned, then thought for a while, and in the end decided to let me have the money. I signed an IOU giving him the right to pay himself back out of my salary in two weeks.

So everything was ready. A beautiful piece of beaver replaced the vulgar raccoon collar. I set myself to make the final arrangements. I couldn't just go and do this hastily. Everything had to be thoroughly, gradually worked out. Gradualness was indeed very important. I must admit, however, that after several attempts, I began to despair: we seemed destined not to bump into each other. One would have thought I had done everything: I was determined, everything was set, we were about to collide —but the next thing I knew, I had moved out of his

way and he had passed without seeing me. I even prayed
to God to give me determination as I approached him.
Once, I was quite decided, but the net result was that I
almost fell under his feet, for my courage failed me at
the very last moment, when I was only two inches from
him. He passed completely unperturbed while I bounced
to one side like a ball. That night I was sick and delirious
again.

Everything ended quite unexpectedly and as well as
could be hoped. During the night I decided to give it all
up and forget my futile plan. So I decided to walk along
Nevsky Avenue to see how it felt, having given up my
plan. I saw him about three steps away from me. Suddenly I decided. I closed my eyes and we banged hard
against each other, shoulder against shoulder. I didn't
yield an inch and walked past him as an equal! He never
even turned around, pretending not to have noticed a
thing. But I know he was just pretending. I'm sure of it
to this day. Of course, I got the worst of the collision,
for he was much heavier. But I didn't care. What I cared
about was that I had accomplished my goal and behaved
with dignity; without yielding an inch, had put myself on an
equal social footing with him in public.

I returned home feeling compensated for everything.
I was in a state of elation. In my triumph I sang arias
from Italian operas. Naturally, I won't describe what happened three days later. If you have read the first part
of this narrative, you should be able to guess for yourselves. The officer was later transferred somewhere. I
haven't seen him for about fourteen years now. I wonder
where my friend is now? I wonder whom he has been
pushing around lately?

II

The phase of petty dissipation was passing; a horrible
nausea came over me. I had pangs of guilt, but I tried to
stifle them, for they made me unbearably sick. Gradually,
however, I got used to this state too. I could get used to

anything—that is, I resigned myself, accepting things rather than really getting used to them. I had an escape that made everything bearable; I took refuge in "the sublime and the beautiful"—in my dreams, of course.

I gave myself over entirely to dreaming—dreaming away for three months on end, huddled in my corner. And believe me, in my dreams, I had nothing in common with the fellow who, in his chicken-hearted panic, had sewn the beaver collar on his coat. I suddenly became a hero who wouldn't even have let my six-foot officer foe into his house. I couldn't even visualize him in my company. What my dreams consisted of and how I was able to content myself with them would be hard to explain today, but at the time, I managed to be content with them. And, in fact, even today, I have to content myself with much the same thing. My dreams were sweeter and stronger after my petty dissipations and were accompanied by remorse, tears, cursing, and ecstasy. I experienced moments of actual intoxication and, I swear, was happy without finding it in the least ridiculous. I had faith, hope, love. That's just it, I had blind faith that, by some miracle, some force would push aside the confining screen, opening up a wide horizon, on which would be a worthwhile life work, useful and sublime, and above all, *all cut out and waiting for me* (I didn't know what kind of work it should be, but it was essential that it should be there ready and waiting for me to perform it). And I imagined that, at any moment, I'd step into the world arena, on a white steed, wearing a crown of laurels. I couldn't even conceive of being second best; that's why, in real life, I resigned myself so easily to being last. I had to either be a hero or wallow in the mud, and that's what turned out to be my undoing. For, while wallowing in the mud, I'd console myself that, at other times, I was a hero. This made it all right, for unlike an ordinary man, a hero couldn't be altogether defiled by mud, so why not wallow in it?

It is noteworthy that I usually thought of "the sublime and the beautiful" during my dissipation, often just when I hit the rock-bottom of abjection. These thoughts came

in little flashes, as if to remind me of the existence of
"the sublime and the beautiful"; but they didn't interfere
with my dissipation. Just the opposite, in fact. They seemed
to spice it up by contrast and, like a good sauce, helped
bring out the taste. This sauce, concocted of contradictions
and suffering, contained painful self-analysis, and the
resulting agonies and torments added piquancy and even
meaning to my dissipation—in short, it was what a good
sauce is meant to be. There was more to it, though, for
without the sauce I could hardly have borne the primitive, vulgar, uncomplicated dissipation of a petty government employee and the soiled feeling it left. Could my
vice have drawn me into the street at night otherwise? No.
But then I had the sauce.

But how much love—ah, how much—I experienced
in my dreams, when I escaped to "the sublime and the
beautiful." Perhaps it was an imaginary love and maybe
it was never directed toward another human being, but
it was such an overflowing love that there was no need
to direct it—that would've been an unnecessary luxury.
Everything always ended safely in a leisurely, rapturous
sliding into the domain of art, that is, into the beautiful
lives of heroes stolen from the authors of novels and
poems and adapted to the demands of the moment, whatever they might be. I, for instance, triumph over everyone, and they, of course, are strewn in the dust, acknowl-
edging my superiority; I'm all-forgiving; I'm a great poet
and court chamberlain; I fall in love; I inherit millions
and donate them to human causes and take advantage of
this opportunity to publicly confess my backslidings and
disgrace which, of course, is no ordinary disgrace but
contains much that is "sublime and beautiful" in it, something in the Manfred style. Everyone is weeping and
kissing me (they could hardly be so thick-skinned as not
to); then I leave, hungry and barefoot, to preach new
ideas and rout the reactionaries at Austerlitz. Then, a
triumphal march is played, an amnesty is declared, the
Pope agrees to leave Rome for Brazil, there's a ball for
all of Italy at the Villa Borghese on the shores of Lake
Como, which lake, for this occasion, is moved to the

vicinity of Rome. Then there's a scene in the bushes, and so on and so forth; see what I mean?

You may say that it's base and in bad taste to drag my confessions out into the market place, after all the raptures and tears I have admitted to. But why is it base? Do you think I'm ashamed of anything, or that my vagaries are more stupid than anything in your own lives? I can assure you that some of these daydreams were quite cleverly concocted. They didn't all take place on Lake Como, you know. But you're right, after all—there's plenty of baseness and bad taste in it all. And what's worse is that I'm trying to justify myself now. And worse yet is the remark I just made. But that's enough, or we'll never finish—there will always be something worse than what came before it.

I could never take more than three months of dreaming at a time without getting an irresistible urge to rush out into the world. In this case, my venture amounted to a visit to my office chief, Anton Antonych. In all my life he was the only true acquaintance I ever had, which I find surprising. But I only went to see even him after I had attained such happiness in my dreams that I felt I had to throw myself on someone's neck and hug all mankind in the concrete person of someone. And since Anton Antonych received only on Tuesdays, I had to adjust my longing to embrace mankind so that it'd fall on a Tuesday. Anton Antonych lived on the fourth floor in a house near Five Corners Square. He had four austere, yellowish rooms, low-ceilinged, each smaller than the next. He lived with his two daughters and their aunt, who poured the tea. The daughters were thirteen and fourteen, had little, turned-up noses, and kept whispering and giggling, which embarrassed me no end. The master of the house usually sat in his study on a leather couch, in the company of some gray-haired guest, a civil servant from some office, ours or another. I never found more than two or three guests there at any one time, and they were always the same. The conversation was always about excise duties, maneuvers in the Senate, salaries and promotions, the head of the department and ways of pleasing him, and so on and so forth. I sat patiently for four hours on end, like a fool, listening to these people, neither able nor daring to contribute to the conversation. My mind became blank; again and again I felt I was sweating heavily; a sort of paralysis kept coming over me; but it was all very good for me. Back home, I could again lay aside, for a while, my eagerness to embrace the world.

Ah yes, I had another acquaintance, a former schoolmate of mine called Simonov. True, I was bound to have many former schoolmates in Petersburg, but I had lost touch with them and we had even ceased to exchange greetings in the street. Perhaps I had asked for a transfer to another department in the service to avoid being with any of them—I wanted to cut off all links with my hateful childhood. Damn school and those horrible years! Anyway, to cut it short, as soon as I was through there, I broke with my schoolmates once and for all, except for two or three fellows whom I still acknowledged in the street. Simonov was one of these. At school there hadn't been anything remarkable about him. He was even-tempered and quiet, but I was able to discern a certain independence of character and, I'd even say, honesty in him. He was not even so very limited. I had spent some pleasant moments with him but they had never lasted, somehow or other always becoming overcast with gloom. His recollections of that time were apparently unpleasant, and he must have been afraid that I might fall back into my old tone with him. I suspected that I was abhorrent to him, but kept going to his place as long as I wasn't certain of it.

So, one Thursday, unable to stand my loneliness and knowing that Anton Antonych didn't receive that day, I remembered Simonov. As I was walking upstairs to his fourth-floor apartment, I thought that my company might weigh on this man and that I really ought not to impose on him. But, as usual, these thoughts only spurred my desire to place myself in an equivocal position, and I went on. Almost a year had passed since I had last seen Simonov.

III

At Simonov's I found two other former schoolmates of mine. They seemed to be discussing something quite important, for they paid almost no attention to me. This was the more surprising in that we hadn't met for years. Apparently I was something like a housefly in their eyes. But even back at school they hadn't treated me like this, although everyone had hated me there. Of course, I realized that they were bound to despise me for my mediocre career in the service and for having let myself go so badly, what with my poor clothes and all that, which in their eyes was a seal of my limited abilities and general lack of importance. But still, I hadn't expected that much contempt. Simonov was even surprised to see me. Although, now that I think of it, he always seemed rather surprised when I came. All this bothered me. I sat down and dejectedly listened to what they were saying.

Gravely and heatedly, they were discussing a farewell dinner party they were giving the next day for a friend of theirs, an army officer named Zverkov who was being transferred to some remote province. Zverkov had been my classmate also. In the senior grades he was a special object of my hatred. In the elementary grades he was just a pretty, playful boy whom everyone liked—although I, of course, hated him even then, precisely because he was so pretty and cheerful. He was always a poor student, and became even poorer as he progressed. He managed to graduate, however, because he had the right connections. In his senior year he inherited an estate with two hundred serfs; since most of us in that school came from poor families, he started showing off. He was terribly vulgar, but there was no real malice in him, even when he swaggered. But the more arrogant Zverkov became, the more most of them fawned on him, despite their lip service to honor and dignity. They fawned on him because he had been favored by the gifts of nature, not to pursue any particular advantage. For some reason

Zverkov was generally accepted among us as an arbiter of elegance and good manners, and that drove me mad. I hated his sharp, self-assured voice, his delight in his own jokes, which were usually hopelessly flat, although very bold; I hated his good-looking, stupid face (although I'd willingly have exchanged it for my *intelligent* one) and his free and easy ways, which he imitated from the officers of that period, the eighteen forties. I hated his boasting about the amorous conquests he would make (he didn't dare have anything to do with women before he got his commission, for which he was waiting impatiently) and the duels he would fight. I remember that once, despite my taciturnity, I got into an argument with Zverkov when, during a recess, I heard him telling the other boys about his future exploits. He was as excited as a young puppy playing in the sun and declared finally that in exercising his *droit du seigneur,* he wouldn't leave a single virgin among the peasants on his estate without his attention. And if the peasants protested, he said, he'd have the bearded animals flogged and fined. Our stupid classmates clapped their hands in approval, so I attacked him—not at all out of sympathy for the village virgins, but because the boys were applauding such an insect. I got the better of him in the argument that time, but Zverkov, stupid as as he was, was cheerful and arrogant and managed to turn the argument into a joke, so that I wasn't really the winner—the laughter remained on his side. After that, he wrenched the upper hand from me several times in that way—without malice, jokingly, casually, laughing. My answers were loaded with scorn. After graduation, he made a friendly gesture toward me; I didn't push him away too obviously for I felt flattered. However, after that, we lost touch.

Later, when he was a lieutenant, I heard about the wild life he was leading and about his conquests, which had already become a barracks-room legend. There were also rumors about the brilliant career he was making.

He no longer seemed to recognize me in the street, and I suspected that he was afraid that exchanging greetings with an inconsequential man like me might compromise him. I saw him once in the theater with his officer's epaulets. He was paying his attentions to the daughters of some ancient general. In the three years or so since I had last seen him, he had gone to seed quite a bit, although he still was handsome and elegant. He was putting on weight and had become rather flabby. One could see that, by the time he reached thirty, he'd be paunchy.

So it was in honor of this man, who was at last leaving town, that my former schoolmates were giving the dinner party. It was obvious that they had continued to see him during these past three years, although I feel certain that, deep down, none of them felt on an equal footing with Zverkov.

Of Simonov's two guests, one was a Russified German named Ferfichkin, a small man with a monkey face, a fool with a permanent sneer, my worst enemy from the lowest grades, a nasty, impudent little braggart who affected a super-acute sense of honor, while he was really a coward at heart. He was one of Zverkov's retinue, who, while pretending to be his disinterested admirers, borrowed money from him all the time. The other man was unremarkable. His name was Trudolubov. He was in the army, was tall, had a cold expression, was quite honest, admired success in all its forms, and talked only about promotion. He happened to be a distant relative of Zverkov's and, stupid though it may sound, that fact lent him a certain prestige among us. He considered me of no consequence whatever, but his behavior toward me was, if not really amiable, at least tolerable.

"Well then," Trudolubov said, "if each of us contributes seven rubles, that'd make twenty-one rubles, and for that sum it's possible to dine decently. Zverkov, of course, won't have to pay."

"Certainly not," Simonov said, "since we're inviting him."

"Do you really imagine," Ferfichkin interjected caustically, with the ardor of a lackey proud of his master's titles, "that Zverkov will allow us to pay the whole bill? Even if he does accept, just not to offend us, he'll contribute half a case of champagne, I'm sure."

"What will we do, just the four of us, with half a case?" Trudolubov objected. All that had struck him was the amount of champagne suggested by Ferfichkin.

"So the three of us, plus Zverkov, makes four. Twenty-one rubles . . . *Hotel de Paris,* tomorrow at five," Simonov, who was organizing the dinner, concluded.

"Why twenty-one?" I said excitedly, perhaps even a little offended. "If you count me in, that'd make twenty-eight rubles."

I thought that to suddenly make such an offer would be very elegant and they'd be quite impressed and look upon me with respect.

"Do you really want to contribute too?" Simonov said gloomily, avoiding my eyes. He knew me through and through, and that made me furious.

"And why not? I'm his classmate too. I'm even rather slighted at your leaving me out," I spluttered.

"And where were we supposed to look for you?" Ferfichkin asked rudely.

"And then you never got along with Zverkov," Trudolubov added, frowning.

But I wouldn't let go now.

"I don't think anyone has the right to decide that for me."

My voice was trembling as if something horrible was happening.

"Perhaps," I added, "it is precisely because I didn't get along with Zverkov that I wish to contribute now."

"How can one ever understand you . . . with all these noble feelings," Trudolubov snorted.

"All right, we'll put you down," Simonov decided. "So, tomorrow at five—*Hotel de Paris.*"

"Let's see the money!" Ferfichkin snarled between his teeth, nodding at me. He wanted to say something more, but broke off. Even Simonov seemed embarrassed.

"That's enough," Trudolubov said, getting up. "If he's that keen on coming, let him come along."

"But I thought we'd have an intimate dinner party— just ourselves," Ferfichkin muttered, fuming as he took his hat. "It isn't a formal gathering, you know," he added, turning toward me, "and it's possible that you're not really wanted."

As they left, Trudolubov barely nodded in my direction, without really looking at me; Ferfichkin didn't even nod, Simonov, with whom I remained face to face, was in a state of irritated bewilderment and looked at me queerly. I didn't sit down, and he didn't invite me to.

"Well, then . . . see you tomorrow then. And the money? Would you like to settle now? I was just wondering . . ." he muttered.

I flushed; at that moment, I remembered that I'd owed Simonov fifteen rubles for I don't know how long. As a matter of fact, I hadn't forgotten it, although I'd never made a gesture to pay him.

"You must realize, Simonov, that coming here I couldn't possibly have known . . . I'm very sorry I forgot to bring . . ."

"That's all right, perfectly all right. It doesn't make the slightest difference. You can pay tomorrow when we meet for dinner. I only mentioned it to make sure . . . You must understand, please . . ."

He stopped short and started pacing the room, looking even more irritated. As he paced, he came down harder and harder on his heels, until finally he was loudly stamping his feet as he walked.

"I'm not keeping you from anything?" I asked him after a two-minute silence.

"Oh no, not at all," he said, starting, "or . . . that is . . . to tell the truth, yes. You see, I have to go and see someone. . . . It's not far, though," he added in an apologetic voice, rather embarrassed.

"Good God, why didn't you tell me!"

I picked up my hat very nonchalantly. I have no idea where I had got all this nonchalance.

"It's not far. . . . It's only a few steps from here," Simonov kept repeating fussily as he saw me off. He was not his usual self. "See you tomorrow at five sharp!" he shouted after me as I was going downstairs.

He really sounded too pleased to be rid of me. I was stung.

"What on earth made me do it?" I muttered through clenched teeth as I walked down the street. "A farewell party indeed! And for a nasty pig like Zverkov, too! Of course, I won't go; I have no obligations toward them. I don't give a damn anyhow! I'll send Simonov a note tomorrow to say I'm not coming."

But what actually made me so furious was that I knew very well that I'd go—I'd go just to spite them, and the more wrong, the more tactless it was for me to go, the more certainly I'd do so.

I even had a tangible reason for not going—I was broke. I had only nine rubles of which seven were due the very next day to my servant Apollon for his monthly wages, out of which he paid for his own board. Knowing what kind of a man Apollon was, it was unthinkable not to pay him. I'll have something to say some other time about that fiend, that thorn in my side.

Still, I knew I wouldn't pay him and that I would go to the dinner.

That night I had the most hideous dreams. And no wonder since, before I fell asleep, memories of my miserable school years kept oppressing me; I couldn't shake them off even in my sleep.

I had been sent to that school by some distant relatives in whose charge I was—I've never heard of them since. I was an orphan and was already embittered by their nagging when they dumped me there. I was silent and brooding, and looked distrustfully at the world around me. My schoolmates took an immediate dislike to someone who was different from themselves and met me with cruel, merciless baiting. I couldn't lie down under their baiting; I couldn't take them in my stride as they took one another. I hated them from the first and withdrew into my timid, wounded, cumbersome pride. Their coarseness revolted me. They laughed openly at my face and my puny figure, although their own faces were incredibly stupid. In that school, children's faces somehow degenerated and turned stupid. Many boys who were attractive when they entered, after a few years, turned into revolting looking creatures. At sixteen, I was already grimly wondering at the pettiness of their thoughts, the inanity of their talk, their games and their preoccupations. They couldn't understand the essential things and were not interested in the most thought-provoking subjects, so I came to consider them as inferiors. This was not due to my offended pride—and please don't come to me with nauseating clichés about how easy it is for me to talk, but while I was still dreaming, those boys were grasping the real meaning of life. They didn't grasp a damned thing, and certainly not the meaning of life—and I swear that that's just what irritated me most about them. On the contrary, they mistook for fancy the most obvious reality in front of their noses and, even at that time, worshiped only success. Disregarding justice, they callously scorned everything that was helpless and oppressed. To them, position in life meant brains, and at sixteen, they were already discussing nice, secure little jobs. I must say, of course, that this attitude was largely due to the bad examples that they had had before their eyes from early childhood.

They were incredibly depraved. Their depravity was, of course, rather superficial, mostly pseudocynical, and the freshness of youth occasionally flashed through it. But even that freshness had an unpleasant edge to it.

I hated them violently, although I was probably even worse then they. They paid me back in kind, not bothering to conceal their loathing for me. But, by then, I didn't want them to like me; I wanted to humiliate them. To escape their jeers, I worked harder and became one of the best students. This impressed them. Besides, they began to realize that I was already reading books well beyond their understanding and was familiar with subjects of which they had never heard (and that were not included in our curriculum). They leered at me in bewildered sarcasm but accepted my mental superiority, especially when the teachers began to single me out on that account. They stopped jeering, but they still disliked me. Cold, tense relations were established.

In the end, I couldn't stand it myself. After so many years, I felt a need for human companionship and friends. I tried to approach some of my classmates, but my attempts were clumsy and contrived and came to nothing. I did make a friend once, but I was already a tyrant at heart and wanted to be the absolute ruler of his mind. I wanted to instill in him contempt for all those around us; I demanded that he break with his world. He was taken aback by my passionate friendship. I drove him to tears and fits of despair. He was a naïve and yielding person, and when I felt I had full possession of him, I began to hate him and finally rejected him. It was as though I'd only wanted his total friendship just for the sake of winning it and making him submit to me. But I couldn't possibly conquer them all—the one I had conquered was a rare exception, unlike the rest.

The first thing I did when I left school was to give up the special position which I had had in store, so I could break all ties with a past I loathed and send it to hell. . . . And I'll be damned if I know what drew me to that fellow Simonov!

Early in the morning I jumped out of bed. I felt terribly excited, as if things were about to start happening. I felt that some radical break in my life would take place that day. But then, perhaps because so few things actually happened to me, I was always inclined to expect some radical break in my existence when something did happen. I went to my office as usual, but slipped away a couple of hours before quitting time. I had to prepare myself for that dinner.

It was important, I thought, not to get there first, lest they think me too eager. But there were so many important considerations of this sort that I drove myself to the point of exhaustion. I had to polish my shoes myself, for Apollon would never have agreed to polish them twice in one day. He'd have considered that beyond the call of duty. To clean my shoes, I had to sneak the brushes from the lobby where they were kept, lest Apollon despise me too much. Then I examined my clothes and found them worn and shabby. "I've been letting myself go too much," I thought. The jacket I'd worn to the office might look decent, but I really couldn't wear it to the party. My trousers were worse: there was a huge yellow spot on one knee. I felt that this spot alone would deprive me of nine-tenths of my dignity. I knew that it was despicable to think this way, but I decided that this was no time for thinking; I had to face reality now, and my heart sank. I knew that I was exaggerating the importance of the party out of all proportion, but I couldn't help it. I was shaking as though I had a fever. I imagined despairingly how that nasty fool Zverkov would greet me; how the moronic Trudolubov would stare at me with unspeakable scorn; how Ferfichkin, the beetle, would giggle insolently at me, trying to please Zverkov; how Simonov would see through all that quite clearly and despise me both for my vanity and my abjectness—and, above all, how miserable the whole business would be. It was all like a piece of bad literature.

Of course, it would have been best not to go at all. But that was out of the question. When something drew me, it really drew me, head first. Had I not gone, I'd have taunted myself for the rest of my life:

"So you didn't have the guts to face *reality,* eh?"

I wanted to show the lot of them that I wasn't the coward I myself thought I was. More than that, in the midst of a paroxysm of cowardice, I dreamed of triumphing, conquering, forcing them to love me for, let's say, the "loftiness of my thought and my incontestable wit." Then perhaps they'd drop Zverkov, and he'd sit all by himself in a corner, crushed and dejected. Later, I'd make it up with him and we'd drink to our eternal friendship. But the worst, the most depressing realization was that I already knew that I didn't really need any of it—I had no wish to crush, tame, or charm them, and the result wouldn't be worth a kopek to me once I'd achieved it.

Ah, how I prayed to God for that day to be over quickly! I kept going to the window, opening the ventilating pane and, with inexpressible anguish, staring out at the wet snow falling.

Finally my cheap wall clock hissed and delivered itself of five chimes. I grabbed my hat and, avoiding Apollon's look—he had been waiting for his wages since morning, but was too proud to mention it first—slipped past him and, jumping into a sleigh I had hired with my last half ruble, drove to the *Hotel de Paris* in grand style.

I V

I'd known from the start that I was going to be the first to arrive, but that didn't matter any more. Not one of them was there, and I even had some difficulty finding the room. They still hadn't finished setting the table. What could it mean? After complicated inquiries among the servants, I found out that dinner had been ordered for six o'clock and not five. This was confirmed at the bar downstairs; I felt too awkward to ask any more questions. It was only 5:25. If they had decided to change the hour, they should've let me know—that's what the post is for —and not humiliated me in my own eyes as well as before the servants. I sat down at the table. A servant continued setting it. I felt even more offended. A little before six, to supplement the lamps that were burning in the room, the servants brought in candles. It hadn't occurred to them to bring them in as soon as I arrived. In the room next door two gloomy-looking men were eating their dinner in silence. Noise was coming from a room further off. A group was dining there. They were laughing and shouting, and I caught some grating, French-sounding squeals. They were having a dinner party with ladies present. Quite nauseating, in fact.

I haven't often been more uncomfortable, so when, at about six, they all arrived together, I was terribly relieved, viewing them as my liberators in a way, and thus forgetting that I was supposed to look offended.

Zverkov came in first, as befitted a chieftain. He and the rest of them were laughing. Seeing me, Zverkov walked casually toward me, with a swaying swagger, and in a friendly but perfunctory way, gave me his hand, a little circumspectly, like a statesman who wishes to keep one amiably at a distance.

I had imagined that as soon as he came in he'd break into his shrill, squeaky laugh and start subjecting us to his flat witticisms and stale jokes. I had been preparing myself for that ever since the previous day, but I hadn't at all expected to be treated like this, with condescending kindness. Did that mean that he now considered himself superior to me in every respect? "If," I thought, "he simply intends to offend me with his airs of superiority, I'll put him in his place yet. But suppose he really has got the idea into his stupid head that he's incomparably better than me and can't help looking down upon me with condescension?" The mere thought of it made me gasp.

"I was rather surprised to hear of your desire to join us," Zverkov said, lisping and drawling, a thing I'd never heard him do before. "We haven't met for a long time. You seem to have been avoiding us. It's a pity. We aren't as horrible as we look. In any case, I'm delighted to renew . . ."

He turned away casually and put his hat on the window sill.

"Have you been waiting long?" Trudolubov asked me.

"I came at five sharp, as I was told yesterday," I answered loudly, with an irritation that promised an early explosion.

"Didn't you tell him about the change in time?" Trudolubov asked Simonov.

"I didn't, I forgot," Simonov said, not sounding in the least sorry, and without even bothering to apologize to me, he went to see about the drinks and appetizers.

"So you've been waiting here for a whole hour, you poor fellow!" Zverkov exclaimed, laughing.

It must have struck him as very funny indeed. Ferfichkin chimed in with his nasty, thin chuckle that reminded me of the yapping of a lap dog. He too found it all very funny and me ridiculous.

"It isn't funny at all," I shouted at Ferfichkin, growing more and more irritated. "It was someone else's fault.

I couldn't help it. No one bothered to tell me. This . . . this . . . is simply absurd."

"It's not only absurd, it's worse," Trudolubov grumbled, naïvely siding with me. "It's plain bad manners. You're too polite about it. It's simply awful manners. Of course, no offense was meant but . . . How could Simonov—I don't know!"

"If anyone did that to me," Ferfichkin said, "I'd——"

"Why," Zverkov interrupted, "you should have ordered yourself something or had dinner served without waiting for us."

"I hope you realize that I could've done so without waiting for anyone's permission," I replied. "If I elected to wait it was because——"

"Let's sit down, gentlemen," Simonov shouted, coming back into the room. "Everything's ready. I'm answerable for the champagne—it's wonderfully chilled. You know, I didn't know your exact address," he said suddenly, turning toward me, without, however, looking at me. "How on earth do you think I could've found you?"

Obviously he had something against me. Probably, since yesterday, he'd decided . . .

Everyone sat down, including me. The table was round. On my left I had Trudolubov, on my right, Simonov; Zverkov was facing me; Ferfichkin installed himself between Zverkov and Trudolubov.

"Tell me, are you working for the government?" Zverkov drawled, continuing to show an interest in me. Seeing that I was embarrassed, he'd decided seriously that he had to be nice to me and cheer me up.

But, in my rage, I thought: "What's he trying to do? Make me throw that bottle in his face?" I was probably so easily irritated because I'd lost the habit of being with people. Still, I informed him abruptly which government department I was working for, without taking my eyes off my plate.

"And are you satisfied with it? Tell me, what made you leave the job you had before?" Zverkov drawled.

"What made me leave the job I had before," I said,

drawling my words out even more than he had done, "was the fact that I'd decided to leave it." I was almost losing all control. Ferfichkin snorted. Simonov looked at me sarcastically. Trudolubov stopped eating and stared at me curiously. Zverkov winced but tried not to show his feelings.

"And how is the remuneration?"

"What do you mean by remuneration?"

"I mean the salary."

"What is this, a cross-examination?"

But I gave him the exact figure. I turned terribly red.

"Not much," Zverkov said ponderously.

"Yes, you can hardly afford to dine in restaurants on that," Ferfichkin commented insultingly.

"It does sound inadequate to me," Trudolubov said seriously.

"And you've grown so thin, you've changed so much. . . ." Zverkov observed, with some venom now, examining me and my clothes with a sort of arrogant sympathy.

"That's enough, stop embarrassing him!" Ferfichkin giggled.

"I'd like you to know, my dear sir, that I'm not in the least embarrassed," I said, at the end of my tether. "Now you listen to me: I'm paying for my dinner in this restaurant myself, Mr. Ferfichkin; no one's treating me."

Ferfichkin went crimson and, glaring furiously into my eyes, snapped:

"What? Do you wish to imply that there's someone here who's not paying his way? You seem to——"

"That'll do," I said, feeling I'd gone a bit too far, "and now, how about having a more intelligent conversation?"

"So you intend to show off your intelligence?"

"Don't worry about that. It'd be wasted around here."

"What's this all about, anyway? What's all the cackling about? Where do you think you are? Remember, this isn't your miserable office."

"That'll do, that'll do!" Zverkov shouted imperiously, "that's enough, fellows!"

"It's all so stupid," Simonov grumbled.

"It's really stupid," Trudolubov agreed. "We wanted to say good-by to a dear friend, and you bring in petty money matters," he added rudely, addressing me alone. "It was you who insisted on joining us yesterday, so please don't spoil the friendly atmosphere."

"Enough, enough, fellows!" Zverkov shouted. "Stop it, gentlemen. It's really out of place. Let me tell you instead how I just escaped getting married a couple of days ago. . . ."

And there followed a stupid story about how Zverkov had almost married. There was nothing much about marriage in it, but plenty of names of colonels, generals, and even various people with court connections were dropped, with Zverkov outshining almost the whole lot of them. The others began to laugh approvingly; Ferfichkin yelped with delight.

They forgot about me, and I sat there crushed and humiliated.

"Good God, what kind of company are they for me!" I thought. "What a stupid light I've shown myself in! And I've let Ferfichkin get away with too much. These lumps think they're doing me a great honor, allowing me to sit down to dinner with them, whereas it's I who condescend to dine with them! So I've grown thin and my clothes are shabby? Ah, the damned trousers! Zverkov probably noticed the yellow stain on the knee right away. Ah, why bother! I ought to get up right away, take my hat, and leave without saying a word. And tomorrow, I could challenge any of them to a duel. The miserable pigs! I don't have to stick it out to get my seven rubles' worth of food. They might think, though—damn it all! To hell with the seven rubles; I'm leaving right now!"

It goes without saying that I didn't leave.

Dejectedly I kept emptying sherry and *Château Lafitte,* glass after glass. I had little experience in drinking, so it quickly went to my head, and my rage grew. I suddenly felt a great desire to insult them all before leaving. I had to find an opportunity to show them. Let them think I was ridiculous, but there'd be no doubt about my superior intelligence and . . . and . . . to hell with them!

I stared arrogantly at them with dilated eyes. *Their* party seemed to be noisy and gay. Zverkov was doing most of the talking. I listened. Zverkov was telling them how he had brought some society lady to a point where she couldn't help admitting her love for him (he was lying like a trooper, of course) and how he was helped in the romance by a friend of his, a prince who owned three thousand serfs, was an officer in the hussars and to whom Zverkov referred familiarly as Nick.

"How is it," I butted in suddenly, "that this Nickie of yours—the one with the three thousand serfs—is not attending your farewell dinner?"

For a moment everyone fell silent.

"You're drunk already," Trudolubov said, finally consenting to acknowledge my existence as he squinted scornfully in my direction.

Zverkov examined me in silence as though I were a bug. I lowered my eyes. Simonov started hurriedly pouring champagne.

Trudolubov raised his glass. All the others except me did the same. "Here's to your health and a pleasant journey!" Trudolubov shouted, "To our school years, gentlemen, and to the future! Bottoms up!"

They emptied their glasses and hurried to embrace Zverkov. I didn't budge. My glass stood before me untouched.

"What? Aren't you going to drink it up?" Trudolubov roared. He seemed to have lost patience and stared at me threateningly.

"I want to make a speech of my own, then I'll drink it."

"Nasty, spiteful creature," Simonov grumbled.

I straightened myself in my chair, feverishly raised my glass, expecting something extraordinary to happen and not knowing myself what I was going to say.

"Everybody quiet!" Ferfichkin shouted. "Watch out now for a display of intelligence!"

"Lieutenant Zverkov," I began, "I wish to inform you

that I can't stand big words, loud mouths, tight waists.
. . . That's the first point I wanted to make. Now, the second."

They all stirred uneasily.

"I hate smut and those who talk smut. Especially the latter. Number three: I like truth, sincerity, and honesty," I continued mechanically, growing cold and wondering in a panic how I could be saying those things. "I like thought, Zverkov; I like true friendship on an equal footing; I don't—but, why not, after all? I'm willing to drink to your health, and good luck to you—seduce young Circassian beauties, Lieutenant, kill the country's enemies, and . . . and . . . to your health, Monsieur Zverkov!"

Zverkov got up, bowed to me, and said:

"Thank you very much."

He had turned pale. He was furious.

"God damn it!" Trudolubov shouted, bringing his fist down on the table.

"Oh no! For things like that people get punched in the face," Ferfichkin squeaked.

"We ought to kick him out," Simonov mumbled.

"Quiet, gentlemen, don't move!" Zverkov said solemnly, controlling the general indignation. "I very much appreciate your reaction, but I assure you, I'm perfectly capable of showing him the value I place on his words myself."

"Now, you, Mr. Ferfichkin, I'd like you to answer me tomorrow for what you said just now," I said in a loud voice.

"You mean a duel? Very good then," he replied. But apparently I was so ridiculous in making this challenge, and it was so incongruous with my physique, that they all burst out laughing; finally Ferfichkin joined them too.

"The best thing to do is leave 'im alone. He's completely drunk," Trudolubov said disgustedly.

"I'll never forgive myself for letting him come," Simonov grumbled again.

And I thought: "Wouldn't it be wonderful to hurl that

bottle at them!" I seized the bottle and filled my glass. "I'd better," I thought, "stay to the end now. They'd be only too pleased if I left. Never. Just to spite them I'll sit here and drink to the very end—just to show 'em that I don't pay the slightest attention to their opinion of me. I'll drink here because it's a tavern and I've paid for my drinks. I'll sit and drink, because they are mere pawns, mere pieces of wood that don't count. I'll sit and drink and sing. . . . Yes, I'll sing if I want to sing, because I've got a right to sing . . . hmmm. . . ."

But I didn't sing. All I did was try not to look at any of them. I affected a nonchalant air, waiting impatiently for them to address me first. But, alas, they didn't. Ah, how I longed to make up with them at that moment! The clock struck eight and finally nine. They moved from the table to the sofa. Zverkov sprawled out, putting a foot on a little table nearby. The wine was moved over there. Zverkov had ordered three bottles himself. He didn't ask me to join them, of course. The others sat around him on the sofa and listened to what he was saying with something bordering on reverence. It was obvious that he was a popular man. I wondered why they should like him so much. From time to time, in their drunken enthusiasm, they'd embrace each other. They spoke of the Caucasus; of what true passion meant; of card games; of jobs that paid well; of the income of some hussar called Podkharzhevsky, which came to such an impressive figure that they were delighted, although none of them knew him personally; about the unbelievable beauty and grace of a Princess D. whom, also, none of them knew or had even seen; and finally they reached the conclusion that Shakespeare was immortal.

I smiled scornfully, pacing up and down by the wall opposite the sofa. I wanted terribly to show them that I could easily do without them, but at the same time, I was stamping my feet on purpose. But to no avail. They *really* paid no attention to me. I had the patience to pace the room in front of them like that, from the fireplace to the table and back, from eight o'clock till eleven, without ever swerving an inch from my course, repeating to myself: "No one can stop me from walking here so long as I feel like it."

The waiter, who kept coming into the room, stopped several times and gaped at me. I was dizzy from the constant turning. There were moments when I felt I was delirious. Within three hours, I managed to get soaked through with sweat and dry again three times. Now and then, with a stabbing, sickening pain, it occurred to me that ten, twenty, perhaps forty years might pass and I'd still remember these, the most ridiculous and painful minutes of my life, with horror and disgust.

One could not have gone further out of one's way than I had to inflict upon oneself the cruelest of humiliations. I realized that, yet I continued pacing the room between the table and the fireplace. "Oh, if only they knew what thought and feeling I'm capable of and how sensitive and complex I am!" I thought, addressing myself silently to the sofa where my enemies were seated. But they behaved as though I weren't even in the room. Once—only once—did they turn toward me: when Zverkov was speaking of Shakespeare and I burst into a scornful laugh. I snorted so affectedly and so nastily that they suddenly interrupted their conversation and, for two minutes, watched solemnly, in complete silence, as I walked, laughing, from the fireplace to the table and back *without paying any attention to them*. But nothing came of it. They resumed their conversation, and two minutes later I was forgotten again. Then it struck eleven.

"Hey!" Zverkov shouted, rising from the sofa, "shall we go *there* now?"

"Yes, yes, let's!" the others agreed eagerly.

I turned sharply toward Zverkov. I was so exhausted, so broken, that I'd have cut my own throat just to put an end to it. I was feverish—my wet hair was stuck to my forehead and temples.

"Zverkov," I said, with determination, in a shrill voice, "I want to ask you to forgive me. You too, Ferfichkin. And the others also—all whom I've offended."

"I see!" Ferfichkin hissed with venom, "you'd rather do without the duel, would you?"

That stab made me wince.

"No, Ferfichkin, you're wrong. I'm not afraid of a duel. I'm prepared to fight you tomorrow if you wish. I even insist, and you can't refuse me. I want to prove to you that I'm not afraid of a duel. You can fire first, and I'll fire in the air."

"He's playing a game with himself," Simonov remarked.

"He's just wagging his tongue," Trudolubov declared.

"Will you kindly let me pass?" Zverkov brushed me off scornfully. "Why are you standing in my way? What do you want?"

They were all flushed and their eyes were glassy with drink.

"I'd like to be your friend, Zverkov. I know I've offended you, but——"

"Offended? You? M-ee? Do you know what, my dear man? *You* couldn't offend *me* under any circumstances!"

"And that's enough from you; now out of the way!" Trudolubov concluded. "Let's go, fellows!"

"But mind you, fellows, I'm reserving Olympia for myself," Zverkov shouted. "You won't forget, will you?"

"All right, all right, we won't fight over it!" the others agreed, laughing.

I stood there feeling as though they had all spat at me in turn. The party was noisily leaving the room. Trudolubov intoned some stupid song. Simonov stayed behind for a minute to tip the waiters. To my own surprise, I walked over to him.

"Simonov, lend me six rubles," I said with the determination of despair.

He turned his drunken eyes on me in utter bewilderment.

"You don't imagine you're going *there* with us, do you?"

"Yes, I'm coming!"

"I have no money with me," he said scornfully. Then he snorted and started to leave the room.

I clutched at his coat. It was a nightmare.

"Simonov, I saw that you have money, so why do you refuse me? Do you think I'm that low? Please, think before you refuse me. My whole future depends on it, all my plans . . ."

Simonov took out the money and almost threw it at me.

"Here, take it if you have no sense of decency," he said mercilessly, and hurried to catch up with the others.

For one moment I was left alone. I glanced at the disorder, the remains of the dinner—a broken glass on the floor, some spilled wine, cigarette ends . . . My head was heavy with drink and delirium, and a horrible anguish was pressing on my heart. A waiter, who had seen and heard everything that had gone on, peered curiously into my eyes.

"I'll go *there*!" I shouted. "And either they'll all get down on their knees and beg me for my friendship, or I'll slap Zverkov's face!"

V

"So this is reality," I mumbled, dashing downstairs, "finally I've met it head on. . . . Yes, it's different from making the Pope leave Rome for Brazil or dancing at that ball on the shores of Lake Como. . . .

"Pig!" the thought flashed through my head, "how can you sneer at that now?

"I don't care!" I answered myself aloud. "All is lost anyway!"

There was no sign of them downstairs, but that didn't matter. I knew where they'd gone.

There was a lone sleigh near the door of the restaurant. The driver wore a coarse peasant coat thickly covered with the wet, warm-looking snow. The street was steamy and stuffy. The small, shaggy, piebald horse was also spattered with wet snow. It was coughing. I remember all that very clearly. As I lifted my foot to get into the sleigh, Simonov's gesture as he gave me the six rubles flashed through my mind, and I fell in a heap into the bottom of the sleigh.

"No, I'll have to do a lot to make up for everything! But

I'll do it or die this very night. Let's go!" I shouted to the driver.

We set off. A whirlwind was raging inside my head.

"They won't get down on their knees and beseech me to be their friend. That is self-delusion, a cheap, disgusting mirage, a sentimental fancy—it's the ball on Lake Como again. So, I *must* slap Zverkov's face. I have to. So, it's decided—I'm rushing over there to slap him.

"Hurry!" I said to the driver, and he flicked the reins.

"I'll slap his face as soon as I get there. But shouldn't I saw a few words, to preface the slap, as it were? No, no need. I'll simply go in and slap his face. They'll all be sitting in the large room, and he'll be with Olympia on the sofa. That damned Olympia! Once she made some cracks about my face and wouldn't have me. I'll drag her by her hair and Zverkov by his ears—no, just one ear. I'll lead him by the ear all around the room. Maybe they'll all set upon me, beat me up, and throw me out. Yes, they're almost sure to do that. Let 'em! I'll still have slapped him first—and so the initiative will be mine and, according to the code of honor, that's all there is to it—he's branded, and no beatings they may inflict upon me will wash off that slap. Nothing but a duel. He'll have to fight. So let 'em beat me up now, the pigs. Trudolubov will do most of the beating, he's so strong. Ferfichkin is sure to catch hold of me from the side and grab me by the hair. Let 'em, let 'em! I've allowed for that. Their fat heads are bound to see the tragic element in it all in the end. As they drag me to the door, I'll shout at them that they're not worth even my little finger. . . .

"Hurry, hurry!" I shouted to the driver so wildly that even he started and whipped up the horse.

"So we'll fight at dawn. It's agreed. I'm through with my office, of course. Ferfichkin was scornful about it. But where will I get a pistol? Nonsense, I'll ask for an advance on my salary and buy one. And ammunition? Ah, that's the concern of the seconds. But how can all that be managed by dawn? And where will I find a second? I don't know anyone. . . . Ah, rubbish!" I shouted, becoming more and more carried away. "The first man I come across in the street can no more decline to be my second than he can refuse to rescue a drowning man. All sorts of things can happen. If I asked the director of my office himself, he'd have to consent, as a matter of chivalry; and he would have to agree to respect my secret. Now, Anton Antonych . . ."

At that very minute, I realized more clearly and more graphically than anyone else in the world the pathetic absurdity of my assumptions, and I saw the reverse side of the coin, but . . .

"Come on, driver, get a move on, get a move on, damn you!"

"Ah, sir . . ." that representative of the laboring masses replied.

An icy shiver suddenly ran down my back.

"Wouldn't it be better—maybe—why—perhaps to turn back home, right now? Oh God, what made me insist yesterday on taking part in this dinner? But it's no longer possible! And that three-hour walk between the fireplace and the table! No, they, and no one else, will have to pay for that walk. They must wash away that disgrace!

"Hey, driver, hurry, hurry!" I shouted.

"And what'd happen if they took me to a police station and lodged a complaint against me? They wouldn't dare! They'd be afraid of the scandal it'd cause! And what if Zverkov, out of contempt for me, refuses to fight a duel? That's most likely, in fact, but I'll prove to them . . . I'll go to the station from which he's supposed to leave tomorrow and grab him by the leg as he gets into the carriage. I'll bite his arm, his hand—'Look, everyone, what a state a man can be driven into!' I'll shout. Let him hit me in the face, and the rest of them with him. I'll shout for all to hear: 'Look at that pig who's going to seduce Circassian girls with my spit shining on his face!'

"After that, of course, everything will be over. My office will have disappeared from the face of the earth; I'll be arrested, tried, dismissed from my government job, and deported to Siberia. But never mind! In fifteen

years, after I've served my time, I'll trace Zverkov
to some provincial town. He'll be happily married by
then, with a big daughter. I'll tell him: 'Look, you mon-
ster—look at these sunken cheeks and tattered clothes!
I've lost everything—career, happiness, art, science, *the
woman I loved*—and all through your fault. Here are the
pistols. I've come to unload my pistol and . . . and I
forgive you.' Then I'll fire into the air and no one will
hear of me again."

This almost brought tears to my eyes, although I realized that I'd taken it all from Pushkin's *Pistol Shot* or
Lermontov's *Masquerade*. And suddenly I felt terribly
ashamed. I felt so ashamed that I ordered the driver to
stop and got out of the sleigh. I stepped out into the snow
in the middle of the street. The driver sighed and looked
at me, bewildered.

What could I do? I couldn't go there because it
made no sense, and I couldn't drop the matter because
. . . "Oh, God, how can I drop it, after all this humiliation? No!" I shouted, jumping back into the sleigh,
"that's the way it has to be! Come on, hurry, let's go!"

And, in my anxiety to get there, I slammed my fist into
the driver's neck.

"What's come over you! What're you fighting for?" the
man shouted, but he whipped up his nag, and it started
kicking with its hind legs.

Wet snow was coming down in large flakes, but I didn't
care; I unbuttoned my coat. I was unaware of anything else,
because I had definitely decided that I was going to slap
Zverkov's face; I felt horrified, as though it were just
about to happen, now and inevitably, and that nothing
on earth could stop it. Isolated street lamps flickered like
funeral torches through the snowy haze. Snow got under
my coat and collar and melted there. I didn't bother to
close my coat—all was lost anyway.

Finally we arrived, I jumped out. With my mind almost
blank, I tore upstairs, and the next thing I knew, I
was pounding and kicking on the door. My legs, especially my knees, felt terribly weak. The door was
opened very quickly, as though I were expected.

As a matter of fact, Simonov had warned them that "one more might come," for in that sort of place warnings and precautions in general were necessary. This was one of the "dress shops" long since closed down by police. During the day, it really functioned as a dress shop, but at night, if you were properly recommended, you could go there as a "guest." I quickly crossed the dark store and went into another room that I already knew. Only one candle was burning there, and I stopped, non-plused: they weren't in there.

"Where are they?" I asked someone.

But, of course, they had left.

The madam of the place, who knew me by sight, was there. She stared at me with a stupid smile. A minute or so later, another creature came in.

Without paying any attention to anything, I walked up and down the room, talking to myself, I believe. I felt as though I had escaped death, and my whole body seemed to rejoice. I would've certainly slapped his face, no doubt about that. But, since they weren't here—it was quite different! I looked around me. I was still trying to figure it out. Unthinkingly, I glanced at the girl who'd just come in. She had a fresh, young face, rather pale, with straight, dark eyebrows and a serious, rather surprised expression. That suited me. I'd have hated it if she'd smiled. I examined her more attentively. I had to make an effort to do so, for my thoughts were still vague. There was something simple and kind in the face before me, but it struck me as uncannily grave. I was sure that that didn't help her in that place, that none of the other fools had noticed her. Anyway, she was no beauty, although she was tall, strong, and well-built. Something nasty made me cross over to her.

By chance, I caught sight of myself in a mirror. My tormented face struck me as unspeakably revolting. It was ashen, vicious, and abject. My hair was disheveled.

"I don't give a damn. So much the better," I thought. "The more repulsive she finds me, the better I'll like it."

VI

Somewhere behind the partition, sounding as if some-one was strangling it, a clock began wheezing. After an incredibly long wheeze, there was a thin, nasty, surpris-ingly hurried chime that made me think of someone leaping suddenly forward. It struck two. I came to. Al-though I hadn't been asleep, I had been in a stupor until then.

The narrow, low-ceilinged room, cluttered with a huge wardrobe, cardboard boxes, and bits of clothing of every description, was quite dark. The stump of a candle on the little table at the other end of the room was about to go out and just flickered faintly from time to time. Within moments, it would be completely dark.

It didn't take me long to regain my senses. Everything came back to me effortlessly, as if it had been waiting for a chance to pounce on me. In fact, all the time I had been in a stupor, there had remained a sort of glowing dot of consciousness which had never disappeared, around which dreamy shadows tramped heavily. But, strangely enough, everything that happened to me that night, now, after I had regained full consciousness, seemed like something out of the very distant past, something I had coped with very, very long ago.

My head was full of fumes. Something was hovering over me, poking at me, exciting and taunting me. Anguish and spite were again accumulating inside me, searching for an outlet. At that moment, I noticed that right next to me, two wide-open eyes were examining me curiously and insistently. The eyes looked at me with a cold, unsympathetic, sullen detachment that made me feel uncomfortable.

A grim thought sprang up in my brain and ran over my whole body with the nasty sensation one gets upon entering a dank, musty hole. There was something un-natural in the fact that these eyes had only now decided to examine me. But I remembered that for two hours I hadn't exchanged a single word with this creature. I hadn't felt the slightest need for it. In fact, I'd rather liked it that way for some reason. Now I suddenly got a general picture of debauchery—inane and as revolting as a spider—that starts without feeling, coarsely and shamelessly, at the culmination point of real love. We looked into one another's eyes for a long time, but she didn't lower hers before mine. Finally I began to feel ill at ease.

"What's your name?" I asked abruptly, to get out of the situation.

"Liza," she answered rather coldly, in a whisper, and averted her eyes.

I remained silent for a while.

"Tonight, the weather . . . snow . . . disgusting!" I mumbled, almost talking to myself, placing one hand under my head and staring mournfully at the ceiling.

She didn't answer. The whole thing was hideous.

"Do you come from around here?" I asked her a moment later, almost angrily, turning my head slightly toward her.

"No."

"Where are you from?"

"Riga," she said reluctantly.

"You a German?"

"No, I'm Russian."

"Been here long?"

"Where?"

"In this house."

"A couple of weeks."

Her tone was more and more abrupt. The candle went out, and I could no longer see her face.

"Do you still have your parents?"

"Yes—they're alive."

"Where are they?"

"In Riga."

"What do they do?"

"Oh, just . . ."

"Just what? What sort of people are they?"

"Tradespeople."

"You used to live with them?"

"Yes."

"How old are you?"

"Twenty."

"Why did you leave them?"

"I just left."

That "just" meant "let go of me, I'm fed up." We fell silent.

God alone knows why I didn't leave. I myself was beginning to feel sick and dejected. Images from the preceding twenty-four hours kept flashing disjointedly through my mind, without the slightest participation of my will. I suddenly remembered a scene I'd witnessed in the morning when, immersed in my preoccupations, I had been ambling to my office.

"Today I saw some people carrying a coffin, and they almost dropped it," I suddenly said aloud, although I didn't feel at all like resuming the conversation.

"A coffin?"

"Yes, in the Haymarket. They were carrying it up from a basement."

"From a basement?"

"From a basement apartment, you know, in a disorderly house . . . It was so muddy all around—eggshells, garbage—it smelled . . . It was quite disgusting."

Silence.

"It was a bad day for a burial," I resumed, just to break the silence.

"Bad? Why?"

"The snow, the slush . . ." I yawned.

"What's the difference?" she said after a while.

"No, it's horrible." I yawned again. "The gravediggers must have been swearing because they were getting wet with that snow. And I'm sure the grave was full of water."

"Why should there be water in the grave?" she asked with strange curiosity, but tossing her words at me even more coldly and harshly than before.

I was beginning to enjoy this.

"Why, I'd say there was at least half a foot of water in there. You can't dig a dry grave in Volkovo Cemetery."

"Why not?"

"What do you mean, 'Why not?' It's all swampy over there. They just lower the coffins into the water. I've seen it myself . . . many times."

I'd never seen anything of the sort. In fact, I'd never been to Volkovo. I'd only heard about it.

"Is it possible that you don't care whether you live or die?" I said.

"Why should I die?" she asked, sounding defensive.

"You'll die all right, some day, and it'll be exactly like that woman I was talking about. She was young too, just like you. . . . She died of consumption."

"A dame like that would've died in a hospital."

She knows all about these things, I thought when she used the word "dame."

"She owed money to the madam," I said, enjoying the argument more and more. "And she kept working to the very end, consumption or no consumption. The cabbies around there had spoken to some soldiers, and I heard it from them. They made fun of her. They even intended to have a party in her memory in a tavern."

I had invented much of this.

A dead silence followed. She didn't even stir.

"And why is it better to die in a hospital?" I added.

"Makes no difference where. Why should I die, anyway?" she said irritatedly.

"If not now, later. . . ."

"Now or later, it won't make any difference."

"No? Just think: Now you're young and pretty, and they value your services. But after a year or so of this life, you won't be the same; you'll fade——"

"After a year?"

"In any case, I can tell you that in a year your price will go down," I went on with vicious zest. "Then you'll move from this establishment to a cheaper one. And, in another year, you'll be moved to a third, still lower; and in about seven years, you'll wind up in a Haymarket basement. And that'll still be nothing. What will you do if they discover there's something wrong with your chest, say, or if you catch cold or something? With the kind of life you lead, it's hard to really get rid of an illness—once you're caught, you won't get loose. That's how you're going to die."

"So I'll die," she said, really angry now and making an abrupt movement in the dark.

"Why, it's a shame."

"Why's it a shame?"

"It's a shame to lose one's life."

Silence.

"Have you ever been engaged to be married?"

"What's that to you?"

"All right, all right, I'm not trying to cross-examine you. Don't get angry. I know it's none of my business. I realize you may have personal troubles. I was just talking. . . . I'm sorry, that's all."

"Sorry for what?"

"You."

"I'm all right," she whispered, hardly audibly, and again I heard her stirring.

This irritated me no end. I was being so kind to her and she . . .

"So you think you're on the right path, do you?" I said.

"I think nothing."

"That's bad too—not to think. Wake up and get hold of yourself while there's still time. Because you do still have time, understand that! You're still young and not bad-looking. You could fall in love, marry, be happy——"

"Marriage doesn't necessarily mean happiness," she interrupted me, resuming her harsh, terse tone.

"Not necessarily, as you say, but it's still better to be married than to be here. No comparison, believe me. With love, one can do very well without happiness. Life is good even in sorrow. It's nice to live in this world whatever your life is like. But here, in this place, there's nothing but foul air. Brrr. . . ."

I turned away in disgust. I was no longer detached. I was involved in what I was saying. In fact, I was getting excited. I was thirsting to lay before her the precious little ideas I'd nurtured in my hole. Suddenly I had an aim.

"Pay no attention to me. I'm here myself, so I can't tell you what to do. Maybe I'm worse than you," I said hurriedly, to justify myself. "But then, it's different for a man, for although I may defile and degrade myself, I'm still no one's slave. I come and go—I'm not stuck here. I brush it off me and I'm another man. But you—you've been a slave from the very beginning. Yes, a slave! You've given up everything. You've given up your freedom, and even if you try breaking these chains one day, you won't be able to—you'll only get further entangled in them. I don't even want to mention other things, because you won't understand me, but tell me this: I'll bet you're already in debt to the madam, right? So you see," I went on, although she hadn't said anything, but simply lay there listening in silence with all her being, "that's the chain. You'll never buy yourself out. It's as though you'd sold your soul to the devil. Now I may be just as miserable as you; I may also be wallowing in filth out of dire misery. Some drink in their misery; my misery makes me come here. Now tell me, what's the point of it? We came in here without saying a word to each other, and afterward, you stared at me like a savage and I stared back at you. Is that the way to make love? Is that the way people are meant to come close to each other? It's hideous, that's what it is!"

"Yes!"

She said it harshly, hurriedly. I was particularly struck by the hurried, emphatic way she said "yes." Maybe she'd had the same thought when she was examining me before? So, she too was capable of thinking to some extent? Damn it, how amusing! Didn't that mean that we were alike in a way, the two of us?

I almost rubbed my hands in joyful expectation. I didn't see how I could fail to cope with this young creature. And what appealed to me most was the challenge it presented.

She brought her head closer to mine, supporting it in her hand, or at least that was the impression I got in the darkness. Maybe she was staring at me again. I would have liked so much to be able to see her eyes. I listened to her breathing deeply.

"Why did you come to Petersburg?" I began with a certain authority.

"I just came. . . ."

"But you were comfortable enough in your parents' home, weren't you? Warmth, freedom, your own corner——"

"Suppose I tell you that it was worse than here?"

"I must catch the right tone," the thought occurred to me. "I won't go far with her using sentimentality."

But, in truth, that thought only flashed through my head. I swear, she really did interest me. Moreover, I felt weak and in the right mood, and besides, shamming so easily coexists with sincere feeling.

"There's no telling," I hastened to reply. "One comes across all sorts of things. I'm quite sure you must've been wronged and that they're more guilty before you than you before them. Understand, I know nothing about you, but I feel somehow that a girl like you wouldn't land in a place of this sort of her own free will."

"A girl like what?" she whispered hardly audibly, but I heard her.

Damn it, I was flattering her. It was disgusting! . . . On the other hand, perhaps it was the right thing to do. . . . She said nothing.

"Let me tell you something about myself. You know, Liza, if I had had a family when I was a child, I'd have turned out quite different from what I am today. I've given it a lot of thought. However bad things may be within a family, I still say that a father and mother are part of you, not your enemies or just strangers. Be it only once a year, they'll still show you their love. Whatever else, you still have the feeling that it is your home. But I grew up without a family, and that's why I'm like this . . . you know, without feelings."

I waited for a while. I didn't think she understood, and anyway, I was being ridiculous with this moralizing stuff.

"If I'd been a father, I think I'd have loved my daughters more than my sons," I began, making an indirect approach as though embarking on something else, just to distract her. I admit I was blushing.

"What's that got to do with it?" she asked.

So she was listening!

"Nothing really. . . . I don't know, Liza. You see, I used to know a strict, stern man who'd go down on his knees before his daughter and kiss her hands and feet —he just couldn't admire her enough. She could spend the night dancing, and her father would stand in the same spot for five hours without taking his eyes off her. He was crazy about her, and I can understand that. At night, she'd get tired and fall asleep, and he'd go and kiss her in her sleep and make the sign of the cross over her. He himself went around in shabby, old clothes and was stingy with others, but he never hesitated to spend his last kopek on presents for her, the most expensive ones too, and he was incredibly happy if she liked them. A father always likes his daughters more than their mother does, and that makes it nice for many a girl at home. I don't think I'd even have allowed my daughter to marry."

"Why is that?" she asked with a slight laugh.

"I swear I'd have been jealous. I couldn't have borne the thought that she'd be kissing another man, that she'd love a stranger more than her own father. It's a painful thought. Of course, that's all nonsense, and everyone is bound to come to his senses in the end. But I believe that, before I allowed her to marry, I'd have found fault with all her suitors one after the other. Finally, I suppose, I'd have let her marry the one she really loved. But, of course, that one would be bound to please a father the least. That's the way it always is, and it often causes a lot of trouble in families."

"But there are people who are willing to sell their daughters, let alone allow them to marry decently," she suddenly declared.

So that was it.

"That, Liza, happens in those wretched families where

there's no God and no love," I went on zestfully. "And
where there is no love, there's no reason either. It's true
that such families exist, but I wasn't speaking of them. It
looks as though you never were happy in your family;
that's what makes you say things like that. You seem to
be truly unhappy. Well, poverty has a lot to do with it."

"Do you mean to say it's better among the well-to-do?
People can be honest and live decently whether they're
poor or not."

"Well, I suppose you're right. But then too, Liza, man
only notices his sorrows; he takes his happiness for granted. If he did take note of it, though, he'd find that he had
his share of happiness also. Now imagine a family that has
been lucky in everything: with God's help you marry a
good husband, who loves you, looks after you, never
leaves you, and all that. Life is good for such a family!
Sometimes there may be sorrows too, but it's still good.
For where is there no sorrow? When you marry, you'll
find out for yourself. On the other hand, take the period
just after marriage—sometimes there's really an incredible amount of happiness then. During that early period,
even quarrels with your husband end happily. In fact,
the more some women love, the more quarrels they start.
I used to know a woman like that. 'You see,' she'd say,
'I love you so, and it's because of my love that I torture
you, so you just take it.' Did you know that one could
deliberately torture a person out of love? Women are
particularly prone to do that. And while they're torturing
you, they think to themselves: 'I'll make it up to you
later with love and tenderness, so torturing you now is
not really a sin.' And everyone looks with joy upon the
happy household—everything is so peaceful, friendly, and
honest. . . .

"Some women are jealous too. I used to know one like
that. She couldn't stand it when her husband went out
somewhere, and she'd follow him into the night to find
out if he wasn't going to see some woman. That's bad, of
course, and she knows it's bad, and her heart stops
beating and she suffers, but it's all because of love. And
how she likes to make it up after a quarrel and be

sorry or forgive! Indeed, both of them are happy, as though they had just met, just fallen in love with each other and just married. And if a husband and wife love each other, it's no one's business what goes on between them. And whatever quarrels they may have, they mustn't allow even their own mothers to judge between them and must never talk about one another. They're their own judges. Love is a divine mystery, and must be hidden from the eyes of the world, as must whatever takes place between lovers. They have respect for each other, and much is based on that respect. And since love existed once, since they married out of love, why should love die? Is it really impossible to keep it alive? It's seldom impossible. If the husband is kind and decent, how can love die? It's true, of course, that the first honeymoon feeling dies, but it's replaced by a better love. In that love their souls merge, they share everything and don't have any secrets from one another. And, when children arrive, even the greatest hardships seem like happiness, as long as there's love and courage. And the children love you later for having accepted these hardships so it's as though you were bearing them for yourself to reap. While the children are growing up, you feel that you're an example to them, something they can rely upon; that, even after you're dead, they'll carry you in their thoughts and feelings all their lives, for they'll have been molded in your likeness. So it is a great human duty, and how can the father and mother fail to come close to one another in it? They say that it's hard to have children. Who says that? It's heavenly bliss, I say. Do you like children, Liza? I love them. Imagine a pink little boy suckling at your breast. What husband wouldn't be moved by such a sight! A little, rosy, chubby baby stretching his tiny arms and legs and snuggling up to you. His little hands with their tiny, clean nails are so soft, and he looks so funny, as though he could already understand. And when he begins teething, he may take a good bite at his mother's breast, squinting at her as if to say 'See, I bit you!' Ah, Liza, isn't it all happiness when the three of them—the mother, the child, and the father—are together? To experience those moments, one should be willing to go through much suffering. No, Liza, we must first learn to live ourselves before we begin to accuse others!"

Those were the right pictures to get through to her, I thought, although I swear I said those things with feeling. I suddenly felt I was blushing. What if she suddenly burst out laughing? Where would I hide myself? This thought made me furious. By the time I came to the end of my speech, I was sincerely excited, and now my pride began to suffer. The silence continued. I even felt like nudging her.

"Why, you . . ." she started, but cut herself off.

But I understood. There was something different in her voice, some new quiver; it was no longer harsh, coarse and resigned, but soft, shy, and ashamed, so that I myself felt ashamed and guilty.

"What?" I asked with tender curiosity.

"Why, you . . ."

"What?"

"Why you're . . . just like a book," she said, and I thought I caught a sarcastic note in her voice again.

That pinched me painfully. It wasn't what I was expecting.

I didn't understand that sarcasm is a screen—the last refuge of shy, pure persons against those who rudely and insistently try to break into their hearts. Until the last moment, her pride prevented her from saying openly what she felt. I should've guessed that, if only from the timid hesitation she had to overcome to make her defensive, sarcastic remark. But I didn't understand, and a nasty feeling pervaded me.

"Wait," I said to myself, "I'll show you."

VII

"Ah, Liza, why should I sound like a book when all this makes me sick just looking at it from the outside. Actually, I'm not completely outside. It has stirred something, awakened something, in me. Now tell me, is it really possible that you yourself aren't sick of being here? Well, I suppose one can get accustomed to anything. Habit can do things to people, I'm sure. But do you really think you'll never grow old, that you'll always be attractive, that they'll keep you here as long as you live? I'm not even talking about what a horrible place this is in its own right. No, wait, let me tell you something about your present existence too. Although you're still young and pretty and nice and have a heart and feelings and all that, I tell you, when I came to just now and found myself here with you, I felt sick. As a matter of fact, people only come here when they're drunk. But if I'd met you somewhere else, and you'd led a decent life, I'd have trailed after you and probably fallen in love with you too. Not even a word but a simple look from you would've been enough to make me feel happy; I'd have waited for you near your house, knelt before you, looked upon you as my bride-to-be, and felt greatly honored to be allowed to look upon you like that. I'd never have dared to have an impure thought about you then, while now I know that all I have to do is whistle and, whether you want to or not, you have to come with me. I don't have to obey your will, but you do have to obey mine. Even the most miserable peasant who hires himself out as a laborer doesn't lose his freedom completely; he knows there's a time limit to his bondage. But you—where's your time limit? Just ask yourself what you're surrendering here, what you're selling into bondage. It's your soul you're selling, your soul, over which you have no power. You're selling it along with your body. You offer your love to the first drunkard who comes along, to tramp upon. Love! But it's everything, it's a jewel, it's a woman's dearest possession! Why, to earn that love, someone might give all his thought, even his entire life. But what's your love worth today? You've been sold, all of you, so why should anyone try to win your love, since everything's possible without it. There's nothing more insulting for a woman. You know, I've heard that they allow you poor idiots to have your own lovers for your pleasure. But, of course, that's nothing but make-believe—a mockery. They laugh at you, and you take it seriously. Do you really imagine that your 'free' lover is in love with you? I don't believe he can be. How can he be when he knows that at any moment, perhaps when you're with him, someone may whistle for you. He'd be too low for words if he did love you. Does he have the least respect for you? What is there in common between you? He just mocks you and robs you, and that's all there is to it. You're lucky if he doesn't beat you—or does he? If you have someone like that, try asking him to marry you. He'll laugh in your face, if he doesn't spit in your eye and give you a beating. He himself probably isn't worth more than a crooked kopek. So in the name of what have you ruined your life here? For the meals, perhaps including coffee, that you're given? Why do they feed you, do you think? A decent woman wouldn't be able to swallow a mouthful at the thought of why they give her her food. You're in debt to them, and you'll remain in debt till the end— till the time when the customers refuse to use you. And that's not as far off as you think, for you'd be wrong to rely too much upon your youth. Time moves very fast indeed here. They'll kick you out soon enough. And they won't kick you out just like that; they'll start by nagging you, heap reproaches and insults upon you as though, instead of giving them your health, your youth, and your soul, you'd ruined them and stolen what was theirs. And don't expect any support from the other women—they'll go for you too, if only to please the madam, because in this place everything has been mortgaged, and conscience and pity have long ago disappeared. These women have sunk too low too, and there's nothing filthier and lower than the insults they'll heap on you. You'll lose everything here; everything will go without return— youth, health, hopes—and at twenty-two you'll look thirty-five, and you'll even have to pray to God that you don't catch a disease. And if you tell yourself that at least you don't have to work and have nothing to do but eat and drink, let me tell you that there's never been any harder, more painful work in the world than this work that makes your whole heart dissolve into tears. And when they chase you out of here, you won't dare say a word nor make a sound in protest; you'll slink away as though you were guilty. You'll go to another establishment, then to another and another yet, and finally you'll land in the Haymarket. And there they'll start beating you in no time, for the customers there don't know how to make love without beating. You don't believe it's all that horrible there? Go and have a look around some time, and perhaps you'll see it with your own eyes. Once —it was on a New Year's morning—I saw a woman there by the door of a house. Her own colleagues had pushed her out as a practical joke—to cool her off for a while because she was bawling—then they decided to lock the door on her. So, at nine in the morning, there she was, completely drunk, unkempt, half-naked, badly beaten. There was a thick layer of powder on her face still, black bruises under both her eyes, and blood streaming from her nose and mouth. Some cabby had just dealt with her, it seems. She sat on the doorstep bewailing her "miseries" at the top of her voice, striking the steps with a salt herring she held in her hand, as a bunch of drunken soldiers and cabbies gathered around her and taunted her. You don't believe that you'll become like that one day too? I wish you were right, but how do you know that ten, or only eight, years before, that woman with the herring didn't arrive in this city fresh and innocent as a little angel, ignorant of evil and full of blushes? Maybe she was just like you—proud, queenlike, quick to take offense, different from the others, sure that she could give happiness to a man if she loved him and he loved her. And you see how it all finished? Well, perhaps that drunken, disheveled woman whipping at the filthy steps with her fish was at that very moment remembering her bygone, innocent years when she lived with her parents, when the neighbor's son waited for her on her way home from school and assured her that he'd love her as long as he lived, that she was the most important thing he had, and then they decided to love one another for ever and ever and to marry as soon as they were grown up.

"It'd be lucky for you, Liza, if you died quickly of consumption in some basement, like the woman in the coffin I told you about. You mentioned the hospital. You'd be very lucky if they took you there. But suppose madam thinks she can still use you? Consumption is a peculiar disease. It's not like a fever, you know. A consumptive keeps hoping and cheering himself up till the very last minute, saying that he's all right. And that works to madam's advantage. Believe me, that's the way it is. You've sold yourself to her and, furthermore, you're in debt to her. So you can't open your mouth. And when you're about to die, they'll all turn their backs on you, for what could they get out of you at that point? They'll even reproach you for taking too much time to die and not vacating your corner quickly enough. When you beg them for a glass of water, they'll swear at you before they give it to you. 'When,' they'll say, 'will you croak at last, you slut? It's impossible to sleep with your damned moaning, and it puts the customers off too!' It's true, you know. I myself have overheard things like that. They'll stow you somewhere in the dirtiest corner of the basement. And as you lie dying in the dank darkness, what will you think about in your loneliness? And when you're dead, strange hands will lay you out, grumbling impatiently. No one will pray for you; no one will be sorry for you—they'll only be concerned with getting you out of the way. They'll buy you a cheap coffin and carry you out just the way they carried out that other miserable creature, then they'll go to the tavern and have a drink to your memory. The grave will be full of mud and slush, and they won't want to take too much trouble with you. 'Lower her in, Ivan. She's out of luck again, the slut, even on her last trip. Come on, take up the slack on your rope, you clod! That's fine now, let's leave it as it is.' 'What do you mean, fine? Don't you see she's on her side. She was a human being after all, wasn't she? Ah well, all right, fill it up.' And they won't quarrel over it, believe me. They'll fill up the grave with wet, gray clay and be off to have a drink at the tavern.

"And that'll be all—you'll be forgotten on earth. Children, fathers, husbands come to the graves of other women . . . but no one will come to your grave, there'll be not a tear, not a sigh, not a prayer over you; nobody will ever come, and your name will be erased from the face of the earth; it'll be as if you'd never even existed. There'll be nothing but a mire of mud around you, and it won't help you to knock on the lid of your coffin like the dead do when they rise at night. You'll moan in vain: 'Let me out; let me back into the world, kind people. My life was no life. It was spent between being used as a doormat and drinking in taverns. Give me one more chance, kind people, to live.' "

I had worked myself up into such a state that there was a lump in my throat, and I had to abruptly cut myself short. I raised myself on my elbows and listened in apprehension, my head bent forward and my heart beating wildly. And there was good reason for my confusion.

For some time, I'd felt that I was turning her soul inside out and breaking her heart, and the more convinced I was of it, the more eager I was to finish what I had set out to do. It was a game I was playing, and I was altogether absorbed in it—although, perhaps, it wasn't only the game.

I knew that what I was saying was contrived, even "literary" stuff, but then, that was the only way I knew how to speak—"like a book," as she had put it. But that didn't worry me as long as I was sure I was getting my point across. In fact, my artificial style may have made the message more effective as far as she was concerned. But now, having attained the effect I sought, I suddenly found I had no stomach for it. The fact is, I'd never, never witnessed such despair. She lay prone on the bed, her arms around the pillow and her face buried in it. Her breast was heaving spasmodically and all her young body was writhing. The sobs compressed in her chest were choking her as they tried to break out. Then suddenly they broke through in horrifying wails as she clasped the pillow even harder, not wanting anyone alive to see her tears and her suffering. She bit the pillow, bit her hand till she drew blood (I saw it later), then clutched at her tangled hair with her fingers, holding her breath and clenching her teeth. I wanted to say something to her, soothe her, but I didn't dare. Then, in a sort of panic, all ashiver, I began groping for my clothes, for I wanted to get out of there as fast as I could. But I couldn't get dressed quickly in the darkness, so I felt around for a box of matches on the night table, where my hand also found a new candle. As soon as the candle lighted up the room, she jumped up. Her face was strangely distorted by an inane, almost mad smile. She looked at me. I sat down next to her and took her hands. She made a movement as if to fling herself toward me, was about to throw her arms round my neck, but didn't dare and lowered her head.

"Forgive me, Liza, I shouldn't have . . ." I began, but her fingers clutched my hands so hard that I realized I was saying the wrong thing, stopped, and said instead: "Here's my address, Liza, come and see me."

"I'll come," she whispered determinedly, without raising her head.

"And now I have to go. Good-by. . . . See you soon."

I got up and so did she. Suddenly she blushed, grabbed a shawl from the chair, and threw it around her shoulders, covering herself up to her chin with it. Then she gave me a strange look, and a tortured smile appeared on her lips. The whole thing was very painful for me. I was in a hurry to get away.

"Wait a minute," she said, catching hold of my overcoat. We were already in the entrance hall. She put down the candle she was holding to light my way and dashed off. Apparently there was something she wanted to show me. When she ran off, I saw that her eyes were shining, that she was flushed and smiling. What could it be? I had to wait. She came back a moment later, looking at me as though she were asking my forgiveness for something. In general, her face was no longer the same as when I'd seen her first—sullen, distrustful, and obstinate. Her eyes were beseeching now and trusting, tender and shy.

She had beautiful, light-brown eyes, full of life—eyes that could express both love and sullen hatred.

Without a word of explanation, as though I were some sort of higher being who could understand everything directly, she handed me a piece of paper. At that moment, her face was shining with a naïve, almost child-like triumph. I unfolded it. It was a letter addressed to her by, I'd guess, a medical student. It was a rather flowery and grandiloquent, but very respectful, declaration of love. I can't recall the exact words now, but I remember that, under the highflown style, I sensed genuine feeling. When I had read it, I met her ardent, curious glance, filled now with a sort of childish impatience. It was fixed on my face—she was impatient to find out what I'd have to say. Briefly, but radiantly, proudly, she told me that she had gone to a dancing party in a private house, "a very, very nice family who still know nothing, absolutely nothing," for she'd only been in this place for a short while and certainly hadn't decided to stay; in fact, she'd leave as soon as she settled her debt. . . . "Anyway, that's where this student was." And the whole evening he'd danced with her and talked to her, and it turned out that they'd met back in Riga, when they were children, that they'd played together—although it was very long ago—that he'd even known her parents. But he had absolutely no idea about *this thing*—he didn't even suspect it. And, the day after that party (three days ago now), he'd sent her this letter through a lady friend of hers who'd been to the party too. . . . "And . . . here we are."

She bashfully lowered her sparkling eyes as she completed her explanation.

Poor thing! She had kept the letter as a precious possession and had rushed to show me that sole possession of hers, not wishing me to leave without knowing that there was someone who loved her honestly and sincerely and addressed her with respect. Most certainly, this letter was doomed to remain lying in her box and would never lead to anything. But that changed nothing: I was sure that she would keep it all her life as a treasure, as her pride and justification. And now, she had thought of that letter and showed it to me with naïve pride, to rehabilitate herself in my eyes, hoping that I would appreciate it and express my appreciation.

But I just shook her hand and left. I was in a terrible hurry to go. I walked all the way home, although the wet snow was coming down in large flakes. I felt exhausted, broken, and confused. But behind my confusion, I could already make out the outline of the truth, a sordid, obscene truth!

VIII

But, in fact, it took me no time at all to accept that truth. When I woke up in the morning, after a few hours of leaden sleep, I reviewed all that had happened the night before and was, if anything, surprised at my *sentimentality* toward Liza, at all those sobs and commiserations that we had shared.

"What a disgusting outburst of nerves!" I decided. "I'm just like an old woman. And why the hell did I have to give her my address? What if she turns up? Ah, after all, let her turn up. We'll see. . . ."

But *obviously* that was not what mattered. The main consideration was to save my reputation in the eyes of Zverkov and Simonov. Yes, that was of major importance.

And there were so many things to preoccupy me that morning that Liza slipped my mind completely.

To start with, I had to pay Simonov the money I had borrowed from him the day before. I decided on a desperate measure: to borrow all of fifteen rubles from Anton Antonych. By chance, he was in an excellent mood and let me have the money as soon as I asked for it. I was so pleased that, while signing the IOU, I told him with a dissipated, nonchalant air that last night, "I had a terrific time at the *Hotel de Paris,* seeing off a former classmate, a childhood friend, an awful rake, terribly spoiled by life, of course, who comes from a distinguished family, quite wealthy, making a brilliant career for himself, witty, charming, a ladies' man, you understand. Of course, we had quite a bit to drink, maybe half a dozen bottles of champagne too much and . . ." And, believe me, all that slipped off my tongue quite easily and sounded self-confident and self-satisfied.

As soon as I got home, I wrote to Simonov.

To this day, I admire the gentlemanly, good-humored tone of that letter. Gracefully, smoothly, without any superfluous words, I took upon myself the full responsibility for what had happened. I gave as an excuse, "if any excuse was admissible at all," the fact that I was unaccustomed to drink and got quite drunk after the very first glass which, I alleged, I had drunk while waiting for them between five and six at the *Hotel de Paris*. My apologies were mainly addressed to Simonov himself, but I asked him to apologize to all the others for me, particularly Zverkov, whom, I wrote, "I remember having insulted, as it were, through the haze of a dream." I wrote that I'd have gone to see each one of them, but I had a horrible headache and felt too embarrassed to face them.

I was particularly pleased with the casual, almost off-hand undertone—oh, not in the least arrogant—that conveyed better than any explanations could that I viewed "the whole mess" with considerable detachment, that I certainly didn't feel annihilated by it, that in my opinion, it wasn't anything for which a young man should be judged too harshly.

"Upon my word," I muttered with admiration, re-reading the note, "there's even a certain aristocratic lightness to it! And all that because I'm a highly developed, civilized man! Another in my place wouldn't have known how to get out of it, but I've disentangled myself and will continue to enjoy myself precisely because I'm a well-educated, sophisticated man of my time. And the more I think of it, the more I believe that it really was my drinking that was at the root of it all. . . . Well, not really. . . . In reality, I didn't have any vodka or anything else while I was waiting for them. I just made that up for Simonov, and now it makes me feel ashamed. . . . Ah, I still don't give a damn! What counts is that I've got out of it."

I placed six rubles in an envelope with the letter and prevailed upon Apollon to take it to Simonov. When he realized that the letter contained money, Apollon became more polite and agreed to deliver it.

Toward evening I decided to go out for a walk. I was still dizzy from the day before and my head still ached. The darker it became, the more confused became my impressions and the thoughts growing out of them. There was something inside me that wouldn't die—that refused to die within my heart and conscience and manifested itself in a stabbing feeling of anguish. I kept to the busiest, most bustling streets, such as Traders' Row, Garden Square, and around Yusupov Park. I've always liked these streets at dusk, when they're filled with all sorts of people, workers, and tradesmen, their faces worried and contracted with irritation, on their way home after the day's work. What I liked was precisely this kopek's-worth bustle, the self-satisfied vulgarity of it all. But that particular evening, the noisy throng only irritated me. I couldn't get hold of myself that day. Something kept oppressing and tormenting me, and wouldn't leave me alone. I arrived home altogether depressed, feeling as if I had some horrible crime on my conscience.

The idea that Liza might come worried me no end. I couldn't understand why, of all the previous day's impressions, her image was the one that tormented me most, with a strange, special torment. All the rest was forgotten by the evening. I'd dismissed it with a shrug and was still very pleased over my letter to Simonov. But I wasn't at all pleased about the incident with Liza; I felt as though she alone had been the cause of all the trouble. "Suppose she comes?" I kept thinking. "Well, so what, let her come! But, I don't like the idea of her seeing how I live. Last night I must have appeared as a kind of hero to her, and now she'll see . . . Yes, that's bad, letting myself go like this. My place stinks of misery. How could I have gone out last night, dressed as I was? And that oilcloth-covered couch of mine with the stuffing sticking out of it!

And my ragged dressing gown that doesn't even keep me decent. . . . Ah, she'll see everything—and she'll see Apollon too. I bet the dog'll be rude to her. He'll find some pretext, just to get back at me, and I won't have the stomach to put him in his place; instead, I'll smile, lie to her, and prance around, trying to keep my dressing gown in place. Brr . . . how horrible! But that's not the worst of it. There's something even lower, even more loathsome: to put on that lying mask again!"

The mere thought made me flare up:

"Why is it dishonest? I was sincere last night. I remember very well—there was sincerity in me too. I wanted to stir up honorable feelings in her, and if she cried, it must've done her good. . . ."

Nevertheless, I couldn't calm down.

All that evening, even after I had returned home well after nine and felt Liza couldn't possibly come then, I couldn't get her out of my head and kept seeing her, always in the same position. One particular moment of the previous night kept returning to me with extraordinary vividness. It was when I lighted the match and saw her pale, twisted, martyrlike face. And what a pitiful, unnatural, distorted smile she wore at that second! I didn't know then that fifteen years later I'd still be thinking of Liza smiling that pitiful, twisted, unappreciated smile.

The following day, I was quite prepared to dismiss the whole incident as nonsense, overwrought nerves, and more than anything, *exaggeration.* I've always known of that weakness of mine and been very wary of it. "My tendency to exaggerate is like a deformity," I repeated to myself every hour or so, but then I'd think in a rage: "She'll come, she'll come, she's sure to come!" I ran up and down the room shouting: "If not today, she'll be here tomorrow, she's sure to find me! Yes, that's only to be expected from these stupid, pure-hearted romantics! Ah, damn them, these filthy, stupid, rotten, sentimental souls! How could she have failed to see through it all?"

But at this point I'd stop, aware of my own terrible confusion.

"And how few words it took," I noted. "How little of

an idyll—especially since it wasn't even a real idyll, but
a literary contrivance—it took to turn a whole human
soul upside down in less than a minute. That's girlish
innocence for you! That's virgin soil!"

Now and then, I'd think of going to see her myself,
"telling her everything," and asking her not to come. This
thought roiled me so inside that I think I'd have crushed
that damned woman if she'd happened to be within my
reach at that moment; I'd have insulted her, spat at her,
struck her, and pushed her out.

But another day, two, three, passed without a sign of
her, and I became almost reassured. I especially felt better after ten o'clock, by which time I was even liable to
slip into rather pleasant daydreams in which I was Liza's
savior. "She comes to me, and I talk to her . . . educate her,
teach her . . . Finally I realize she's in love with me, passionately. I pretend I don't understand. . . ." I don't really
know why there had to be that pretense—just to make it
prettier, I suppose. "Finally she comes, embarrassed and
beautiful, shivering and sobbing, and throws herself at my
feet, telling me I'm her savior and that she loves me above
all else in the world. So I'm taken aback, but 'Liza,' I say
to her, 'do you really imagine I haven't noticed your love?
I saw and guessed everything, but I didn't dare force
myself upon you first, because I know I have some influence upon you and was afraid you might try to force
yourself to reciprocate my love out of sheer gratitude
and generate within yourself a feeling of which I want
no part because it is . . . well, it's a despotism of sorts.
. . . It would be a lack of discretion. . . .' " At this
juncture, I'd entangle myself in such European claptrap,
permeated with the refinements so dear to George Sand,
that I'd have to skip. " '. . . But now you're mine; you're
my creation; you're pure and beautiful; you're my beautiful wife.

" 'Boldly and freely enter my house
To be its mistress, my sweet spouse.'

After that, we live happily ever after, go abroad, etc.,

etc." In brief, it'd make me sick finally, and I'd stick my tongue out, taunting myself.

"Ah, they won't even let the slut out," I thought. "They surely aren't allowed to go out for a little stroll when they feel like it, especially not in the evening." I felt certain, for some reason, that she'd turn up in the evening, and what's more, at seven. "But then, she said they still didn't have full control over her, that she still had special rights. So, well . . . yes. . . . Ah, damn it, I'm sure she'll come!"

It was a good thing Apollon was around to take my mind off her. His rudeness stretched my patience to the limit. He was my ulcer, my plague, imposed upon me by fate. We'd been squabbling for years, and I hated him. I don't think in all my life I'd ever hated anyone as much as I loathed him, especially at certain moments. He was a middle-aged, ponderous man who also went in for part-time tailoring. For some reason, he despised me beyond measure and was impossibly overbearing with me, although I must say that he looked down upon everyone else, too. Just a look at his firm mouth compressed into a butterfly and his blondish, carefully brushed head, with its forelock fastidiously arranged and slicked down with vegetable oil, was enough to tell you that this creature had never had any doubts about himself. He was the most pedantic man I'd ever met and, on top of that, possessed a vanity that might perhaps have been excusable in Alexander the Great. He was in love with every button on his coat, every one of his fingernails—yes, he seemed to be madly in love with them! He treated me rather tyrannically and talked to me very little, and when he happened to look at me, it was always with a firm, supercilious, sarcastic expression that drove me mad. He performed his functions as my servant as though he were bestowing the greatest of favors upon me, although in fact, he hardly ever did anything for me, for he didn't feel that he was obliged to. There's no doubt that he considered me the greatest fool on earth, and if he refrained from firing me, it was only because he got his monthly wages from me. He was willing to do nothing for me for seven rubles a month. I'm sure that many of my sins will be forgiven me because of what I put up with from him. At times, my loathing for him reached a point where the sound of his steps alone would throw me into convulsions. But what disgusted me most about him was his lisp. I believe his tongue was a little too long or something like that, and that gave him a lisp and a slobbery way of talking, of which, I believe, he was inordinately proud, fancying that it gave him an air of great distinction. Usually he spoke in quiet, measured tones, clasping his hands behind his back and looking at his feet. Another thing that infuriated me was his habit of reading a psalter aloud in his cubicle. I fought many a battle over it, but he relished his evening reading too much. His smooth, sing-song voice sounded as though he were chanting the psalms over the dead. Curiously enough, this is the way he wound up in the end: he now hires himself out to chant psalms at wakes. He also exterminates rats and manufactures boot polish.

But, at that time, I couldn't get rid of him; it was as though he were a chemical necessity for my existence. Anyway, he never would have agreed to leave then. I couldn't move to furnished rooms. My apartment was my private corner, my shell, my sheath, where I could hide from men. And I'll be damned if I can explain why, but Apollon just happened to be an integral part of it, and for seven whole years, I couldn't bring myself to remove him from there.

It was unthinkable, for instance, to put off paying him his wages, even for a couple of days. He would make such a fuss about it that I wouldn't know where to hide. But now I was so angry with the whole world that I decided to *punish* Apollon anyway and not pay him his wages for another two weeks. I'd been toying with the idea of doing something like that for a long time, perhaps two years, to prove to him that he had no reason to take himself so seriously and that, if the fancy took me, I could just withhold his pay. I promised myself not to talk to him about it and make him swallow his pride and be the first to approach me on the subject.

Then I'd take seven rubles out of my drawer, show them to him to prove that I had them, and tell him I didn't wish to pay him, simply because I didn't want to, just because I didn't feel like it, because that was the way *I wanted it,* because I was the master, and because he was rude and insolent. But, if he asked me politely, I might relent and give it to him. Otherwise, he might have to wait another two or three weeks, and maybe a month. . . .

But, angry though I was with him, it was he who won out in the end. I couldn't even hold out for four days. He acted just the way he usually did in such cases—for I'd tried this before, so I knew his contemptible stratagems. He would fix his stern gaze on me for several minutes, especially when I went out or came in. If I managed to stand up to it, pretending not to notice the way he was looking at me, he turned to other ways of persecuting me. For instance, he would enter my room noiselessly, while I was pacing up and down or reading, stop by the door, and remain standing there with one foot thrust forward and one hand behind his back. On these occasions, his gaze was no longer stern but outright contemptuous. And if I asked him what he wanted, he wouldn't answer, but would stare at me for a few seconds more, pursing his lips, and his face would take on an indescribable expression. Then he'd turn around and slowly shuffle off to his cubicle. Two hours later, he'd emerge again and once more impose himself upon me in the same manner. Sometimes, in my fury, I didn't even ask him what he wanted but instead turned sharply toward him, glaring back at him haughtily. We'd stare into each other's eyes for a couple of minutes, then he'd slowly turn around and leave, only to reappear two hours later.

If all that failed to subdue me, he resorted to his sighing trick: he'd suddenly look at me and sigh very deeply, measuring the extent of my moral degradation. In the end, it goes without saying, he always got his way. I ranted and raved and hollered at him, but I was forced to do as he wished.

This time, however, he had no sooner started with his routine—first-phase "stern looks"—than I flew at him like a madman. I was already too irritated—I just couldn't stand it.

"Stop!" I shouted at him, as he was turning slowly away, with one hand behind his back, ready to retire to his cubicle. "Stop, come back here, I tell you!"

I must have really yelled, because he did stop, staring at me with something that could have passed for surprise. But he still didn't speak, and that was what made me especially mad.

"How dare you come in like that without permission and stare at me? Come on, answer me!"

But he again just looked at me for half a minute or so without a word and then started turning away once more.

"Stop!" I roared like a wild beast, rushing up to him. "Don't you dare move! Now then, will you tell me what you came here to stare at?"

"If you wish to order me to do something, it is my duty to do it," he said, after another silence, quietly, evenly, lispingly, raising his eyebrows and bending his head first to one side then the other—and all that with murderous self-control.

"That's not what I asked you, you vicious bully!" I screamed, shaking with rage. "So I'll tell you, you murderer, why you came in here; it's because I haven't given you your wages. You think you're too good to ask for them, so you came here trying to punish me with your stupid stare, without even suspecting how stupid you are, how stupid you look—how stupid, stupid, stupid."

He started to turn away in silence, but I caught hold of him.

"Listen," I shouted, "here's the money, see?" I took the bills out of the desk drawer. "See? Seven rubles, right? But you won't get 'em! At least, not until you come to me and humbly apologize. Do you hear me?"

"Impossible," he answered, with a sort of uncanny self-assurance.

"I'll show you it's possible! I give you my word it is!"

"I have nothing to apologize for," he said, ignoring

my shouting. "On the contrary, I could complain to the police, because you called me a murderer, and that's an insult."

"Go on! Complain!" I continue to holler. "Go there this very second! I still say you're a murderer! Yes—murderer, murderer, murderer!"

But he only glanced at me and, no longer paying any attention to my shouting, glided toward his room without turning his head.

"If it hadn't been for Liza," I muttered to myself, "none of this would've happened." I let a minute go by, then went gravely, solemnly, but with a wildly beating heart, to his room.

"Apollon," I said with quiet dignity, despite the choking feeling I had, "go out and fetch me the police sergeant. At once!"

He had installed himself at his table in the meantime, had put his glasses on, and was preparing to sew something. When he heard my order he gave a snort of suppressed laughter.

"Go! Go at once, or you can't imagine what'll happen!"

"There must really be something the matter with you, sir," he said with his usual slow lisp, without raising his head and still trying to thread his needle. "Whoever heard of a man complaining against himself? As for your threats, sir, you're wasting your efforts, I dare say, for nothing will ever come of them."

"Go!" I screamed, grabbing him by the shoulder. I felt I was on the verge of hitting him.

I hadn't heard the entrance door open, but someone had entered the apartment, seen us, and stopped in bewilderment. I looked up, almost died of shame, and rushed to my room where, clutching my hair with both hands, I leaned my head against the wall, remaining there motionless.

A couple of minutes later, I heard Apollon's slow steps:

"There's *a person* wants to see you," he said, staring at me with special severity. Then he stepped out of the way and let Liza in.

It didn't look as if he intended to leave—he kept looking us over with a sneer on his face.

"Go on, go on, on your way!" I said, completely at a loss.

Just then, the clock on the wall strained, wheezed, and struck seven.

IX

Boldly and freely enter my house
To be its mistress, my sweet spouse.

I stood in front of her, crushed, branded, sordidly overcome with shame, and I think I smiled, trying to close my ragged, stuffing-shedding old dressing gown. . . . It had all happened exactly as I'd imagined it in my moments of depression. Apollon, having had his fill of looking at us, left the room. But that didn't make me feel any better. Worse yet, she too suddenly became more embarrassed than I could have imagined. And it was looking at me that embarrassed her.

"Sit down," I said mechanically, offering her the chair by the desk while I installed myself on the sofa.

She sat down obediently, never taking her eyes off me. It looked as if she expected me to do something, and this naïve expectation brought back my fury, but I controlled myself. She should've known better, pretended she hadn't noticed anything, that all was as usual, but instead she . . . And I felt, though still rather vaguely, that I'd make her pay dearly *for everything*.

"You've found me, I'm afraid, in a rather strange predicament, Liza," I began lamely, well aware that it was the wrong way to start. "No, no, don't start imagining things!" I exclaimed, seeing that she was blushing. "I'm not ashamed of my poverty. In fact, I'm proud of it. I'm poor but honorable—it's possible to be poor and honorable at the same time," I went on mumbling, "but . . . perhaps you'd like some tea."

"No . . ." She started to say something, but I interrupted her.

"Wait."

I leaped up and rushed to Apollon's cubicle. I felt I had to get out of her sight.

"Here, Apollon," I whispered feverishly, throwing down on his table the seven rubles that I had kept in my fist all that time, "here's your money. You see, I'm letting you have it, but for that, you must save me—go and get me a pot of tea and a dozen cookies from the tea shop. If you refuse, you'll make me the unhappiest man in the world, for you have no idea what sort of a woman she is! That's all. Now, you may be imagining something, but . . . Ah, you have no idea who she is!"

Apollon, who had put his glasses back on and resumed his work, at first squinted at the money, without putting down his needle. Then, without answering or paying any attention to me, he went on trying to thread his needle. I stood waiting for three minutes or so, my arms folded on my chest in a Napoleonic pose. My temples were covered with sweat and I could myself feel how pale I had turned. But, thank God, he must have taken pity on me. When he was through fiddling with his needle and thread, he got up, slowly pushing back his chair, slowly removed his glasses, slowly counted the money, and finally asked me over his shouulder if he should ask for a pot of tea for two. Then he slowly shuffled out.

As I was going back to my room, where Liza was waiting, it occurred to me that I might run away, no matter where, just as I was, in my tattered dressing gown, and come what may.

But I returned and sat down. She looked at me worriedly. For some moments we remained silent.

"I'll kill him!" I shouted suddenly, banging the desk with my fist and splattering ink over the top.

"But why, why?" she said, shivering.

"I'll kill him, I'll kill him!" I screamed, pounding the desk with my fists in a fit of rage, but clearly realizing how stupid my fit was. "You can't imagine, Liza, what a murderous bully he is. He's torturing me, Liza. Now he's gone to get the cookies, he——"

And suddenly I burst into uncontrollable sobs. Between my sobs, I was terribly ashamed, but I couldn't stop.

"What's the matter, what's the matter?" Liza said in agitation. She was frightened.

"Water! Get me some water. . . . Over there!" I mumbled weakly, knowing very well that I could easily have done without the water and didn't really have to mumble like that. But, although my sobbing fit had been quite genuine, I had to play a part to save appearances.

She handed me a glass of water, looking at me at a loss. At that moment, Apollon returned with the tea. I suddenly felt that this ordinary, everyday tea would be quite inappropriate after what had happened. It made me turn red. Liza glanced fearfully at Apollon, who left without even glancing at us.

"Do you despise me, Liza?" I asked her, trembling with impatience to know what she thought of me.

She didn't know what to say, she was so embarrassed.

"Drink your tea," I said irritatedly.

I was furious with myself, but, of course, I took it out on her. Vicious resentment against her was rising in my breast. I believe I'd have killed her if I'd had a chance. To punish her, I swore to myself that I wouldn't address one single word to her. I had decided that it was all her fault.

The silence had already lasted five minutes. Neither of us had touched the tea. I wouldn't touch mine just to make her feel even more embarrassed, and she felt too awkward to drink hers alone. Several times I caught her sad, perplexed glances. Stubbornly, I remained silent. Of course, it was I who suffered most, because I realized how loathsome my perverse stupidity was, even though I couldn't help it.

"I want," she began, feeling she had to break the silence somehow, "to leave . . . that place . . . for good . . ."

Ah, poor, silly thing; that was the very last thing to say at such an inappropriate moment to a fool like me. Even my heart bled for her at this show of artlessness and unnecessary frankness. But something ugly inside me nipped in the bud any pity I may have had and even exacerbated my spite. Ah, to hell with everything! Another five minutes went by.

"Maybe I'm disturbing you," she said, hardly audibly, and made a motion to get up.

As soon as I recognized this first sign of resentment at the way I was treating her, I began shaking with anger and burst out:

"I'd like to know the purpose of your coming here. What was it?" I began, gasping for breath, unable to care about getting my words in logical order. I was in such a hurry to blurt out everything that was pent up inside me that it made no difference to me where I started.

"Why did you come? Answer me! Come on, answer me!" I shouted in a blind rage. "All right, my girl, I'll tell you why: you came because of all the 'touching' things I said the other night. But, for your information, I was laughing at you then, just as I'm laughing at you now. Why are you trembling? Yes, I say I was laughing. I had been insulted at a dinner party just before I came by the fellows who preceded me. I came to your place to take a punch at one of them, the officer, but I was too late. I had to vent my spite on someone else, and you happened to be around, so I poured my resentment out on you and had a good laugh. I'd been insulted, so I wanted to insult back; I'd been made a doormat, so I wanted to show my power and wipe my feet on someone else. That's all there was to it, and you imagined I came specially to save you, isn't that right? That's what you imagined, wasn't it? Wasn't it?"

I knew she'd get confused and details would be wasted on her; however, I felt she couldn't miss the essence of what I was saying. And that's exactly what happened. She went ashen, pale as her kerchief; her lips twisted painfully, and she collapsed back in her chair as though felled by an axe. From that moment on, she remained there, shivering, eyes wide open, mouth agape, and listened to me. My cynicism had crushed her.

"Save you, indeed!" I resumed, jumping up and tearing back and forth across the room. "Save you from what, I'd like to know! Suppose I myself am lower than you? Why didn't you ask, when I was lecturing you on morals, what I was doing there myself, and whether I'd come especially to preach morals? What I was really after at that moment were power and a role to play, and your tears, your humiliation, and your hysterics. That's what I was after! But I couldn't keep it up because I'm garbage myself; I lacked the stomach for it and, I'll be damned if I know why, gave you my address. Even before I got home that night, I cursed myself for giving it to you; I hated you already because I'd lied to you. I can only play with words or dream inside my head; in real life, all I want is for you to vanish into the ground! I need peace. I'd give up the world like a kopek just to be left in peace. If given a choice between letting the world go to pot or going without my tea, I'd let the world go to pot so long as I could always have my tea. Were you aware of that or not? Well, I know that I'm no good, perverse, self-ish, and lazy. I've been shaking with fear these last three days because I thought you might come. And shall I tell you what it was that worried me most? The thought that I had tried to pass myself off as a hero to you and you would come and find me in my lousy dressing gown, penniless and repulsive. I just told you I wasn't ashamed of my poverty. Well, I am ashamed of it—more ashamed of it than of anything else; I'm more afraid of it than of becoming a thief, and I'm as hypersensitive as if I'd had the skin peeled off me, so that contact with the very air hurts. Can you still fail to see that I'll never forgive you for catching me in my dressing gown just as I was snapping at Apollon like a vicious little lapdog? Your savior, your erstwhile hero, throws him-self at his flunky like a lousy, mangy cur, and the flunky just laughs in his face! Nor will I ever forgive you for the tears that I couldn't hold back in front of you just now, like a stupid woman put to shame. And the fact that I'm confessing all this to you now—that, I'll also never forgive you. Yes, you and you alone are responsible for everything because you happened to be at hand, because I'm a louse, because I'm the most disgusting, most laughable, pettiest, most stupid, and most envious of all the worms of the earth—which are in no way better than me, but which, hell knows why, never feel embarrassed. But me—all my life I've let all sorts of scum push me around—that's just like me! And do you think I care if you don't understand all this? What concern of mine are you? What concern is it of mine whether or not you rot in that house? Don't you realize that when I've finished telling you all this, I'll hate you just because you were here and listened to me? Why, a man only bares his soul like this once in a lifetime, and even then, only when he's in hysterics. What more do you want? Why do you still stay here after all this? Why are you pestering me? Why don't you leave?"

But, at this point, a very strange thing happened.

I was so used to imagining everything happening the way it does in books and visualizing things falling somehow into the shape of my old daydreams that at first I didn't understand what was going on. What actually happened was that Liza, whom I had humiliated and crushed, understood much more than I had thought. Out of all I had said, she had understood what a sincerely loving woman would understand first—that I myself was unhappy.

Her fright and resentment gave way, at first, to sorrowful surprise. Then, when I explained how base and despicable I was, with the tears flowing from my eyes (they flowed during my whole tirade), her face started twitching convulsively. She wanted to get up and stop me, and when I was through, she wasn't struck by my cries of "Why are you pestering me? Why don't you leave!"; instead, she was concerned over the pain it must have caused me to say all that. And then, the poor thing had been so humiliated before and felt so much my inferior that it was beyond her to be angry or take offense. Suddenly she was standing, and in an irresistible impulse, with her whole being drawn toward me but too shy to take a step forward, she stretched her hands out to me. I couldn't stand it any longer. . . .

Then she flung her arms around my neck and burst

into tears, and I too lost all control and sobbed as I never had in my life before.

"They don't let me . . . I can't be good. . . ." I mumbled, stumbling to the couch. I threw myself on it, face down, and remained like that for at least a quarter of an hour, sobbing hysterically. She knelt near me, put her arms around my shoulders, and froze in this embrace.

But the trouble was that these hysterics couldn't go on for ever. And so—for I'm writing down the truth in all its disgusting ugliness—as I lay on that couch of mine with my face buried in the greasy oilcloth cushion, I began to realize, at first distantly, that it would be terribly awkward for me to lift my head now and look Liza in the eyes. I'm not sure what I was ashamed of, but I was ashamed all right. The thought also flashed through the turmoil in my head that we had definitely changed places, Liza and I, that she now had the heroic role, and I was the beaten-down, crushed creature she had been that night over there. . . . All this occurred to me while I was still lying face down on my couch.

Good God, was it possible that I envied her?

I can't answer that to this day, and then, of course, I understood even less than I do now. I cannot live without having someone to bully and order around. But, since nothing can be explained by reasoning, why reason?

Anyway, I managed to overcome my feelings, and since I had to raise my head sooner or later, I raised it. And to this day I'm sure that, precisely because I was ashamed to look her in the eye, new feeling flashed in my heart —the need to dominate and possess. Passion burned in my eyes as I fiercely clasped her hands. Ah, how I hated her, and how furiously I was drawn to her at that moment! And the one made the other stronger. This was like avenging myself! Her face expressed first bewilderment, perhaps even fear. But only for a moment. Then she threw herself at me in rapture.

X

A quarter of an hour later, I was darting impatiently up and down the room, again and again stopping by the screen and peeping at Liza through the slits. She was sitting on the floor crying, her head leaning against the edge of the bed. But she wasn't leaving, and that was what irritated me. By now, she knew everything, for I had subjected her to the ultimate insult, but . . . no need to go into detail. She had guessed that my outburst of passion had actually been an act of revenge, a new effort to humiliate her, and that now, to my almost impersonal hatred, there was added a *personal* hatred for her.

However, I'm not completely certain that she did understand everything clearly, beyond the fact that I was a loathsome creature and, most important, that I couldn't love her.

I know they'll tell me that it's incredible for a person to be so spiteful and stupid; they might add that my failure to fall in love with her or at least appreciate her love is incredible too. But why is it incredible? In the first place, I couldn't fall in love because, for me, loving means bullying and dominating. I have never been able to imagine any other way of loving and have reached a point where, to me, love consists of a voluntary concession by the object of my love of my right to bully it. Even dreaming in my mousehole, I never visualized love as anything but a struggle, starting with hatred and ending in the subjection of the loved object, after which I was unable to think up anything. And why is reproaching her for coming to see me just to hear my *touching* words—without it ever occurring to me that she'd really come, not for my lousy words but to love me—so incredible, since I had reached such a stage of moral disintegration, had so completely lost the habit of *living?* For a woman, all resurrection, all salvation, from whatever perdition, lies in love; in fact, it is her only way to it. But, in truth, I didn't hate her so much as I darted around the room and peered at her through the cracks in the screen. Her presence there simply weighed on me heavily. I wanted her to vanish. I wanted *peace;* I wanted to be left alone in my mousehole. The whiff of real life had overwhelmed me, and I couldn't breathe.

But more minutes passed without her stirring, as though she were unconscious. I had the nerve to tap on the screen to remind her. . . . She shuddered, jumped up, hurried to take her shawl, her hat, her coat, anxious to get out of my sight, anywhere. . . .

A couple of minutes later, she emerged from behind the screen, looking fixedly at me. I grinned viciously (although, in fact, I forced myself to grin like that *for appearances' sake*), but I had to turn away from her stare.

"Good-by," she said, walking toward the door.

I rushed after her, caught her hand, opened it, slipped something in . . . then closed it again. Then, I turned away, tore over to the opposite corner of the room, so I wouldn't see, at least . . .

I was about to lie just now and write that I did it accidentally, not knowing what I was doing, acting in a sort of daze. But I don't want to lie, so I say candidly that I opened her hand, and it was spite that made me put that into it. . . . I got the idea while I was darting up and down the room and she was sitting behind the screen. But I can say one thing for myself: in doing this cruel thing, I wasn't prompted by my heart but by my stupid head. This cruelty was so contrived and such *bad literature* that I couldn't bear it myself and leaped away to a far corner of the room; after that, full of shame and despair, I rushed after Liza. I opened the front door and listened.

"Liza, Liza!" I called down the staircase. But I kept my voice hushed.

There was no answer. I thought I could hear footsteps downstairs.

"Liza!" I shouted, louder this time.

But no answer came. At the same moment, I heard the squeaking of the heavy glass door downstairs. Then it shut with a bang.

She had left. I returned to my room deep in thought. I felt terribly sad.

I stopped by the desk near the chair on which she had sat and stared blankly in front of me. A minute passed, then suddenly I saw on the table, right in front of my eyes . . . well, in short, I saw the crumpled five-ruble bill I had pushed into her hand. It was that bill. It couldn't be any other—there wasn't another one in the house. That meant that she'd managed to throw it on the desk at the moment I'd rushed to the opposite corner of the room.

So? I might have expected her to do something of the sort. Really? Well—no. I was so egotistical, I despised people so much, that I'd never imagined she'd do it. It was too much. The next moment I was pulling on any clothes I could find and was off after her. She couldn't have gone more than about two hundred yards when I burst into the street.

There was no wind, and the snow was coming down almost perpendicularly, piling a soft layer on the sidewalk and on the empty street. There were no people and not a sound to be heard. The street lamps twinkled sadly and pointlessly. I ran a couple of hundred yards or so and stopped.

"Where is she going? Why am I running after her?" I thought.

"Why? To go down on my knees before her, to sob with remorse, to kiss her feet, to beg her to forgive me. . . ." I was longing to do it, my breast was bursting, I never again thought of that moment without emotion. "But what for?" I thought. "Won't I hate her even more tomorrow, just because I've kissed her feet today? As though I could give her any sort of happiness! As though I hadn't found out today for the hundredth time what I'm really worth! As though I could prevent myself from torturing her!"

I stood in the snow, staring into the blinding haze and thinking all that.

"And isn't it much better," I mused later, back at home, trying to soothe the living pain with my fantasies, "for her to bear this humiliation as long as she lives, because humiliation is purification, because it causes the most corrosive, the most painful awareness? I'd have soiled her soul and tired her heart no later than tomorrow, but this insult and humiliation will never be extinguished in her; whatever filth surrounds her, my insult will elevate her, purify her through . . . through hatred . . . well . . . maybe through forgiveness. . . . But will it really be easier for her now?"

No. But let me ask a question now on my own behalf: what's better—cheap happiness or lofty suffering? Well, tell me—which of the two is better?

That was what I was musing about sitting at home that evening, hardly able to bear my sadness and despair. Never before had I gone through such anguish and remorse. But, when I rushed out of the house after Liza, had there ever been any doubt that I'd come back without catching her? I never met her again—never heard of her. I must also add that I was very pleased with my phrase about the beneficent effect of insult, humiliation, and hatred, although I myself, at that time, almost fell sick with despair.

Even now, after all these years, this memory remains strangely vivid and unpleasant. I have many unpleasant memories, but . . . why not stop these notes right here? I feel it was a mistake to start writing them in the first place. However, I've at least felt ashamed all the time I've been writing this story, so it isn't literature, but a punishment and an expiation. Of course, spinning long yarns about how I poisoned my life through moral disintegration in my musty hole, lack of contact with other men, and spite and vanity is not very interesting. I swear it has no literary interest, because what a novel needs is a hero, whereas here I have collected, as if deliberately, all the features of an anti-hero. These notes are bound to produce an extremely unpleasant impression, because we've all lost touch with life and we're all cripples to some degree. We've lost touch to such an extent that we feel a disgust for life as it is really lived and cannot bear to be reminded of it. Why, we've reached a point where we consider real life as work—almost as

painful labor—and we are secretly agree
is presented in literature is much better.
this fuss about? What are we turning ou
What are we demanding? We don't kn
We would be the ones to suffer if our wh
were granted. Well, try it yourselves—a   ...ore
independence. Take anyone and untie his hands, open up
his field of activity, relax discipline, and . . . well, believe me, he'd immediately want that discipline clamped
down on him again. I know that what I'm saying is
liable to make you angry; that it may make you stamp
your feet and scream:

"Talk about yourself and about your own miseries
in your stinking hole, but don't you dare say *all of us.*"

But listen to me for a moment. I'm not trying to justify myself by saying *all of us.* As for me, all I did was
carry to the limit what you haven't dared to push even
halfway—taking your cowardice for reasonableness, thus
making yourselves feel better. So I may still turn out to
be more *alive* than you in the end. Come on, have another
look at it! Why, today we don't even know where real
life is, what it is, or what it's called! Left alone without
literature, we immediately become entangled and lost—we
don't know what to join, what to keep up with; what to
love, what to hate; what to respect, what to despise!
We even find it painful to be men—real men of flesh and
blood, with *our own private bodies;* we're ashamed of it,
and we long to turn ourselves into something hypotheti-
cal called the average man. We're stillborn, and for a long
time we've been brought into the world by parents who
are dead themselves; and we like it better and better. We're
developing a taste for it, so to speak. Soon we'll invent
a way to be begotten by ideas altogether. But that's
enough, I've had enough of writing these *Notes from
Underground.*

*Actually the notes of this lover of paradoxes do not
end here. He couldn't resist and went on writing. But we
are of the opinion that one might just at well stop here.*

The Dream of a Ridiculous Man

A FANTASY

ᛁᚾᚩᛁᚳᚱᛁ

I

I'm a ridiculous man. Now they call me a madman. That would be a promotion if I weren't just as ridiculous as before in their eyes. But it no longer makes me angry. I find them all nice now, even when they laugh at me—indeed, if they do, they're somehow particularly dear to me. I'd even laugh with them—not really at myself but out of sheer love for them—if looking at them didn't make me so sad. Sad, because they don't know the truth, while I do. Ah, it's so hard to be the only one to know the truth! But they won't understand it. No, they won't.

And yet, looking ridiculous used to upset me very much. In fact, I didn't just look ridiculous—I *was* ridiculous. I've always been ridiculous, and I think I've known it from the day of my birth. Perhaps I became fully aware of it at the age of seven. I studied at school, then at the university, and the more I studied, the more I realized that I was ridiculous. For me, in the final analysis, higher learning amounted to explaining and proving my ridiculousness. And in life it was the same as in my studies: every year I became more conscious that I looked ridiculous in every respect. Everyone has always laughed at me, but no one has ever suspected that the one person in the world who knew just how ridiculous I was was none other than myself. And that was what hurt me more than anything. But then, I had only

204

myself to blame: I was proud, and never wanted to admit it to anyone. And my pride kept growing with the years. If I had admitted to anyone that I knew I was ridiculous, I believe I'd have shattered my skull with a bullet that very night. Yes, I worried terribly during my adolescence that I would break down one day and admit it to my schoolmates. But once I reached adulthood, although I found out more and more about this horrible peculiarity of mine, I somehow became more resigned to it. I say "somehow," because to this day, I cannot account for it. Maybe it was the result of the conviction that dawned upon me quite independently of my will that nothing made any difference in this world. I had suspected this for a very long time, but I only became fully aware of it during this past year. I suddenly felt that it really made no difference to me whether or not the world existed. I began to feel with my whole being that *nothing had happened while I'd been alive*. At first I felt that, to make up for it, many things had happened before. Later, however, I realized that this was an illusion—nothing had happened before either. Little by little, I discovered that nothing will ever happen. Then I stopped getting angry at people and almost stopped noticing them. This change manifested itself even in the smallest things. When I walked along the street, for instance, I would bump into people. I was certainly not absorbed in thought, for what did I have to think of by that time? I just didn't care about anything any more. If only I could've answered some of the many questions that tormented me, but I hadn't found a single answer. Then I became indifferent to everything, and all the questions faded away.

It was only later that I learned the truth. I discovered it last November—November 3, to be precise; since then I remember every moment. It was a gloomy evening, as gloomy as they come. I was returning home at night, between ten and eleven, and I remember remarking that it was impossible to imagine a gloomier moment, even in its physical aspect. Rain was pouring down and it was the coldest, gloomiest rain possible. In fact, it was *awesome*. I remember that clearly; it was awesome and obviously hostile to man. And then, before eleven, the rain stopped and was replaced by a monstrous dampness that was even damper and colder than the rain had been. A strange steam billowed from every object, from every stone, every sidestreet as one looked down it from the corner. I suddenly felt that if all the gaslights went out at once, everywhere, the picture would be more cheerful, because it was by gaslight that all these sad things could be seen.

I hadn't dined that day. I had sat since early evening in the house of an engineer. Two of his friends were there too. I had been mostly silent, and I believe they were rather bored with me. They were discussing something that excited them, and at one point, their discussion became heated. Yet, they didn't really care—they got excited for the pleasure of it. And I said so.

"Good God," I said, "don't you realize that you yourselves don't really care one way or the other!"

They weren't offended. They just laughed at me. They laughed because I hadn't spoken reproachfully but simply because everything was all the same to me. They saw that it was all the same to me and it made them laugh.

When I had that idea about the gaslights in the street, I glanced at the sky. It was very dark, but I could make out torn clouds and bottomless black gaps between them. Suddenly I noticed a little star in one of those gaps. I looked at it intently. That star reminded me that I wanted to kill myself. I decided I would go through with it that very night. The idea of killing myself had implanted itself firmly in my mind two months before and, poor though I was, I'd bought myself an excellent revolver and loaded it that first day. But two months passed, and the revolver was still lying in my desk drawer. Killing myself was a matter of such indifference to me that I felt like waiting for a moment when it would make some difference. I can't tell you why I felt that way. Anyway, I kept waiting for the right moment. Now that star gave me the idea of going through with it that very night. Without fail. Why the star gave me that idea, I cannot say.

But just as I was looking at the star, along came a little

girl and grasped me by the elbow. The street was quite deserted. At a distance, a cabman was asleep on his box. The little girl was about eight. She had a scarf tied round her head and wore a ragged overcoat. She was all wet from the damp, but what struck me especially were her battered, wet shoes. I remember them to this day. She started tugging at my elbow, trying to make me pay attention to her. She wasn't crying, but she was spasmodically shouting some indistinct words which she couldn't pronounce too clearly, as she was shivering with cold. Something must have frightened her, for she kept repeating, "Mummy, Mummy!" and there was terror in her voice.

I just glanced at her and, without saying a word, started walking away. She ran after me, tugging at my sleeve. I discerned a note in her voice that indicates despair in badly frightened children. I know that note well. And, although she spoke indistinctly, I gathered that her mother was dying somewhere or that something had happened to her and she'd rushed out to get help. But I wouldn't follow her. In fact, I decided to chase her away. I started by telling her to go and find a policeman. But she clasped her little hands together and trotted along at my side, sobbing, trying to catch her breath. Finally I stamped my foot and shouted at her. She whimpered, "Mister, mister . . ." turned away, and darted across the street. Someone else had appeared there and she apparently had left me for him.

I reached the fifth floor where I live. I have just one room. It's small and poor, and has only a semicircular skylight for a window. There's an oilcloth-covered sofa, a desk loaded with books, two straight chairs, and an old but very comfortable armchair. I lit a candle, sat down, and began to think.

Behind the wall, in the room next door, there was bedlam. A retired army captain lived there. He had, as usual, some half-dozen visitors drinking vodka and playing cards with an old, greasy pack. The night before there had been a fight, and two of them had pulled each other's hair for a long time. The landlady had wanted to complain to the police, but she was too afraid of the captain.

There's only one other tenant on this floor—a thin, smallish lady married to some army man. She came from out of town with her three children, who took ill, here in the house, immediately upon their arrival. She and her children are also terribly afraid of the captain. Every night they shake with fear and cross themselves; the youngest child once even had a fit out of sheer terror.

I know for certain that, from time to time, the captain stops people on Nevsky Avenue and begs them for a handout. He cannot get a job. Strangely enough (and that's why I'm telling all this), I haven't once felt any resentment for the captain during the month that he's lived here. Of course, I've avoided his company, and besides, he got bored with me practically as soon as we met. But I don't mind all that racket behind the wall in the least—let them do what they want—it's all the same to me. I can sit up all night without hearing them, completely forgetting that they exist. I haven't gone to sleep before dawn for a year now; I just sit throughout the night in my armchair doing nothing. I read books only during the day. At night I just sit without even thinking, just allowing shreds of thoughts to wander at their leisure. I use up a whole candle every night.

I sat down quietly at the desk, took the revolver out of the drawer, and placed it in front of me. As I put it down, I remember asking myself, "Is this really it?" and answering categorically, "It is." That is—I'd shoot myself. I knew I'd shoot myself that night. I didn't know, however, how long I'd sit at my desk first. And there's no doubt that I would have shot myself had it not been for that little girl.

II

You see, although I didn't care one way or the other, I still felt pain. I'd have felt physical pain if someone had hit me. And the same applies to mental pain. If

I'd witnessed something sad, I'd have felt pity just as much as I would have before I ceased to care about anything in this life. I felt pity that night, most certainly enough to help a child. Then why hadn't I helped that little girl? Well, I hadn't helped her because of a thought that occurred to me at that moment. It was a question I couldn't answer—an idle question, but it made me lose my temper. I grew angry because I'd come to the conclusion that if I'd decided to end my life that night, then everything in this world should be, more than ever, a matter of complete indifference to me. Why then had I suddenly realized that it wasn't and felt sorry for the little girl? I remember how sorry I felt for her—so sorry that it hurt. And this was incredible in my state. I really don't know how to convey how I felt then, but the feeling persisted after I got home and sat down at my table. I was irritated, as I hadn't been for a long time.

I reasoned: it seems obvious that if I am still a man and not a zero, then as long as I haven't turned into a zero, I am living; hence, I can suffer, get angry, and feel ashamed of my actions. That's so—but if I'm to kill myself in, say, two hours, what concern of mine can that little girl possibly be, and how can I care about notions like shame or, for that matter, anything else in the world? I'm about to be turned into an absolute zero; so how is it possible that the knowledge that I'm about to stop existing *completely*—and, therefore, that everything else will stop existing—did not diminish in the least my pity for the little girl or my shame over committing a despicable action? When I stamped my foot and shouted at the poor child, it was as if I wanted to say:

"Here, see! I don't feel any pity, and, what's more, even if I commit an unspeakable crime now, it will be all right, because inside of two hours, everything will be extinguished."

Can you believe that that was why I shouted? I'm almost certain of it. It seemed obvious to me that my life and, with it, the whole world were at the mercy of my whim. I could even put it this way: it looked as if the world had been made especially for me alone; if I shot myself, the world would stop existing, at least for me. To say nothing of the possibility that indeed there wouldn't be anything or anyone left after me, and as my consciousness sputtered out, the whole world would vanish like a phantom, like a mere figment of that consciousness of mine. For it is possible that all the world and all the people are nothing but me.

I remember that, as I sat and reasoned like that, I kept rephrasing and twisting all the questions, one after another, that occurred to me. And in the end, quite new and unexpected considerations started cropping up.

At one point, I wondered how it would be if, after living on the moon or Mars and committing some horribly shameful deed there that dishonored and disgraced me in a way that can be imagined only in a nightmare—if, after that, I were transported to earth and remained conscious of what I'd done on the other planet—to which I'd never return; would it then be *all the same* to me as I gazed at the moon from the Earth? Or wouldn't it? Would I feel ashamed of the base act I'd committed there or not?

These questions were idle and useless since the gun lay on the table in front of me, and every bone in me knew that I was going to use it. Still, they tormented me, and that drove me mad. It was as if I could no longer die without deciding something beforehand. In short, that girl saved me, because the questions she'd stirred up delayed the shot.

Behind the wall, in the captain's room, things were growing quieter. They had finished playing cards and were trying to settle down and drop off to sleep, lazily winding up their arguments and swearing drowsily at one another.

It was then that I suddenly fell asleep, something that had never happened to me before while sitting in my armchair at my desk. Sleep crept up on me and caught me completely unawares.

A dream is a strange thing. Pictures appear with terrifying clarity, the minutest details engraved like pieces of jewelry, and yet, we leap unawares through huge abysses of time and space. Dreams seem to be controlled by wish rather than reason, the heart rather than the head—and yet, what clever, tricky convolutions my reason sometimes makes while I'm asleep! Things quite beyond comprehension happen to reason in dreams!

My brother, for instance, died five years ago. Sometimes I dream of him. He shares in all my worries and takes a great interest in everything, despite the fact that throughout my dream I'm fully aware that he is dead and buried. Why, then, doesn't it bother me that, although dead, he's still worrying and busy by my side? How can my reason allow it?

But enough of that. Now I'll speak of my dream.

Yes, I had the dream on November 3. They tease me now, reminding me that it was nothing but a dream. But what difference does it make since the dream revealed the truth to me? Once you've found Truth, you know it's the truth and that there isn't and can't be any other truth, whether you're asleep or awake.

So let it be a dream. Yet that waking life that you praise so much—well, I was about to extinguish it by killing myself when my dream, that dream of mine, revealed a new, great, regenerated, powerful life to me.

Listen then!

III

I said I had slipped into sleep without noticing it, still juggling with the eternal questions. Suddenly I saw myself reach out for the revolver and, without getting up from my armchair, point it at my heart. Yes, at my heart and not at my head, despite the fact that I had resolved to shoot myself in the head, or to be more precise, in the right temple. So I pointed the revolver at my breast and waited like that for perhaps a couple of seconds. The candle, the table, and the wall started to sway before my eyes. I hurriedly pressed the trigger.

In a dream, you may fall from a great height, you may be slashed or punched without ever feeling pain—unless you actually hurt yourself in your bed, in which case you'll experience pain and almost always wake up. So it was in my dream. I felt no pain, but I fancied that my shot shook everything around me. Then all light sputtered out, and it turned horribly black. It was as if I'd turned blind and mute. I was supine on something hard. I couldn't see or budge. Around me people were moving to and fro and shouting. I could make out the captain's deep voice and the screams of the landlady . . . Then there was a gap and I was carried off in a closed coffin. I felt the coffin swaying. Then I was suddenly struck by the thought that, after all, I was dead now—dead for good. There was no doubt about it in my mind. I could neither move nor see, but I still felt and I thought. Soon, as is usual in dreams, I began to accept things without question.

Then they buried me. They left, and I was all alone. I didn't stir. Previously, when I had imagined how they'd bury me in my grave, I had always associated sensations of cold and damp with it. Now, indeed, I had an acute sensation of cold, especially in the tips of my toes. But that was all I felt.

I lay there, strangely enough, waiting for nothing, accepting as a matter of fact that a dead man has nothing for which to wait. But it was damp. I don't know how much time went by—an hour, a few days, or many days, but suddenly a drop of moisture that had seeped through the lid of my coffin fell on my left eye. Then, a minute later, a second drop fell, then, after another minute, a third, and so on and on, always at one-minute intervals. Unexpectedly, this made me terribly indignant, and I felt an acute pain in my heart.

"It must be my wound," I decided; "the bullet must still be in there."

And moisture still dripped every minute on my closed left eye. Suddenly I called out to the Creator, who ordained all that was happening to me, not with my voice, for I couldn't move my tongue, but with my whole being:

"Whoever You are—if You do exist—if there is anything more sensible than what's happening here, make it happen. But if You are avenging Yourself for my unreasonable suicide by inflicting upon me the inane disgrace of existence beyond life, be sure that no suffering inflicted upon me can equal the silent contempt that will be in me throughout millions of years of martyrdom!"

I made this appeal and fell silent. The dead silence lasted for almost a full minute; another drop fell; but I knew—I had unshakable faith—that things were about to change.

Then my grave opened. I couldn't tell whether it was dug open or what, but some dark, mysterious creature seized me—and then we were in space. Suddenly I could see. It was dark all around, darker than I'd ever seen before! We were moving through space at a fantastic speed and were already quite far from Earth. I asked no questions of the creature that was carrying me off. I was too proud. I waited. I assured myself that I wasn't afraid, and the thought that I wasn't afraid made my heart vibrate with tremendous self-satisfaction. I don't remember how long we went on flying like that; I haven't the faintest idea. It was the way it always is in dreams —we leap over space, time, the laws of reason and existence, and stop only at points dear to our hearts. I remember suddenly seeing a little star in the darkness.

"Is it Sirius?" I asked, forgetting I wasn't going to ask questions.

"No, it is the star you saw in the gap between the clouds on your way home," the creature carrying me said.

The creature bore a human resemblance. I didn't like it. I even felt a deep aversion for it.

Having fired at my heart, I had expected to cease to be completely; instead, I had put myself in the hands of a creature that, although of course not human, still did *exist*.

"Ah, so there is life beyond the grave!" I decided with the puzzling light-heartedness of a dream, but it didn't change anything in me deep down. "If I must *be* again and live according to someone's omnipotent will," I thought, "I don't want to be vanquished and humiliated."

"You know very well that I'm afraid of you, and that's why you despise me!" I said suddenly to my companion, unable to prevent myself from making this admission, and feeling a scorching humiliation.

He didn't answer, but it suddenly dawned on me that I was not being despised or laughed at or even pitied, that our journey had an unknown, mysterious purpose, concerning me alone. Fear mounted in me. My silent companion mutely communicated something that permeated the whole of me. We soared through dark, unknown spaces. I had long since ceased to see any constellations familiar to the eye. I knew that there were stars in the celestial spaces whose rays took millions of years to travel to the earth. But we had probably passed beyond them by now. I was waiting for something in terrible anguish; I was completely exhausted.

Suddenly a familiar and unbelievably nostalgic feeling shook me: I saw our sun! I knew it couldn't be *our* sun, the sun that gave birth to *our* earth; I knew we were infinitely far from our sun, but somehow everything inside me knew that this sun was exactly the same as the other, its copy, its double. A delightful nostalgia filled me with rapture: light kindred to that which had given me birth warmed my heart and brought it back to life. And, for the first time since the grave, I felt alive.

"But if this sun is exactly similar to our sun," I cried, "where is the earth?"

My companion pointed to the little star twinkling with an emerald light in the darkness. We were flying straight toward it.

"Are such duplications possible in the universe?" I asked. "Is this the law of nature? And if that star is earth, can it really be like our earth—wretched, yet eternally dear to the hearts of her most ungrateful children?"

Overwhelming love for the earth I had left made me tremble. A vision of the little girl I had wronged flashed before me.

"You'll see!" my traveling companion said, and I detected a note of sadness in its voice.

In the meantime we were rapidly approaching the

planet. It grew before my eyes. I could already make out the oceans, the outline of Europe, when suddenly a strange, powerful, holy indignation exploded within me.

"How can there be such a duplication, and what is its purpose? I love and can only love the earth I left behind, the earth I stained with my blood when, ungrateful man that I was, I shot myself through the heart to snuff out my life. I never ceased to love that earth, not even the night I left it. In fact, my love for it then was probably more poignant than ever.

"Is there any suffering on this new earth? On our old earth, we can truly love only with suffering and through suffering. We don't know how to love otherwise; we don't know any other love. I want to suffer so that I may love. I want—I'm longing this very minute to kiss the earth I left behind with tears streaming down my cheeks. I don't want any other earth. I won't consent to live on any other planet! . . ."

But my companion had already left me. I suddenly found myself standing on that other earth, wallowing in the bright, gorgeous sunlight of a day in Paradise. I believe I was on an island of the Greek archipelago or perhaps somewhere on the coast of the Greek mainland. Everything was exactly as it is on our earth, but there was a holiday air about, an aura of supreme triumph. A tender, emerald sea splashed quietly, kissing the shore with love that seemed almost conscious. Magnificent tall trees stood in the full glory of their blooming, and I felt that their luxuriant, innumerable leaves were welcoming me with their gentle rustle, whispering words of love. Bright, fragrant flowers blazed in the lush grass. Flocks of birds flew through the air. They were not afraid of me and alighted on my shoulders and hands; I felt the joyful beat of their fluttering little wings against my body.

Finally I met the people of this happy earth. They came toward me, pressed around me, and embraced me. And, oh, how beautiful were these children of the sun— their own sun, that is! I'd never come across such beauty in human beings on our earth. Only, perhaps, in children in their very first years would it have been possible to find a remote suggestion of that beauty. The eyes of these happy people were radiant and their faces were intelligent, expressing the serenity of those who have supremely fulfilled themselves. But there was also simple, childlike joy in their faces and voices. Yes, after one glance at their faces, I understood everything! This earth hadn't been desecrated by the Fall of Man; its inhabitants still lived in a paradise such as that of Adam and Eve before they sinned. Only here paradise extended over the entire earth.

These people laughed happily, thronged round me, and lavished kindness upon me. They took me to their homes. Each of them was anxious to make me happy. They didn't ask me any questions, appearing to know everything already. They were in a hurry to remove the signs of suffering from my features.

IV

All right, suppose it was nothing but a dream; still, the sensation of love left in me by those pure and beautiful people has stayed with me always. I still, to this day, feel their love flying out to me. I saw them myself, I understood them, and I'm certain that I loved them, that I suffered for them afterward. Of course, I realized even then that many things in them were beyond my grasp. For instance, being a modern Russian believer in progress and a vulgar denizen of Petersburg, I couldn't see how they could know so much when there was no indication that they had any knowledge of the achievements of our modern science. But I soon realized that their knowledge fed upon different revelations than ours and that their aspirations were quite different. They didn't want anything and were absolutely serene; they didn't strive to find the meaning of life, because their own lives were full of meaning. Their understanding was of a higher order and deeper than that provided by our science. Science tries to explain what life is in order to teach us how we should live; they didn't need science to tell them how to live—they knew by themselves. I understood that, although I couldn't account for their knowledge. They pointed at their trees, and I couldn't comprehend the intensity of the love with which they looked at them; it was as if they were communicating with beings like themselves. In fact, I don't think I'd be wrong in saying that they talked to them! Yes—they'd found the language of the plants, and I'm sure they could understand them. And these people were like that with all nature. The animals lived in peace with them, never attacked them, loved them; they were subdued, as it were, by love.

The people pointed out stars to me and spoke to me about them. I couldn't understand what they said, but I'm certain they had some sort of communion with the stars, a live, direct knowledge of them rather than a rational, scientific understanding.

Those people never even tried to make me understand them. They loved me anyway. And I knew that they'd never understand me; that's why I hardly ever mentioned our earth to them. I simply kissed their soil in front of them and mutely adored them; they let me adore them without any embarrassment, for they themselves had so much love for me. They didn't suffer for me when, with tears in my eyes, I kissed their feet, for they knew the strength of the love in their hearts with which they returned my love. I used to stop and wonder now and then why they never once caused me to feel offended and never aroused envy or jealousy in a man like me? Why did a braggart and a liar like me never once feel like parading my knowledge of science and philosophy, about which they obviously had no idea? I was never impelled to surprise them and teach them what I knew—not even out of love for them.

They were as playful and gay as children. They strolled through their beautiful woods and meadows singing their sweet songs, gathering honey and the fragrant fruit of their forests, and sipping the milk of the friendly, loving animals. Obtaining food and clothing required little effort.

They knew love and begot children, but I never detected among them those outbursts of *cruel* sensuality that are so common on our earth and are almost the sole source of our sins. They rejoiced in their newborn children as new sharers of their bliss. They never had any quarrels and were never jealous of one another; they didn't even understand what jealousy meant. Their children were the children of all, for they were all one family.

Illness was almost completely unknown among them, although death existed. But their old people died peacefully, as though falling asleep, surrounded by people taking leave of them, blessing those staying behind, smiling at them, and receiving their bright smiles in return. I never witnessed any sorrow or tears on these occasions —only love that reached the point of rapture, a sort of calm, contemplative rapture of fulfillment.

One might have thought they maintained contact with their people after death, that the earthly link wasn't severed by it. They seemed puzzled when I asked them about eternal life, for apparently it was beyond all possible doubt to them. They didn't have any temples; instead they had a sort of tangible, live, and constant communion with the universal Whole. They had no faith, but had instead a firm knowledge that when their earthly happiness was filled to the limit, there would come for the living and the dead a day of even closer communion with the universal Whole. They waited for that day with joy, but without impatience, without longing, as though they had a foreknowledge of it that they shared with one another, in their hearts.

In the evenings, before retiring, they formed magnificent, harmonious choirs, and in their songs they conveyed all the impressions of the departing day, praising it and bidding it farewell. They praised nature, earth, sea, and forests. They composed songs about one another and in them showered childlike praise upon their friends. Their songs were very simple, but they came straight from the heart and penetrated other hearts.

And it wasn't only in their songs—they really spent

their whole lives admiring one another, as though they were all in love with one another. Some of their rapturous and solemn songs were completely beyond my understanding. Even when I understood the words, I couldn't grasp their entire meaning. It was beyond my brainpower. But my heart seemed to soak it in. I often told them that I'd had a presentiment of all this for years; that, while still on my original earth, I had experienced their joy and glory as a nostalgic feeling that at times reached a pitch of unendurable torment; that I'd sensed them in their glory in the visions of my heart and mind; that back on our earth I'd often been unable to look at the setting sun without tears; that my hatred for the people of our earth had always contained a feeling of despair—why couldn't I hate them without loving them? As they listened to me I saw very well that they couldn't imagine what I was talking about. But I wasn't sorry that I had told them those things, for I knew that they felt through my words how terribly I yearned for all those I had left behind me. Yes, as they gazed at me with their eyes so full of love, I felt I was becoming as pure and truthful as they were, and that it didn't matter whether I actually understood them or not. A feeling of the fullness of life seized me by the throat, and I adored them in silence.

Now, of course, people laugh at me and assure me that I couldn't possibly have noted all those details in my dream, that I must've had some vague, feverish sensation engendered by my own heart and that I invented all the intricacies only after I woke up. And when I suggest to them that perhaps everything really did happen, you should hear them laugh! Yes, they laugh in my face.

There's no doubt, of course, that I was completely overwhelmed by my dream and that the sensation it left lingered on in my torn, aching heart. But then, the actual images—that is, those I really did see during the hour while I was dreaming—were so harmonious, so overwhelmingly enchanting, and so true that, when I awoke,

I found words were too feeble to express them, and so they were bound to become blurred in my mind. Perhaps then, I was forced, without being aware of it, to invent details later, distorting them, of course, in my anxiety and hurry to communicate them somehow. But how could I help believing that everything had actually happened? Perhaps it was even thousands of times better, happier, more radiant than I could convey.

Call it a dream, but it must've happened all the same. But, as I said, maybe it wasn't a dream at all. For something happened there, something so frighteningly real that it couldn't have been a dream image. Let's assume that my heart generated the dream; how could my heart, after that, have generated the horrible things that happened? How could I have invented it or dreamed it up? How could my petty heart and my puny mind arrive at such a revelation of truth? Judge for yourself, for I'm going to tell you about that truth which, up to now, I've refused to reveal.

The truth is that—well, that I ended up by corrupting them all. . . .

V

Yes, in the end, I corrupted the lot of them! How I managed to do it, I can't say; I don't remember too clearly. My dream flashed through eons, leaving in me only a general impression of the whole. All I know is that I caused their fall from grace. Like a sinister trichina, like a plague germ contaminating whole kingdoms, I contaminated with my person that entire happy, sinless planet. They learned how to lie, they came to love it, and they grew to appreciate the beauty of untruth. It may have started with a joke, innocently, playfully, with a flirtation, but the germ of the lie penetrated their hearts, and they took a fancy to it.

Then came voluptuousness. And voluptuousness begot

jealousy, and jealousy begot cruelty. . . . Ah, I don't know how soon, but it wasn't long before the first blood was shed. Those people of the other earth were shocked and horrified and they started to break up and disperse. Alliances were formed only to be directed against other alliances. Recriminations and accusations flew to and fro.

They learned about shame and they made a virtue of it. The concept of honor appeared, and each alliance hoisted its colors. They started to torture animals, and the animals escaped into the forests and became their enemies. They fought to secede, for independence, for individual advantages, for what's mine and what's yours. They ended speaking different languages; they experienced suffering, and came to love it; they declared that suffering was the only way to Truth. Then science spread among them.

As they became evil, they talked about fraternity and humanitarianism and came to understand those concepts; as they became criminal, they invented justice and drew up voluminous codes of laws to enforce their justice—and built a guillotine to enforce their laws.

They only dimly recalled the things they had lost and refused to believe that there had been a time when they were pure and happy. They even dismissed as ridiculous all possibility of return to that lost bliss, branding it a pipe dream. They were unable to visualize or conceive of it.

And a strange thing happened: while they ceased completely to believe in their lost bliss, dismissing it as a fairy tale, they longed so much to become happy and innocent once more that they capitulated to their own wishes and, like small children, proceeded to worship their longings. They built countless temples, deified their own wishful thought, and prayed to it. And although they were certain their wishes could never come true, they worshiped them with tears in their eyes.

Probably, however, if they had been given a chance to regain their lost state of innocence and bliss, if someone

had pointed it out to them and asked them whether they
wanted to return to it—they'd have refused. They told
me:

"We are false, cruel, and unjust. We know it, we deplore
it, and we torture ourselves because of it—punish ourselves perhaps even more cruelly than the merciful Judge
who will sit in judgment over us and Whose name we do
not know. But then, we have science, and with its
help we shall discover Truth once more; then we shall
accept it in full knowledge. Knowledge is of a higher
order than feeling; awareness of life is of a higher order
than life. Science will give us wisdom, wisdom will reveal
to us the laws of nature, and knowledge of the laws of
nature will confer upon us a happiness beyond happiness."

That's what they said, and after these words, each of
them began to love himself more than anyone or anything else in the world. And how could it be otherwise?
Each became so jealous of his individuality that he had
to do his best to belittle and humble the individuality
of others, seeing therein the purpose of his life.

Slavery made its appearance, even voluntary slavery
in which the weak submitted to the strong of their own
free will, if only in order to gain their support to op-
press those who were even weaker than themselves. Saints
came to those people and preached to them about their
pride, their loss of a sense of proportion, their loss of
shame. The saints were laughed at and stoned. The blood
of the saints splattered the doors of the temples.

Then came men who started to toy with ideas on how
to reunite people. They tried to devise a society in which
each individual, while continuing to love himself above
everyone else, would at the same time abstain from inter-
fering with others. Thus, they imagined, men could live
together in a harmonious society.

Whole wars were fought over that idea. Those who
fought firmly believed that science and wisdom and the
instinct of self-preservation would finally force men to
unite in a harmonious, reasonable society. And, in the
meantime, these wise ones were in a hurry to exterminate

the unwise who couldn't grasp their Idea, and thus prevent them from hindering its triumph.

The feeling of self-preservation began to give way; soon there arrived the proud and voluptuous, who wanted all or nothing. To obtain all, they didn't hesitate to commit crime, and if that didn't work, they were prepared for suicide.

Religions appeared worshiping the nonbeing and self-annihilation for the sake of an eternal repose in nothingness.

Finally these people grew tired in their senseless efforts, and suffering appeared on their faces. Then they proclaimed that suffering is beautiful because suffering alone contains thought. So they praised suffering in their songs. I walked among them wringing my hands in despair and crying over them. I believe I loved them even more than before the suffering had appeared on their features, when they were still so pure and beautiful. I loved their degraded earth more than I had loved it when it was a Garden of Eden, if only because sorrow had made its appearance in it. Alas, though I've always welcomed sorrow and torment for myself, I was not happy to see them struck by it, and it made me cry. I stretched out my hands toward them, cursing and loathing myself in my despair. I told them that I was responsible for everything that had happened to them—I alone—that it was I who had introduced falsehood, contamination, and vice among them. I beseeched them to crucify me and explained how they should prepare the cross. I couldn't—I didn't have the strength to kill myself, but I longed to be martyred at their hands. I longed for martyrdom—I wanted them to shed my blood, drop by drop to the last drop.

But they merely laughed at me and ended by taking me for a feeble-minded fool. They exonerated me, explaining that they had asked for whatever they had and that it had been bound to happen. Finally they warned me that I was becoming dangerous and that they would have to lock me up in a madhouse if I didn't shut up.

That hurt me terribly. Sorrow compressed my heart, and I felt I would die, and then . . . Well, then I woke up.

It was morning already. The sun hadn't risen, but it was after five. I found myself in my old armchair. My candle had completely burned out. Next door, in the captain's room, they were all asleep. Everything was very quiet, a very rare state in this house.

I immediately jumped up. I was absolutely stunned, for nothing like that dream had ever happened to me—I'd never even fallen asleep in my armchair before. As I stood there regaining my senses, my eyes fell upon the loaded gun lying ready on my desk. But I immediately pushed it away from me. Now I had a great thirst to live. I raised my hand to call out to eternal Truth—but I didn't call out. I began to weep instead. I was overcome by boundless rapture. Yes, I wanted to live and to preach. At that very instant, I decided to preach, and of course, I'll go on preaching as long as I live. I'll go from place to place preaching. I want to preach . . . I'll preach the Truth, for I've seen it with my own eyes, I've seen it in all its glory!

And so, since then, I've been preaching. Moreover, I love everybody—those who laugh at me even more than the rest. Why, I don't know. I can't account for it, but so be it. They say that even now I don't make much sense; that in fact, I make less and less sense. They wonder where I will end up. What they say is true. I'm becoming confused, and things may get even worse. There's no doubt about it—I'll often get muddled up before I find the right words to preach and the right deeds to perform, because it's terribly difficult. Why, I'm very much aware of that at this very moment. But then, who doesn't get confused? Still, we're striving for the same things; we're all, from the sage to the worst criminal, making our way toward the same objective. Only we're trying to get there by different roads. That's an old truth, but here's something that's new about it: I can never stray too far from my course.

You see, I've seen the Truth. I've seen it, and I know that men can be happy and beautiful without losing the ability to live on earth. I cannot—I refuse to believe that wickedness is the normal state of men. And when they laugh at me, it is essentially at that belief of mine. But how can I not have faith, since I've seen Truth? I didn't arrive at it with my intellect; I saw it in its entirety, and it is inconceivable that it could not exist. So how can I lose my path? Of course, I may wander off it a few more times and speak in alien words perhaps, but it'll never be for long; the vivid picture of what I saw in my dream will always guide me and correct my course. Ah, I'm fresh and cheerful, and I can go on like this for another thousand years.

You know, at first I wanted to conceal the fact that I'd corrupted them. But it was a mistake, it was the first mistake! And Truth whispered in my ear that I was guilty of deception and saved me and showed me my way. But I don't know how to organize a paradise on earth, because I cannot convey it in words. After my dream, I lost the words that could convey it. At least the most important, indispensable ones. But never mind, I'll go and speak tirelessly, for I've seen it with my own eyes, although I'm unable to tell what it is I've seen.

But here's something that those who laugh at me cannot see. They say, "So he had a dream, a hallucination." Well, is that really such a wise objection? Why are they so proud of it? A dream. What's a dream? And what's our life if it isn't a dream? And I may say, moreover: "All right, suppose it never happens, let's say paradise will never come about! I know myself it won't—yet I'll still go on preaching."

And, on the other hand, it would've been so simple. . . . In one day—in a single hour—everything could've been arranged. The key phrase is, "Love others as you love yourself." And that's all there is to it. Nothing else is required. That would settle everything. Yes, of course it's nothing but an old truth that has been repeated and re-read millions of times—and still hasn't taken root.

"Awareness of life is of a higher order than knowledge

of the laws of happiness." That's an adage that we must fight.

And I shall fight it.

And if everyone wanted it, everything could be arranged immediately.

Afterword

Dostoyevsky was a sick man. He was spiteful, intolerant and irritable. Turgenev once described him as the nastiest Christian he had ever met.

He had plenty of provocation. His father, a staff physician at a Moscow charity hospital, was a cruel, hard-drinking, and dissolute man. His mother died when he was sixteen. Fyodor Dostoyevsky, one of seven children, grew up in a cramped private apartment in a wing of the hospital and on a small country estate where, eventually, his father was murdered by his serfs. The serfs had been infuriated by his brutality and debauchery, which included the retention of a regular harem of peasant girls. The family did not report the real cause of death to the authorities. Imprisonment of the serfs would have entailed too great a financial hardship.

It would be reasonable to assume that Dostoyevsky's early sympathies went to the oppressed masses in reaction to paternal cruelty as well as out of compassion for the suffering of the humble he'd witnessed all around him. His early writings placed him politically and were greeted enthusiastically by Russian liberals. The ranking Russian critic, Belinsky, hailed his first novel, *Poor Folk,* which was full of pity for the underdog, detecting even in this rather maudlin effort a great literary talent.

His humanitarian feelings led Dostoyevsky to join a liberal circle of enthusiastic young men who met to discuss socialism, mostly of the utopian variety of Fourier. During one such meeting of the Petrashevsky group, Dostoyevsky and his companions were surprised by the police. They were imprisoned and sentenced to death. This sentence, however, was nothing but a gruesome farce,

227

devised by the tsarist authorities for the edification of subversives.

On December 21, 1849, the prisoners were taken to a city square for public execution. The death sentence was read to them, they were given the cross to kiss, a sword was symbolically broken over their heads, and they were ordered to don special white shirts. They were to be shot three by three. The first three were bound to the execution posts. Dostoyevsky was the sixth in line, that is, he was to be executed in the second batch. . . .

Suddenly the tsar's messenger appeared on a foaming horse and announced that the tsar was graciously making them a present of their lives. There was a beating of drums. The retreat was sounded. The men already tied to the posts were untied and sent back to rejoin the others. Some prisoners fainted. Two went permanently insane. The effect on Dostoyevsky, too, was shattering. The epileptic fits to which he had been subject since his childhood became incomparably worse.

He was sentenced to eight years in the Omsk penitentiary in Siberia, a sentence which, again thanks to the tsar's magnanimity, was reduced to four years, followed by a stretch in the army as an enlisted man and an interdiction against living in either Moscow or Petersburg. Dostoyevsky was twenty-eight at the time of his conviction.

In Siberia, Dostoyevsky found himself among the "crowd." They were criminals, perhaps, but, above all, they were simple Russian people, such as up till then he had only been able to observe from, as it were, his middle-class balcony—not too high but still a balcony. Now he was among them, aware of their physical presence, of their smell. They fascinated him, and his concern for them was as great as ever. But his attitude had changed. All liberalism had left him; he was no longer a revolutionary, nor even a would-be reformer.

It is possible to account quite reasonably for the political change of heart that occurred in Dostoyevsky after his arrest. Sensitive, highly impressionable and delicate as he was, he must have reached the point of nervous breakdown, a point which later was studied and clearly defined by another Russian, the physiologist Ivan Pavlov.

Pavlov observed that after subjection to certain physical and mental stress, the animals upon which he was experimenting uniformly showed symptoms of nervous disintegration, reaching a state resembling that of hypnosis. He soon realized that in this state the animals were highly receptive to suggestion. Subsequently these findings have been applied, in various countries, to human beings. Men are brought to the breaking point, and those in command then impose upon them the notions they think fit. Today this technique, applied in full awareness, is by and large referred to as "brainwashing." But it seems clear that the same results have been achieved, more haphazardly—stumbled upon, one might say—throughout the ages.

After the scene on the execution square, the shattered, broken prisoners were probably highly receptive to any further demonstration of the ruthless power of the tsarist regime and readily convinced of its invincibility and inevitability. At the same time, they were filled with abject gratitude for its magnanimity in sparing them. In any case, Dostoyevsky was. Although he always remained responsive to human suffering, he now felt that all resistance to the order of things causing it was irremediably doomed to failure, and that the only course for mankind was Christian submission.

His attitude was sarcastically described by Alexander Herzen, one of those with whom Dostoyevsky had previously shared his views: "Compassionate love may be very strong. It sobs, it burns, then it wipes away its tears—and it does nothing."

When he had served his four years in the penitentiary, Dostoyevsky was sent to a small Siberian garrison town as a private in the army. There he married his first wife, a moody, passionate, consumptive woman with a pronounced streak of cruelty in her. They had violent quarrels and he was often unfaithful, although he was really quite attached to her.

Only in 1859 was Dostoyevsky fully pardoned and

allowed to return to Petersburg. He immediately resumed his writing, which now included a great deal of journalism on the reactionary side of the political argument.

His poor health was a pretext that frequently sent him abroad to various spas: Medicine at the time subscribed most emphatically to a belief in the curative powers of various mineral springs. At these resorts, Dostoyevsky, always short of money and always under pressure from his publishers to deliver, took to gambling, which developed into a full-fledged passion and complicated his existence still further.

In 1864 Dostoyevsky suffered two new shocks, one after the other: First his wife died, and then his brother Mikhail, who was closer to him than anyone.

A relieving break came in Dostoyevsky's life three years later when he married his young secretary, Anna Snitkina. She was a plain woman with "her nostrils too far apart" and not particularly brilliant, but she remained to the end a good and loving wife, bore him children, looked after his manuscripts and his interests. She was to survive him by almost forty years. After his death in 1881, she lived quite comfortably off the royalties from his works, of which the major novels had been written while they were married. She died in misery, however, in 1920. The Soviets had come to power and summarily dismissed Dostoyevsky as a "mouthpiece of reaction and obscurantism."

Now they have once again recognized him as a "great Russian classic," although they say he was given to frequent errors because he couldn't help reflecting the tottering beliefs of a decaying class.

Indeed, the regime would have found it hard not to rehabilitate him. Throughout the time he was banned, old, much-thumbed copies of Dostoyevsky's works were secretly circulated and enthusiastically discussed by small, clandestine groups.

It is no wonder that Dostoyevsky should have been discussed in solemn secrecy during the period when he was under a cloud in the Soviet Union, somewhat as he himself had discussed socialist utopias in his youth. For in the many things that have been said about him, one word has recurred again and again: "prophet."

This word misled many who saw in Dostoyevsky a sort of spiritual Jules Verne. He was no expert on the "shape of things to come." But perhaps, in the Biblical sense, the word "prophet" is suitable.

Often writing carelessly and hurriedly, borrowing devices from Eugène Sue's *romans feuilletons*—the precursors of the thrillers—thinking nothing of contriving quite unlikely situations and coincidences, guilty of many lapses into maudlin, tear-jerking sentimentality, Dostoyevsky nevertheless managed to achieve peaks hardly ever equaled in Russian or, for that matter, in world fiction.

His uncanny insight into human motivation, combined with a fearless willingness to dig into the human soul, made many stop and gape. Among others, of course, it attracted droves of zooming simplifiers, would-be metaphysicians, philosophical poets, professors of literature and affirmers of various faiths. They got hold of tidbits from his writings, commented upon them, read intricate implications into any irritated grunt Dostoyevsky happened to make, and in their elaborate efforts, became deaf to his music.

He was picked up by great specialists like Freud and Sartre, and by humble students of Russian literature who often owed their acquaintance with him to genteel Victorian renditions—sometimes quite unfortunately revised by contemporary literary experts. They discovered that Dostoyevsky was an obvious case of parricidal tendencies, that he was a forerunner of today's existentialists, that his idea of death anticipated that of André Malraux, that it was very appropriate to compare *The Brothers Karamazov* and *Hamlet*, and so on and on, in suitably obscure language. This is not to say that all these links are necessarily totally false, but rather that they are often nothing more than an intricate elaboration of the fact that the author in question had read Dostoyevsky. Or, to put it differently, that Dostoyevsky touched upon many aspects of universal problems which have also concerned later writers.

What has made it difficult to discuss in normal tones a writer who showed such piercing understanding of certain aspects of human psychology is that, on the strength of his great talent as a novelist, he has been quoted *ad nauseam* as a religious and even as a political prophet, and his political and metaphysical views have been taken almost as revelations handed down by someone in a state of grace.

There is even a special, scornful word in Russian for particularly cheap interpretations of Dostoyevsky's thoughts and feelings: *dostoyevshchina*. However, today, the sad fact is that the Soviets dismiss as *dostoyevshchina* just about anything said about Dostoyevsky that does not jibe with Marx, although, of course, they think Dostoyevsky had a point when he asserted that the Russians were the real Chosen People.

And here, to return to that word "prophet." In his *Aspects of the Novel,* E. M. Forster, one of those applying this term to Dostoyevsky, is very careful to define it:

Prophecy . . . is a tone of voice. It may imply any of the faiths that have haunted humanity—Christianity, Buddhism, dualism, Satanism, or the mere raising of human love and hatred to such a power that their normal receptacles no longer contain them; but what particular view of the universe is recommended—with that we are not directly concerned.

Dostoyevsky's prophetic quality is precisely not what he says but the tone in which he says it, not his ability to solve metaphysical problems but his uncanny ability to convey the torments people go through in trying to solve them.

It is impossible to make a philosophical system out of Dostoyevsky's world. It is full of contradictions, inconsistencies, absurdities. It is a universal projection of the human soul speaking in many clashing voices.

Dostoyevsky, after he had renounced the possibility of an ideal social organization, felt (it was a feeling rather than an idea) that the whole point of life is redemption through suffering and love, which is a very Christian approach indeed.

Of course he is fully aware of the cruel, vicious streak in man and of his desire to inflict suffering and to dominate. But although he acknowledges the existence of these things—and, indeed, describes them in striking detail —he always disapproves. Nietzsche, who is often loosely associated with Dostoyevsky, was very scornful of this Christian stand and held Dostoyevsky in contempt for his "morbid moral tortures," his rejection of "proper pride." He accused him of "sinning to enjoy the luxury of confession," which Nietzsche considered a "degrading prostration." Dostoyevsky was, in Nietzsche's words, one of the victims of the "conscience-vivisection and self-crucifixion of two thousand years" of Christianity.

The vague linking of Dostoyevsky with Nietzsche illustrates the way many people have hung their own theories on any of the many convenient pegs in Dostoyevsky's writings and then labeled the peg Dostoyevsky himself. One finds, too, constantly reiterated suggestions and suspicions that he committed or came close to committing some of the misdeeds of his characters, perhaps the price of exceptional intuitive understanding of *other* people.

Thus, having taken his Christian stand, having renounced any attempt to alleviate the human condition through practical, man-made measures (he had tried and the tsarist authorities had taught him that there was nothing to be done in that direction), Dostoyevsky preaches submission and the acceptance of suffering, recommending it as the way to redemption and salvation. As he does so, however, he is still trying to convince himself of the existence of God. This internal debate throbs like a pulse throughout his major novels, for he is painfully aware that without God, the acceptance of suffering in the name of the soul's redemption would not make much sense. Yet, if we add up the final score of these arguments, it must be said that the rational skeptic winds up ahead with a comfortable margin, although the author's sympathies are on the losing side. The surprising thing here is that it is not only a matter of Dostoyevsky's reason outarguing his deep feelings on the rational level—on that level reason is bound to win anyway—it is that Dostoyevsky's doubting side also wins, as it were, artistically: his doubters are much more convincing, and by far better artistic portrayals, than his believers.

But does it really matter whether Dostoyevsky's tormented characters use strong or quite inadequate arguments in their discussions of universal themes? Whether Dostoyevsky's "prophecies" come true or not? Whether it is likely that the world at large can only be saved by the "God-bearing Russian people" inspired by the Russian Orthodox version of Christianity? What if some of these thoughts do sound just as silly today as Hegel's incarnation of the timeless Divine Absolute in the nineteenth-century Prussian monarchy?

Dostoyevsky's vision is so striking because of his ability to create a universe, a crazy, impossible universe, perhaps, but one in which the most incredible details, the strangest thoughts and feelings, are governed by certain universal laws which Dostoyevsky reveals to us through his art.

Dostoyevsky's writings included in this volume belong to distinct periods of his life. *White Nights* was written before his political change of heart. The three excerpts from the *The House of the Dead* cover the period of transition. *Notes from Underground* is a passionate rejection of his former beliefs and an attack on his former political associates by another character of whom Dostoyevsky doesn't approve either. *The Dream of the Ridiculous Man,* written toward the end of his life, is an internal religious dialogue in which Dostoyevsky gropes for a positive answer.

These writings may give a general idea of Dostoyevsky's evolving outlook on man's fate, of which so much has been said with and without reason and under every pretext. They also contain a fair sampling of human hearts that Dostoyevsky was able to probe to such surprising depths—a whole range from the primitive peasant, who kills without really understanding that he is extinguishing a life, to the hypersensitive neurotic who experiences a whole gamut of emotions, from elation to bottomless despair, over fluctuations of everyday life so minute that another would hardly notice them.

The earliest of the stories, *White Nights* (1848), which in style (especially in the developed metaphors) shows the strong influence of Gogol, was written before Dostoyevsky's arrest, sham execution and exile. He still hoped at the time that human society could be organized in a way that would alleviate the suffering of the humble and the weak. He hoped that some form of socialism would provide an answer.

Actually, Dostoyevsky's *White Nights*—midsummer nights at the sixtieth latitude north—are not very white or very summery. The moon and stars are plainly visible. It often rains. But somehow the *I* is in a state of midsummer exaltation. His flimsy substitute world of fantasy shaken by the general summer exodus from Petersburg, he momentarily establishes contact with the real world when his city-bound eyes are filled with the beauty of the countryside in spring. Thus jolted awake, he is able to make friends with Nastenka.

His meeting with this ethereal, lovelorn girl, herself trying to escape the plight of being pinned to her stern grandmother—a plight which, although it has a dream-like, nightmare quality, is nevertheless a real one from which she makes a real escape—affords him moments of such exaltation that all his complex, heroic fancies appear by comparison bloodless and sterile. And so, although his "romance" with the girl comes to nothing, he feels rewarded forever: even a fleeting contact with life means more than all his dream world.

White Nights, then, despite the loneliness and sadness of the narrator, is an affirmation of life. It is also an affirmation of self-sacrifice and brotherly love, for it is the gentle *I* who saves the girl from despair, convincing her that she must write to the man she loves, thereby giving up his own claims to her love.

The three excepts from *The House of the Dead* (1859–1861)—a book based on the prison experiences that wrought such drastic changes in Dostoyevsky—deal with a side of man's nature that exerted an irresistible fascination upon the author: the violence and cruelty in man that come out both in murder and in the chastisement of criminals.

Although the two first-person accounts of murder are as different as the two murderers, both men seem in a way to glide into the killing, watching it as it were from the outside, paying a terrible tribute to the Devil in his unceasing struggle against God for the human heart.

As to Dostoyevsky's brief study of the executioners, it seems especially interesting in the light of the world's further experimentation in the infliction of suffering during the twentieth century.

Incidentally, Dostoyevsky himself is careful to note in the book that corporal punishment was abolished in Russia, along with serfdom, in 1861, during the reign of Alexander II, the Liberator.

Notes from Underground (1864), generally classified as a novel, whose Russian title would be more accurately if less dramatically translated as *Notes from a Hole in the Floor,* i.e., from a mousehole, is, by Dostoyevsky's standards, a relatively compact protest against the nineteenth century's oversimplified, optimistic visions of the future. It is hard to tell which irritated Dostoyevsky more: the Victorian representation of the universe as a sort of clockwork with all the implied optimism of the watchmakers, or the maudlin enthusiasm of the Russian followers (notably Chernyshevsky) of Fourier and other French utopian socialists whose views he had once shared and who now seemed so unbearably smug, neat and shallow to him.

In *Notes,* the main argument is that man's desires are not reasonable and often make him act against his own interest and common sense, but they are what makes him human. In the second part of the book, this irrational streak is shown in action. And it is interesting to note that while in *White Nights* we have a spontaneous "sacrifice" of self-interest, the *I* of the *Notes* sacrifices his secret longing for the woman's presence and affection to deal her one more blow. Even before the traumatic experience of his life Dostoyevsky was quite acutely aware of the complexity of human psychology. What changed was his angle of vision.

In *Notes from Underground,* Dostoyevsky attacks the Crystal Palace, *i.e.,* man-made, socialist utopia, on the grounds that man is a fickle, unreasonable animal who could never live in an edifice based on reason: man's whims and wishes are bound to clash with his enlightened self-interest. Thus, Dostoyevsky explains, man is unlike the ant which, as some might say today, is totally integrated in its group—the anthill—and feels physically, and in whatever other way an ant feels, fulfilled in acting for the general good of the anthill.

While the anthill is the ant's end in itself, to man its equivalent is only a never-attainable mirage, and the meaning of his life lies in building a road toward it. But being too lucid, the underground man knows this, and so can find no solace in road-building.

For those who pretend to reach out for the Absolute through aesthetics by claiming to "devote their lives to the good and the beautiful," he has nothing but scorn. Here, while he is at it, Dostoyevsky takes a few sideswipes at some of his contemporaries with whom he disagreed and who irritated him (the painter Gué, the critic Chernyshevsky, the writer Saltykov-Shchedrin, etc.) but these appear only as incidental allusions in double references which have an overriding general import.

In this translation, the general aspect has been rendered and here a word of explanation on the allusions may be helpful, although they are nothing but private references to the quarrels of the day.

Two are contained in the following passage:

> Then I'd have turned everything under the sun into goodness and beauty. I'd have uncovered it in the most unmistakable piece of rubbish. Tears would have oozed

out of me like drops squeezed out of a sponge. *An
artist paints a picture of s*—All right, let's immediately
drink to the health of that artist, because I'm a lover
of everything that's "good and beautiful." *Some author
writes something that will be to everybody's liking,* so
let me drink to everyone's health, because I stand for
"the good and the beautiful!"
[My stress—A. MacA.]

The first stressed sentence reads in Russian "an artist
paints a picture of Ge." The Russian letter G is the first
letter of the word whose equivalent in English is a four-
letter word meaning excrement. But there was also a
painter named Gué (in Russian transliteration Ge).
Although syntactically and contextually it would make the
sentence meaningless, it seems likely that Dostoyevsky
was taking a passing dig at the artist, of whose work he
disapproved. Similarly, in the second stressed sentence,
the words "to everybody's liking" are italicized in the
original, possibly a reference to an article of Saltykov's
under that title, although what matters here is that Dostoyevsky has in mind hack writing, *i.e.,* an "unmistakable piece of rubbish."

Oddly enough, one rendition gives the sentence as
"some author writes *As You Like It,*" thus inferring that
Dostoyevsky considered Shakespeare's play a *typical*
example of rubbish—a source for scholarly speculation
on Dostoyevsky's scorn for Shakespeare.

Also a target of Dostoyevsky's sarcasm was Chernyshevsky, whose symbol for utopia, the London Crystal
Palace, he uses throughout the *Notes.*

In *The Dream of a Ridiculous Man* (1877), the last
short story Dostoyevsky wrote, he again denounces a
society in which, while continuing to love himself more
than anyone else, man will nevertheless find a satisfactory
modus vivendi, based on reason, with other self-loving
men. Instead, he presents a dream society based on love
for others and an unquestionable, tacitly implied belief in
God and eternal life. But, when one comes to think of it,
the people in that dream world behave very much like
the ants: they do everything for each other and

look collectively after the group's children. We may say they love one another in the Absolute or the Supreme Being, whichever way one looks at it, which is to them just what the anthill is to the ants.

In *The Dream*, relations are based on love, the happy people know nothing about "science," they live in a world of the *heart* as opposed to the world of the *head* which Dostoyevsky had already repeatedly rejected. Is this then Dostoyevsky's answer to the woes of the world? Well, yes and no.

Yes, in that the story reiterates again and again the importance of heart over head. The narrator's *rational* decision to commit suicide, based on his *rational* conviction that life has no sense, fails to obliterate pity for the little girl in him, thus proving to him that the universe has a real, objective existence outside him and his logical constructions. He falls asleep, and in his dream, to his surprise, finds that he has shot himself in the heart instead of the head as he had planned. Awake, he had contemplated a rational suicide, while in his dream he knew it was his feelings he must kill.

But the twist that follows shows that Dostoyevsky still is not satisfied with the answer. It transpires that this paradise based on love is also impossible, for once realized, there would be nothing for man to reach out for, no meaning to life in the flesh if the soul is not to be purified through suffering. And indeed, it turns out that on that happy replica of earth, the ridiculous man, instead of being converted, corrupts the childlike, saintly people. In their earthly paradise, he plays, as it were, the role of Christ in reverse: dooming them, begging for crucifixion, which they refuse.

Once back on *our* earth, however, the ridiculous man takes up the preaching of salvation through love, which is so simple, which is just around the corner and yet, he knows himself, never attainable. Nevertheless he goes on preaching because he has had a glimpse of the Absolute.

And so, probably, had Dostoyevsky.

—ANDREW R. MACANDREW

SELECTED BIBLIOGRAPHY
Works by FYODOR DOSTOYEVSKY

Poor Folk, 1846
The Double, 1846
An Honest Thief, 1846
White Nights, 1848 (Signet Classic 0-451-520130)
Uncle's Dream, 1859
The Friend of the Family, 1859
The Insulted and the Injured, 1861
The House of the Dead, 1862
Notes from Underground, 1864 (Signet Classic 0-451-520130)
Crime and Punishment, 1866 (Signet Classic 0-451-519957)
The Gambler, 1866
The Idiot, 1868-69 (Signet Classic 0-451-063708)
The Eternal Husband, 1870
The Possessed, 1871-72 (Signet Classic 0-451-519183)
A Raw Youth, 1875
The Dream of a Ridiculous Man, 1877 (Signet Classic 0-451-520130)
A Diary of a Writer, 1873-81
The Brothers Karamazov, 1879-80 (Signet Classic 0-451-520904)
Letters of Fyodor Dostoyevsky

Selected Biography and Criticism

Berdyaev, Nicholas. *Dostoyevsky*. Trans. Donald Attwater. New York: Meridian Books, 1960.

Carr, Edward H. *Dostoyevsky, 1821-1881: A New Biography*. London: Allen and Unwin, 1949.

Grossman, Leonid. *Dostoyevsky: A Biography*. Trans. Helen Mackler. Indianapolis: Bobbs-Merrill, 1975.

Jackson, R. L., ed. *Twentieth Century Interpretations of Crime and Punishment: A Collection of Critical Essays*. Englewood Cliffs, N.J.: Prentice-Hall, 1974.

Magarshack, David. *Dostoyevsky*. New York: Harcourt, Brace & World, 1963.

Mochulsky, Konstantin. *Dostoyevsky: His Life and Work*. Trans. Michael A. Minihan. Princeton, N.J.: Princeton University Press, 1967.

Modern Fiction Studies (Dostoyevsky Number), 4 (Autumn, 1958).

Simmons, Ernest J. *Dostoyevsky: The Making of a Novelist*. London: Oxford University Press, 1940.

Steiner, George. *Tolstoy or Dostoyevsky*. New York: Knopf, 1959.

Wasiolek, Edward, ed. *Dostoyevsky: The Major Fiction*. Cambridge, Mass.: M.I.T. Press, 1964.

Wellek, René, ed. *Dostoyevsky: A Collection of Critical Essays*. Englewood Cliffs, N.J.: Prentice-Hall, 1962.